INVISIBLE THREAT

ROBERT L. HIRSCH

INVISIBLE THREAT

iUniverse books may be ordered through booksellers or by contacting:

iUniverse
1663 Liberty Drive
Bloomington, IN 47403
www.iuniverse.com
1-800-Authors (1-800-288-4677)

Because of the dynamic nature of the internet, any web addresses or links contained in this book may have changed since publication and may no longer be valid. The views expressed in this work are solely those of the author and do not necessarily reflect the views of the publisher, and the publisher hereby disclaims any responsibility for them.

Any people depicted in stock imagery provided by Getty Images are models, and such images are being used for illustrative purposes only.
Certain stock imagery © Getty Images.

ISBN: 978-1-5320-9658-7 (sc)
ISBN: 978-1-5320-9657-0 (hc)
ISBN: 978-1-5320-9656-3 (e)

Library of Congress Control Number: 2020910154

Print information available on the last page.

iUniverse rev. date: 07/14/2020

Truth is by nature self-evident. As soon as you remove the cobwebs of ignorance that surround it, it shines clear.

—Mahatma Gandhi

FOREWORD

Oscar Wilde wrote "Decay of Lying—An Observation" in 1891. In his essay Wilde states among many things "life imitates art far more than art imitates life."

I mention this as I publish my novel during the 2020 Covid-19 worldwide pandemic. I conceived and wrote this story well before the horrible coronavirus outbreak, and as the plot unfolds, you will note many parallels between fiction and reality.

RLH

PROLOGUE

JULY 3, 2012

Dr. Alan Mazer completed rounds on an early July morning at the Johns Hopkins Hospital in Baltimore, Maryland, just before the holiday weekend. He had a lot of office work to complete before the Fourth of July and hoped to get out of the office at a reasonable time. The new crop of interns and residents had just come on board. Alan wanted to meet some of the new faculty and staff, but that was doubtful considering the frenetic pace in the hospital. As he headed back to his lab and office, he noticed that most of the televisions in patient rooms were tuned to CNN or Fox News. He ducked inside a room as a group of students rounded with a chief resident and attending physician. He watched the television, paying no attention to the students or patient, who apparently had not seen the news. Several explosions had just rocked highways leading into and out of the Washington and Baltimore corridors. From what he could gather by reading just the news scroll, as the television was muted, it appeared as if several eighteen-wheeler trucks had been crashed intentionally. The trucks then exploded, blocking both local roads and major arteries in both directions. There were numerous roadside casualties, but no numbers were posted yet. It looked like all the interstates and major local highways, including I-95, I-270, I-295, Route 50, and both beltways around DC and Baltimore, were affected. First responders were frozen in place on the ground. Although reports were slow to come in, calls to local stations that were fed back to the networks showed that response times for ambulances, rescue, and fire equipment were sluggish because of the massive traffic stalls. Helicopter runs were now being tested, but landing locations were tight because of huge blazes and traffic.

Alan and the rest of the country knew right away that, once again, the world had changed. This was a sign of a coordinated terrorist attack. It did not take long for fear to strike in the minds and hearts of every American citizen. This was a local event, but just like 9/11, it had national and worldwide repercussions. No, towers were not brought down, but thousands of people were now stuck in their cars and could not move. What was next? Could something be in the air? Was the traffic jam just the beginning?

Panic was setting in as thousands of Washington and Baltimore commuters sat trapped in their cars. It did not take much to sabotage the commerce and economy of the mid-Atlantic states—lost workdays, stores not receiving goods, food wasted, and the list went on and on. A coordinated attack like this on any highway or highways around major cities ripped the economy to shreds. Dow futures were now down seven hundred points and falling fast. The government had missed this and needed a quick and defining response.

MASSACHUSETTS

1981

Ghaffar Khorasani rounded the exit ramp at the intersection of the Mass Turnpike and Route 30 to head home after a rather boring day. Ghaffar headed the physics department at Weston Country Preparatory School, an elite high school where many of the students in the area competed for the top college slots in the country. Ghaffar had been in Framingham and Natick shopping on Route 9 earlier in the afternoon and was now headed back home on the Pike, against the flow of most homebound traffic from Boston. He could have taken back roads or Route 9, but after being in Massachusetts for just under two years, he had already become an impatient driver. He had his hand on the horn nonstop and could not deal with lights or oddballs who drove at the speed limit. So it was on to the Mass Pike and hopefully at least seventy miles per hour, even though it was only eleven miles to his exit.

Massachusetts was a long way from Iran. Ghaffar wondered how it was possible that he could be across the world. He and his family had survived two revolutions in Iran. First, the United States came in and backed the Shah's monarchy in the White Revolution. Despite huge benefits to the country, the poor did not benefit. It took time, but Westernization was antithetical to Islam. Despite large revenues from oil money, which continued to flow to the rich, a big turnaround happened in the 1970s. An underground of anger developed. Eventually the Shiite clergy, merchants, and students helped lead the support of Ayatollah Ruhollah Khomeini in 1978.

The next revolution, the 1979 Revolution, changed everything for Ghaffar. With a doctorate in physics from the University of Tehran, in a stable country, Ghaffar should have been teaching at a university in Tehran. However, he saw the writing on the wall. Ghaffar escaped before the Shah and his regime tumbled. He unwillingly left his poor farmer parents behind and sought asylum in the States. So he found himself in the cold northeastern United States. Except for December and January, when the temperature might slip to as low as 40 degrees in Tehran, Ghaffar was not used to the bitter, wet, cold weather of Boston and New England. But he had a nice job and could not really complain.

Many of his professional friends from the university or in other situations in Iran who could find the ways and means to immigrate to the United States could not get a job worthy of their prior station in life. A physician friend was bathing patients as a practical nurse in a local hospital. Most wealthy Iranians seemed to have gone west to California and found a better and more hospitable place. The Boston area had relatively few Iranians. Again, the weather wasn't great, and the word was that, except for few places in the northeast United States, Iranians were not welcome. Most Bostonians kept to themselves and their little cliques.

But, as it was now, Ghaffar was not going anywhere. He had a nice, secure job; a place to live; and colleagues and students who seemed to respect him. Weston Country Prep was good enough for now. As he pulled into his apartment complex just off Brookline Avenue, he found a parking place a chilly two hundred yards from his door. He grabbed his briefcase and sport coat and jogged only as fast as a two-hundred-fifty-pound man with asthma could. As he approached the unsecured door to his apartment building, he felt so glad to have found this place when a first-floor pad was available. There was no way that his five-foot, eleven-inch frame carrying this weight could take on two or even three flights of stairs at the end of the day.

Ghaffar took a few deep breaths as he paused in the lobby and dug out the keys to his apartment and mailbox. He opened his mailbox and pulled out a few pieces of junk mail, a couple of bills, and a free newspaper, something similar to *The Phoenix*, a free paper that had been a staple for years in the Boston area. He liked to look through the personal ads; maybe someday he'd respond to one of those "SWF seeking SM looking for adventure and ..." ads at the back of the paper. The warmer humid air in the foyer felt soothing to his wheezy lungs as he relaxed for a minute, scanned the junk, and threw it in the garbage. A young, fair-skinned, brunette woman, appearing to be of college age or a little older, opened a mailbox, grabbed several envelopes and the paper, and slammed the metal door shut. She then proceeded down the hallway on the right, apparently not cognizant of Ghaffar or anyone else entering the lobby.

Ghaffar sauntered to his apartment just a few steps down the left-side hall extending off the apartment lobby. There were no elevators in this building built in the early part of the twentieth century, but a central, small, circular stairway led to the second floor, and stairways off each of the small hallways went to the second and third floors. This was not an elegant building but had been kept up nicely. It had a dozen one- and two-bedroom units total. With the yearly flood of college and graduate students from many Boston-area schools and a few longtime residents, the property provided an excellent income for the owners, who kept the property in reasonably working condition.

Ghaffar opened the remainder of his mail, but it didn't take long for him to fall asleep on his couch. He was exhausted from his long day at school and side trip to Framingham. He awoke and began thinking about what he would do for dinner. He must have been dreaming during his dozing about back home and how he could have left his parents in Iran. He was feeling guilty and devastated now. Lonely, without any real friends, Ghaffar came home to this empty apartment every night.

Depressed, he would eat for sure. That was the only way to take his mind off his dejected feelings. It was now after eight o'clock. He called Papa Ginos for delivery of a large cheese pizza, and by nine thirty he was stuffed, having consumed all but one slice of the pizza designed for more than one adult. Having also consumed a beer in the process did not help. He had forgone his Muslim upbringing and allowed himself the indulgence of alcohol in his depressed state.

After eating and drinking, he awoke with a start again, with his television on, to the all-too-familiar voice of Ted Koppel, ABC's *Nightline* host ever since the beginning of the Iranian hostage crisis in 1979. Koppel reviewed what had happened over the last two days. Fifty-two Americans who had been held hostage in Iran for 444 days by student revolutionaries were finally released, with the support of Ayatollah Ruhollah Khomeini. It happened to be January 21, 1981, the day after America had inaugurated President Reagan. The hostage release was all done to make former president Jimmy Carter look even worse than before he lost his reelection bid. Ghaffar was glad that the American hostages had obtained their freedom, as he was well on his way and committed to becoming an American citizen. But he was not at all happy about the transition in Iran. His parents, who had labored to get him educated, were downtrodden and lost in the Iranian struggle.

Ghaffar slept restlessly. It might have been the pizza, and it might have been the news from Iran. It could have been the relentless mixed sleet and snow on his bedroom windows overnight. In any case, as he awoke early on Wednesday morning, he was not ready to face his rambunctious physics students, who were only interested in moving on to their next class. He put the coffee on and took a shower. By the time he dried off and got dressed, the aroma of the coffee drew him into his small kitchen and he felt a little better about the day. Ghaffar quickly finished his coffee and turned off the pot. He figured he would grab another at Dunkin' Donuts on the way to school and probably a donut or two as well. He headed out his apartment door.

Leesa Mazer slipped on the ice-covered sidewalk leading to the stairs to her building. It was just after dawn on an early, cold January morning. As she went down, she first slammed the right side of her body hard and then her head onto the concrete walkway. She never lost consciousness, but she did see stars. She ached all over and could not move. The street was quiet except for the noise of a garbage truck and early-morning trash pickup a block away. The ice must have formed from the quick moving front of sleet and snow that morning, followed by a fast freeze when a cold front came in with the Canadian high. No storms were in the area now, just frigid weather. Leesa cried out in pain. The front door to the apartment building opened, and Ghaffar Khorasani walked out bundled up in his coat, heavy scarf, gloves, and rubber-soled shoes on his way to work at Weston Country Prep. He quickly but carefully made his way down the slippery steps, which had not yet been sanded or salted. He looked down and then saw the woman he had previously noticed several times in his apartment lobby retrieving her mail. However, now it looked like she needed serious help. He knelt down gingerly next to the woman.

"Can I help you?" Ghaffar asked. "I am Ghaffar Khorasani, and uh, I live here in this, uh, building."

"Please, yes. I am in a lot of pain. My name is Leesa. Please help me get into the building. It is freezing out here. Can you get me into the building? I am freezing and aching," pleaded Leesa.

"Leesa, I don't want to move you because you might have a very serious injury. Can you move your legs and arms?" asked Ghaffar.

"I am a nurse, and I'm pretty sure I don't have any serious injuries. Just help me. I cannot get up from the ice without your help. I'm in a lot of pain. But thanks for being cautious," Leesa said.

Ghaffar stood Leesa up carefully, and with his large frame he grabbed her under her arms and pulled her up to a standing position. Even though she weighed only on the order of 125 pounds, or half his weight, it was not an easy task to move her. Everything was still covered with ice, as the temperature was still well below freezing. Ghaffar, with some help from Leesa, slowly walked the fifteen feet to the stairway and then up the ten steps to the door of the apartment while she held onto the cold, wrought-iron banister with her left hand. Thankfully, ice had not formed on the iron. Ghaffar could not recall any standard physics principles under stress. He dragged Leesa across the large lobby and foyer and helped her as she collapsed onto the couch. She unbuttoned her overcoat and gasped. Her white pant suit was now stained and her white shoes scuffed up. Ghaffar thought she looked like an angel. To anyone else, she looked just like an injured and exhausted nurse. Ghaffar now finally deduced what Leesa had been doing outside on the front walk in the early morning hours. She was obviously returning from work at one of the nearby hospitals. He also was in a huge quandary. He needed to continue to help this woman he had just met, but he also had his obligation for work. He needed to head out soon for his early-morning classes at Weston.

"How are you feeling?" inquired Ghaffar.

"I am in a lot of pain. I slipped on the ice and hit my whole body on the right side, then I banged my head. I was rushing home, and I know I should have slowed down. I had worked a double shift and ..."

Leesa broke down and started crying. She could not take it any longer; the pain and exhaustion were too much, and she just continued to sob. Ghaffar offered her a blanket from the chair across the room. She accepted and smiled while continuing to sob. Ghaffar had almost no experience in handling the emotions of others. Teaching physics did not give him much opportunity to hone such skills. But his gut said it was time to call the school.

"I will be right back," he said.

He decided to take the day off. He walked down the hall and past the mailboxes to the pay phone on the wall and called the school office. This was going to be his first missed day from work in one and a half years.

"Leesa, I cannot leave you here on the couch in this condition. I will stay with you until you can move around or get to a doctor or emergency room to be checked out."

"I have already caused you enough headaches for the day, for the week. Please, I can handle this from here," implored Leesa.

"No, I have already called the secretary at my school; they will bring someone in today to handle my classes. It will not be a problem. And it will give me an extra day to prepare for exams I am working on for my students," he joked.

"If you insist," Leesa said. "Then let's wait here for an hour until rush hour is over, and then we can go over to Beth Israel, where I work. I can get right into the emergency department there and get checked out. I cannot thank you enough, Ghaffar."

"Can I bring you some coffee or something to eat? You must be hungry and cold after that spill and working for the past day," Ghaffar said.

"Coffee would be great, thanks," Leesa replied. "I would normally go right to sleep for a while, but it looks like I will be staying up for a bit."

"I am just down the hall on this floor and will bring you a cup of some strong coffee that I made this morning."

After resting in the lobby for a while, Ghaffar called a taxi. It took about fifteen minutes, but finally, a yellow cab arrived. Ghaffar and Leesa walked carefully down the steps, but the extra caution was really not needed. Leesa's pain was still quite intense. However, the day had warmed up to above forty degrees, and the ice that had formed on the streets and sidewalks the night before was a thing of the past. Ghaffar accompanied Leesa in the cab to her emergency department, where she walked in the side entrance with Ghaffar's assistance, her identification card in hand. She was happy to see some friendly faces. An intern who had rotated through her medical floor was now working in this unit; he recognized her and came over to assist her immediately.

"From the way you hobbled in her with your friend," the intern said, "I would say we need to send you over to radiology after checking you in and examining you."

"I slipped on the ice as I was walking home from work this morning. That happened about two hours ago. I have been resting since. I just want to make sure there is nothing wrong and then, please, I want to go home," Leesa moaned.

"Understood, but please be patient and a patient for me," said the young intern. "Let's just take time to check all systems."

Ghaffar interjected, "Yes, let's make sure you're okay, and then I'll get you home." Ghaffar was happy he had called in to take the day off. He spent the next three hours waiting for all testing to be completed, a lengthy time despite Leesa's connections. She was released with a warning to take a few days off.

A week later Ghaffar knew he wanted to change his look. He was motivated. He was tall, dark, and handsome. On the other hand, he knew he was also a good thirty pounds overweight. After his encounter with Leesa the previous week, he had an incentive to get in better shape. He had hoped her spill on the ice might lead to a social interaction or two—but if not with her, maybe someone else. It was certainly time for a social life beyond monitoring school events. Ghaffar had read recently about a diet craze. The Atkins diet was well researched by a US cardiologist, and it seemed to have worked wonders for obese individuals. He thought he would give it a shot. It was basically a high-protein diet that had few side effects. Ghaffar took his own initiative on the diet plan, but it was not an easy one. He loved breads, pizza, pasta, and all things sticky and gooey. He was not sure how he would get by without his late-night Papa Ginos and Chinese takeout, but he needed to try. Alcohol was not at issue, as he rarely imbibed. He knew his health and his looks needed it now. The Atkins diet was not really a low-calorie diet, but it did restrict a lot of what Ghaffar would want. Early on, he ate almost exclusively proteins. The diet allowed more calories and some carbohydrates as the weeks went by, but restrictions on all the "good stuff" remained. It was brutal. He was tired, and his breath smelled stale even after brushing his teeth and using breath mints. But after two weeks, he had some positive reinforcement. He had already lost twelve pounds, and his clothes were feeling loose on him. This diet, although difficult, seemed to be quite a miracle.

He continued on his journey to lose more weight, and as the weather warmed even more as February pivoted to March, he walked around the school campus at lunchtime on the few days when the weather allowed for it. Ghaffar had a spring in his step and felt good about himself for the first time in a very long time. He began to enjoy his life in America and began teaching with more enthusiasm. Ghaffar starting using humorous models to explain physics principles—models that he had developed himself. Students were no longer bored in his classes and ventured up to him after class to speak with him. This was a new experience. After almost two years at Weston, he was feeling good about his position.

Two months into his new regimen, down eighteen pounds and looking great, Leesa approached Ghaffar in the lobby as she was retrieving her mail.

"Ghaffar, I have not seen you lately. I guess we have been working different shifts. I know you are a nine-to-five type of guy. Wow, you look great. Are you working out?" she asked as she touched his shoulder.

"Yes, a bit. I am walking every day at lunch," Ghaffar explained.

"Well, I took one week off after my fall, then I worked evenings for four weeks, and this week is a scheduled vacation week," Leesa remarked. "And believe me, I need this time off."

"What are you doing with your week off?" he inquired, looking past the outside door, not making much eye contact.

"I am off to the Washington, DC, area to see my parents for the Jewish holidays," she replied. "This, however, is my least favorite holiday. I really don't see why I need to eat matzah for eight days in recognition of the Hebrew slaves getting the hell out of Egypt and not being able to have their bread rise. I am glad they got out, yes, but come on—matzah? In addition, I will be constipated the whole week. I know—too much information."

"Well, before you go, you could spend a couple of days showing Boston to me," Ghaffar replied, looking at her now. "I have been here almost two years and have really never ventured around town. I had been so out of shape I was afraid to walk the Freedom Trail. I thought I would not make it very far."

"Sounds like a plan. I would like that very much," she said. "Let's do it."

It was just after the morning inbound rush hour to Boston when Leesa and Ghaffar walked at an easy pace the few short blocks to the Brookline Village green-line station of the T. The T, or MBTA, was Boston's longstanding and well-worn subway system. Ghaffar was also pleased to have the week off and to be going out with Leesa for the day. They hopped on board the train that arrived just as they approached the station. As expected, it was standing room only even though it was after nine thirty in the morning. They had looked at a map of the famous two-and-a-half-mile Freedom Trail over coffee earlier that morning and decided the best place to start was, of course, at the beginning. They took the green line directly to Park and didn't have to change trains. As they arrived at the top of the stairs out of the Park Street station, it was evident that spring had already sprung in Massachusetts. Boston

Common seemed to be overflowing with people. This might not have been the best of weeks to be vacationing, as many families had the same idea. The grass was shaking off its wintry brown and turning green. At the Commons were plenty of dog walkers and hundreds of nasty pigeons. School was on break in many areas of the Northeast, and it was the beginning of a beautiful day. On top of that, the Sox had a game at one thirty, another excuse for people to take a day off from work. It wasn't a Yankees or Orioles game, so tickets at Fenway could be easily found for a game against a lowly Eastern Division team.

Freedom Trail was a must for any tourist to Boston. And if one was not out at Boston Harbor or at Lexington and Concord (and Walden Pond) to the west, the Freedom Trail was a good way to quickly get a perspective of the beginnings of the Revolutionary War.

The first stop on the redbrick Freedom Trail for Leesa and Ghaffar was the capitol building. Looking up from the Commons, the gold-gilded dome was an amazing sight in the brilliant morning sun. Leesa told Ghaffar that they were looking at American history here. Paul Revere worked on the dome and originally covered it with copper. They spent the whole day meandering through the streets of historic Boston. Having been on several tours with friends and relatives who came to Boston, Leesa knew most of the key sights and avoided the on-and-off bus tours. They took their time walking the Freedom Trail. Ghaffar was so happy to be seeing and hearing firsthand the history of his new country. He was even more excited to be with Leesa, who also seemed upbeat and in a cheerful mood. But walking and shopping all day was quite exhausting, even in his new body. At the Old South Meeting House, where the Sons of Liberty dumped tea in the Boston Harbor to protest the king's taxes, Leesa and Ghaffar decided to end their Freedom Trail walk early. They dragged themselves to their last stop, Faneuil Hall. Although the Faneuil Hall was a center of protests, it was now a perfect place for a repast, filled with more shops and eateries. Leesa wanted Ghaffar to continue to see Boston at its "finest." Unbeknownst to him, he would see and taste some real, original Boston food and service. Leesa led him down to Durgin-Park, a restaurant that had been in business probably as long as there have been nasty servers.

It was historic, and the food was good. But Leesa explained as they entered that they had better know what they wanted pretty darn quick.

At the restaurant, a not-so-typical middle-aged waitress put down two glasses on the red-and-white-checked tablecloth and gruffly asked what they wanted. Leesa looked quickly at Ghaffar and then turned to the waitress, who had already disappeared. The place was dimly lit in several corners, probably so patrons did not have to look so closely at the unknown diners at their elbows. Leesa told Ghaffar that he had to try the "chowda"; she would have a lunch-size portion of pot roast. When the waitress returned, Leesa made sure to quickly place her order.

"I'll have the chowder and the baked scrod," Ghaffar pronounced. The waitress quickly barked the order back in her distinct accent, waited unpleasantly for a nod, and then took off for another table. Despite the typical service at long wooden tables in this historic restaurant open for over 150 years, the food was excellent. It was unlikely that, after their two o'clock lunch, either Leesa or Ghaffar, who was still trying to lose weight, would be eating much of a dinner. For that matter, they were pretty much done with touring as well.

Walking out of the restaurant, Leesa's eyes locked onto Ghaffar's and his onto hers. She had felt an attraction to him all day. It was definitely strong and not at all a reaction of gratitude for what he had done for her when she fell in January. They were full from the late lunch, and the thought of even a five-minute walk to the T was unsettling. Ghaffar hailed a cab, and they headed back across town through the afternoon traffic toward their apartment building. On the circuitous journey to avoid ballgame and tourist traffic, Leesa slipped her hand into Ghaffar's. She looked at him with a wide smile, and he smiled back. No words were spoken, but they could hear the silence of contentment throughout the backseat. Leesa did not let go of his hand until Ghaffar had to pull his wallet out to pay the cabbie.

Climbing the steps to the apartment building's front door, Ghaffar got an awkward feeling. It did not last long. Leesa took his hand and pulled him toward her apartment. They walked down the right-side hallway to her place. After entering her apartment, she pushed the door shut and kissed him passionately. He returned her kiss with equal intensity. She threw her light coat onto the couch in the living room and led him into her bedroom straight ahead.

"I'll be right back; I am going to the bathroom," declared Leesa.

Ghaffar took off his sports jacket and awkwardly took off shoes, placing them under a chair in the corner of the bedroom. Leesa returned from the bathroom in what seemed like seconds dressed in a see-through black negligee. Ghaffar was not quite ready for this but was excited beyond his wildest expectations.

Leesa whispered in a sexy voice, "Ghaffar, you are a little behind me. Come over here and let me help you undress."

Ghaffar walked toward the bed where Leesa had taken a seat. She unbuttoned his shirt and noticed that his chest muscles were much more defined than she ever would have thought. It raised her sense of pleasure even more. She threw his shirt onto the floor toward the chair and undid his belt. Ghaffar helped her, and as he did she quickly unzipped his pants and pulled them down as he stood at the bedside. His penis poked straight out through his boxers. Leesa bowed her head from the bedside, gently held onto his large erect shaft, and started to lick his penis. Ghaffar could not remember the last time he felt this good. He reached down and felt Leesa's smooth vagina, and it was so very wet. He gently massaged her clitoris, and he then inserted two fingers into her vagina as her juices flowed. Leesa moaned and shook as he had never seen or heard a woman act before. After a few moments, Ghaffar gently pushed her head off his organ. He grabbed her underneath her buttocks and lifted her onto the bed. She lay down, and he inserted himself into her well-lubricated vagina. Before long they both reached a wondrous climax together. When Ghaffar rolled over, he saw the huge smile on her face, and she saw his. She could not remember being so happy. She was in a place she had not been, ever. So was Ghaffar. This was the end of a magical tour of Boston, he thought.

NARI LEE

JUNE 2012

Nari Lee drove her little used red 2009 BMW Z4 toward 495, so looking forward to a day at the beach on the Cape. She was hoping to find a small spot on the beach in Falmouth, not too far out on the Cape; lay down; read a book; and rest. She thought she had left early enough to avoid the traffic from Providence and everywhere else inland, but it was a slow go. How did a California girl—not your usual blond-haired, blue-eyed, model surfer—get here to the East Coast? As she listened to her satellite radio station playing lots of sixties Beach Boys hits, she thought, *This has to be a dream.* How did a Korean girl from San Francisco, a bright kid and a pretty damn good golfer, end up here?

The life for Koreans coming to America depended on timing. And coming to America from a different culture where a different language was spoken made such a move taxing no matter when it happened. Most Koreans immigrating to America in the early 1900s came en masse to work the pineapple fields and sugar plantations in Hawaii. It was a great opportunity for plantation owners to get cheap labor. Koreans coming to America later in the twentieth century came often as mail-order brides for the many plantation workers already in Hawaii and who had difficulty adjusting. Nari's parents came to America in 1980, after the revocation of the Immigration and Naturalization Act in 1965, eliminating the quota system. The United States realized a need for recruiting experts from various fields.

In 1980, the home computer age was just starting to take off. The Apple II came onto the market in 1977. The Radio Shack TRS80 was right there too, and IBM was trying to compete at the higher end in the home PC market. Commodore 64 would take everyone by surprise in a few years' time. But in 1980, Nari's mother and father, Sung Kim and Hoon Lee, were computer experts and spoke perfect English. They landed in America and engaged with a busy startup tech company developing a low-cost but relatively high-end home computer—a copycat is what they would call it. The market would be blitzed with these machines in the next few years, but whoever had the speediest processors and the best looks and graphic cards for games would win out. Nari's parents worked every day, it seemed, for twelve to sixteen hours a day. They did not get much in the way of salary but took a big chance and grabbed a big piece of equity. If things went well and the company was bought out or went public when the computer was developed, then they could achieve the American dream in a very short time. Their focus was only on work and nothing else.

Their focus paid off. After two years, the small computer startup Techbrands became a well-known Bay Area company and was taken over by a Japanese giant in business. For the Japanese megacompany, it was an affordable risk. They wanted a piece of the American PC business as soon as possible and took a gamble on Techbrands fast, small PC. It was a bet that paid off in spades for the employees of Techbrands. The hard work with little pay but lots of stock was well worth the short wait for the workers. Employees were required to stay with the new company for at least one period, and then they could leave after their stock vested. If they did, many would be worth millions.

Both Sung Kim and Hoon Lee stayed with Techbrands for exactly one year after their year of retained responsibility was completed and cashed in their chips. The company was not the same under the direction of the large Japanese conglomerate. Further, the foreign marketing group tried to push the PC directly against the giant Apple. That would never work. Others had already tried and failed miserably.

Sung and Hoon were on their way to financial independence. It also happened that Sung was on her way to having a child. In the spring of 1984, the Lees welcomed a healthy baby girl to America, a natural-born citizen of the United States. They were so proud, and they themselves were well on their way to becoming citizens as well. With their newfound wealth and baby on board, they moved from their apartment to a modest home in Palo Alto.

Nari Lee walked at nine months of age and was running around their new house by the time she was one year old. The Lees had moved to this area to be near good schools and near Stanford. They figured that if they wanted to start their own company in the future, it would be a good place to find the right talent. Being close to other high-tech companies and Stanford drew lots of venture capital money into the region. With plenty of money in the bank as a runway to developing their own venture, Hoon and Sung took their time planning their own company and nurturing their daughter. They were a very well-to-do couple now.

Their home was an exclusively English-speaking home, and Nari was a motormouth. She started with a few words at seven months of age and was putting together three- and four-word sentences by the age of eighteen months. By two years of age, Nari let everyone know what she wanted and probably had a spoken vocabulary of a hundred words. It appeared that this little tyke was something special. With some of their free time and freedom to pursue their next steps, her dad and mom thought very hard about what they wanted for their daughter and their own future. Sung worked out what she thought would be the future in home computers and automation. In her mind, communication via the internet, which was so slow at the time, needed some giant leaps forward. She thought she could unite her ideas of faster communication with graphics and computer automation. She worked diligently on a business plan. In the meantime, Hoon concentrated on Nari's education before she entered preschool. She was beyond bright. At four she was reading through books that were grade levels above her age and always asked for more and more.

Dad was also working hard, and not just with Nari. Hoon had quite a lot of time on his hands, and he was always a man for self-improvement. Since Sung was usually busy bouncing ideas off him about the business plan or taking Nari to various play groups or activities for toddlers, Hoon needed a distraction. To keep on top of the electronics and the computer technology industry, and to develop a better understanding of some new areas that might help a new computer business, he enrolled in two courses at Stanford in a part time master's program. One was in machine-based learning, and another was in the development of new computer languages. These courses became a major focus of Hoon's time, and he found himself spending hours studying and at the library. Even so, he always made sure he spent plenty of time with his wife and his beautiful little Nari.

Over the next few months on campus, Hoon walked by the Stanford Golf Club frequently. It was a good thirty-minute walk to the club from the library, but he needed the exercise. And he did a lot of thinking on these long walks. He decided one spring afternoon to ask the golf professional if he could have a lesson.

"What about right now? There's no time like the present," the pro responded.

"Am I dressed appropriately?" Hoon replied.

"You're all set. What's your shoe size?"

"Eight medium," said Hoon.

"I've got some loaner clubs and some shoes in the back," replied the pro. "Let's go out to the practice facility—doctor?"

"No, I'm Hoon Lee, master's degree student."

"I'm Howie Pierce. I'll be back in a minute."

The golf lesson was fun. Hoon was no natural but would definitely have fun out there. Howie said he showed promise, and for now all he had to do was practice his grip and stance. If Hoon got those two basics down, then Howie would get him swinging the club in a couple of weeks. Hoon went to Sears, bought an inexpensive set of starter golf clubs, and even picked up a short kids club for Nari. In two weeks' time, he felt at ease holding the grip. Howie told him that the only thing between the ball and him was the club, and his grip on the club was the key. He had to practice his grip every day until it felt natural.

With her child-sized club, Nari went outside and mimicked her dad every evening after dinner. She stood outside with him and gripped her club just like Daddy. She was not sure what this was all about but had fun spending time in their small yard with her dad. One Saturday afternoon, Hoon said to Nari, "Bring your golf club to the car. We will learn how to hit golf balls."

"Mommy, I'm going with Daddy to play golf!" she shouted through the screen door. After a brief conversation with Sung, Hoon drove off to the Stanford Golf Club where he had scheduled his second lesson with Howie. He figured Nari would watch and maybe learn as well. But at four years of age he did not have very high expectations for himself or for Nari either.

Nari sat on the wooden bench behind dad and the pro. Howie was impressed with Hoon's grip and posture, and Hoon was ready to learn to hit a golf ball. The pro pulled an iron from Hoon's bag and asked him to try to swing it backward and forward while the pro showed him how to turn his shoulders and hips back and then toward the target. Hoon did this several times and then tried with a ball in the path of his swing. To his delight, he made contact. The ball didn't go very far, but he got a big cheer from Nari. Howie asked Nari if she wanted to try with her club, and she jumped off the bench.

"Oh, yes, thank you, mister golf man!" she exploded with excitement. Howie smiled and saw that she had almost a perfect grip on the club. He took her hand and guided her to the hitting area next to her dad.

"Nari, I want you to just get up here and try to hit this ball. I am not going to tell you how to do it. If you need some help, I'll help you out. Okay?"

"Okay, I am ready, Owie," Nari said confidently. As Hoon watched from his station, Nari gripped the club as she had learned but swung wildly, hitting the grass way behind the ball. The ball remained on the tee. She tried again with the same result. The third time was also a miscue. Howie stepped up, said a few words to Nari, and took her through one swing in slow motion. He controlled her swing smoothly going backward and had her turn more quickly toward the ball. Nari then tried it on her own a few times. She then hit the ball, and this time it traveled a fair distance. A huge smile spread across her face. Howie went back to working with Hoon and left Nari on her own. After twenty-five more minutes, the lesson was over, but Nari was still swinging and trying, usually successfully, hitting balls about thirty to fifty yards. She seemed enthralled with the idea of blasting these white balls onto the green range.

On the drive home, Nari told her dad how much she liked playing with him and wanted to "do golf" again tomorrow. It appeared that she was infected with the golf bug at the very young age of four. Her dad was not so sure about his own pursuit of this game, but with Nari's enthusiasm, he knew there was probably no cure for this virus. This was just the beginning of a great father–daughter relationship built on not only love but the love of sport.

The golf craze was being reawakened in America. It was 1986, and Jack Nicklaus had just captured the hearts and imaginations of every middle-aged man when he won his eighteenth major at the Masters at age forty-six. Also, the country was being invaded by male and female superstars from around the globe. A few years later, South Korean men were starting to make their mark in the world and on the US PGA tour. Hoon kept his eye on this development, thinking that maybe his Korean-American born daughter might have a future in golf. She was bright and seemed to have natural talent. After a few lessons with Howie, Hoon decided, his money would be better spent on Nari. She had the talent and honestly seemed to love the game. Hoon was a better spectator. The next week, Howie took Nari to the range and spent an hour on the basics with her.

Every week it was the same—working on different clubs and different aspects of the swing. A young child typically wouldn't understand much of what was being said, but Nari was not your typical young kid. She absorbed everything. Plus, she loved every drill he gave her to practice at home. Furthermore, Hoon had to be at the campus twice a week for classes. He dropped Nari off under Howie's supervision, and he let her go to the range and practice for a couple of hours twice a week. This was a great time to be a five-year-old kid.

By the time she was ten, Nari was not only a top student in her private school, she was doing well in junior golf tournaments in her city and placed twice in the top ten in two statewide junior tournaments. Hoon decided it was time to get her a top-rated swing coach when she was thirteen. This sped up her improvement, and by the time she was fifteen she was the ninth-best junior girl in California. On top of that, Nari's excellence in and love of academics continued. She excelled in science and loved biology. In fact, she enjoyed it so much that she preferred to do after-school projects to practicing her golf game. Her father was not pleased that she was focusing less on golf. Her game slipped in her junior and senior years in high school, but she was still the best player in the Bay Area by far. She won every girls school tournament but lost several slots in her national ranking as she did not place in any of the junior tournaments. Despite her lackluster performance compared to her sophomore year, several universities scouted her at her high school and junior golf tournaments. Nari did not seem to play with the same enthusiasm as in prior years, but despite her apparent lack of interest in golf, she played well enough to garner a lot of attention. So when it came time for college admissions in the spring, it was not a surprise that offers were abundant. Most scholarship offers Nari received were related to her golfing ability. The universities all assumed she was a Korean-born golfer now living in the United States. It probably did not hurt that Korean Se-Ri Pak took the LPGA by storm in 1998 at the age of twenty. She won two major championships in her rookie year, including the US Open. Her success brought a tidal wave of great Korean women and men golfers to the States.

The offer Nari really liked came out of left field and was far and away something she could not resist. It was a full golf scholarship to Brown University—on the other side of the world to most Californians—in Providence, Rhode Island. Not only that, but in their acceptance letter, they acknowledged her academic achievements and indicated that if she had not been an athlete, she would have been offered a full academic scholarship. There was no question in her mind that she was going to this Ivy League school. Yes, it was far away from family and friends, and she would have a short golf season in the fall and spring. She was not so sure about how she would make the adjustment—the winter wardrobe she would have to buy, or the snow and ice she would have to tolerate. But after she had been there for a while, she not only tolerated the area, she grew to love the Northeast. Growing up in northern California, snow is something you only see if you go to a ski resort; snow became part of her life in New England. Nari graduated with the highest honors from Brown, and then she went on to obtain her doctorate in immunology from this institution. As if that were not enough, she spent another two years getting her doctor of pharmacy degree from the University of Rhode Island.

The traffic was heavy at the Bourne Bridge, but Nari knew it would thin out soon and she would have smooth sailing to Falmouth, Massachusetts. It was only mid-June, so most local school systems had not let out and in-season rentals had not yet started. It had been an unseasonably warm spring, and the ocean temperature was rising more quickly than usual. The day also just happened to be an unseasonably warm day. The high was going to be in the low eighties, and with New England weather, Nari knew she had to jump on any good day. There were plenty of beaches at Falmouth, and she was sure to find a good spot. It was only ten in the morning, and the recent shark attack and shark sightings might also have decreased the early summer weekend beach crowds on the cape. With a relaxing day ahead, Nari looked forward to her first days on the job outside of academics in July at Immunoviratherapeutics.

NEW MEASLES
VACCINE SELECTED
MAY 2013

Excitement ran through the officers' suites at Immunoviratherapeutics. After many years of testing and development, the company was coming down the home stretch in its final candidate selection for its new measles virus vaccine. The measles virus had been around for centuries, and it reared its ugly head in many countries where vaccines were not available or areas where it was not used. The company was developing a new vaccine to protect children that would be given only once instead of twice. One injection would hopefully increase compliance and improve protection and vaccine delivery in developing nations.

The company made mutations in two regions of the H and F regions of the measles proteins, key areas for attachment and penetration of the virus into the host cell. Company scientists conducted multiple tests on over two hundred virus mutants until they found viruses that behaved like the normal measles virus. Scientists then injected several of the strains into animal hosts to look for a rapid and increased immune response. This decision on which strain to choose for development in humans was based on the growth in tissue culture and responses in the animal models.

These preliminary tests then led to a six-year development campaign at Immunoviratherapeutics. Two single-point mutations in the genetic code of the measles virus were made. In the case of the measles virus, RNA, or ribonucleic acid, was the infectious code material that was inserted into the human cell, not DNA, or deoxyribonucleic acid. These changes were made to intensify the immune response so that only one injection would be needed, eliminating the currently required booster injection.

Before any new virus vaccines could be injected into humans, no less children, the US Food and Drug Administration required a panel of many safety tests. The company went well beyond the requirements and tested the selected virus mutations in three animal models to assure themselves that there would be no ill effects. Two candidate mutant viruses were tested in parallel. It seemed reasonable at the time to spend the extra money on two possible candidates. If one failed, the company would have a backup candidate and would not have lost a full year in the development process. The extra expense at this time, especially as revenue was just beginning to come in from their first novel product, the MPV (metapneumovirus) vaccine, would keep the investment community at bay. This was a wise decision. In a matter of two months, bad news hit. The outside vendor performing the testing sent a preliminary report to the company: their number-one vaccine candidate had induced a neurological problem in one of the animal models. In the juvenile mouse model, 25 percent of the animals developed hind-limb paralysis by two weeks of age. This strongly suggested that the virus was invading the brain or spinal cord. Also, one of the primates injected, a rhesus macaque, had an acute seizure that was thought unrelated to the vaccine. Other than that, the other two models were fine. But this one finding clearly knocked this candidate out of the selection process. Thankfully, the company's planned strategy of running two side-by-side mutants in the animal testing was genius. The second vaccine candidate was perfectly clean in all three models. Further, the testing showed enhanced immune responses as predicted. Not only that, but detailed pathology of the brain and spinal cord showed no pathology in animals injected with the second candidate vaccine. The company would obviously discuss all these results with the FDA before moving ahead with their application for human testing. At this point in time, they felt confident they had a strong candidate for a new and better measles vaccine.

4
DEFINING ALAN
1995

Alan remembered the many weekends he spent with his father. From the time he was five or six until he graduated high school, he would see his father, Ghaffar, every two weeks. He developed as strong a bond as could be expected from such a relationship. For the first five years of his life, he had known his dad as a kind and loving man. His dad would be the first to hug him when he came into their apartment. He had only one very strong early childhood memory. His father ran to him when he hit his head on the playground and then carried him home to patch up his bleeding forehead. He also remembered his mom reeling and shouting at his father for letting this happen to her boy. As he looked back, he wondered if that event could have been the beginning of a failure. Supposedly, children were not the real cause of marriages gone bad. But they brought him into this world almost nine months to the day after their wedding, and they were together only six months before they wed. They couldn't really have known each other that well, or the vast differences between them and how these differences would affect their relationship.

Mom was such a contrast to Dad. She was raised in a conservative Jewish home in Potomac, Maryland, a well-to-do suburb of Washington, DC. In Boston now, Leesa rarely visited her parents, who were only an hour away by plane. Dad had grown up in relative poverty in Iran and had huge guilt about leaving his parents behind when he left for America. He had great respect for what his parents gave him—an education and an ability to get to this point in life. On the other hand, Alan's mom did not seem to respect her parents or their religion. Leesa didn't force Alan to go to Sunday school or synagogue. He was on his own and left to his own devices. He learned later that, according to Islamic law, if a Muslim man marries a Jewish or Christian woman, the woman has the right to continue practicing her faith but their children must always be raised as Muslims. No Muslim is permitted to convert to another religion. Any such act is viewed as abandonment and is punishable, including by death in some Islamic jurisdictions. As it turned out, they gave Alan his choice, and this was in fact quite a liberal view of Islam by his father.

Ghaffar had been raised on a farm, and his parents struggled to get by. He was their only child, and education was very important to them. He was a bright child, and they pushed him in school. His academic achievements allowed him to enter the highest secondary schools available and eventually the University of Tehran. His future was very bright, and in time he became a doctoral-level physicist. When the politics in Iran hampered his ability to attain a position at the university, he knew it was time to leave. He fled the country, seeking asylum in the States.

When Alan was with Ghaffar on weekends, Ghaffar took him to pray. They attended a mosque in the suburbs of Boston at least once each visit, and Ghaffar tried to teach him some basic stories in the Quran. He tried to instill in his son that peace was a key message and cornerstone of the Quran and Islam. Alan had matured physically and intellectually at an early age. By the time he was thirteen, he stood close to six feet tall and could have shaved every day. However, emotionally his maturation lagged somewhat. He was confused about his heritage but began to take a strong stand in his early teen years. He recognized early on that he would need to keep his Western name if was going to have any sort of career. He never thought of changing his name as he perceived much prejudice and hatred.

As he grew older, he saw both similarities and differences between his mother's and father's religions. Alan had a very strong recollection of one visit to his mother's parent's house during the Jewish High Holy Days. Leesa and Alan arrived at Leesa's parents' house on the day before the Jewish New Year. It was the end of September and a beautiful day in the Washington, DC, area. Leesa knew she would be in for "discussions" about going to temple that week. In the end, she would only share in what amounted to festivities at the house. She agreed to partake in the huge amounts of traditional foods—her mom's chicken soup with knaidlach, brisket that one wouldn't need a knife to cut, sweet potato pie, grilled vegetables, and desserts that would go on and on.

Alan was thirteen, and he made his own decision about religion. Many of his contemporaries were "becoming adults" at this age, having bar and bat mitzvahs and big parties. What it meant for most of them was an end to the drag of after-school Hebrew education and more time for sports and play or mall hopping. A few might take it seriously and go on to further their education. Alan's mom had raised him to think for himself. He could be what he wanted to be and think how he wanted to think. She was ahead of her time with respect to religion and really did not care much for the holy this and holy that. She was a secular Jew. Leesa marked the holidays on the calendar and visited her parents, like today, on the High Holidays. Marrying a Muslim man and splitting after five years had not gone over well in the Mazer household, but Leesa was trying to restore some semblance of grace with her parents. She did not want her son to be blamed for her mistake. Alan had to make his own choices about religion.

"I'll go with you and Poppy tomorrow," Alan said. "I've been to a few services recently when my friends had their bar mitzvahs."

"That's great!" exclaimed his grandma. "We will go around ten o'clock and pray for a couple of hours. I want to show you off to my friends."

Alan blushed a bit and turned to his mom, thinking, *What have I done?*

At the temple the next day, Alan followed all the rabbi's instructions and read along in English. He did not know a word of Hebrew, but he noticed that the printed letters looked very similar to the Arabic in the Quran he had learned to read at the mosque with his father. What interested him most was a card that he found in his prayer book on his assigned seat. In the book was a card with his grandparents' names and the description of the importance of investing in Israel. As he looked down the empty row where no one had yet been seated, each book had a card as well. The card suggested a donation amount for bonds for Israel; it was a High Holiday appeal for Israel. Basically the card described how much money each member would want to invest in Israel and requested that they do so. The range was from $72 to $10,000 or more. The member could fold down the tab to indicate that he or she wanted to invest in Israeli bonds. After a ten-minute speech by the president of the congregation on the importance of investing in Israel, men came down the aisles and collected the cards from the congregants. Poppy had folded down the thousand-dollar tab. It looked like almost everyone passed a card toward the center aisle, where they were collected. Alan could not believe what he was seeing. He thought this might be occurring at every synagogue and temple everywhere that day and that this might happen every year. *The amount of money being invested in Israel by US citizens must be huge*, he thought. Later on, his grandfather told him that he never intended to collect his investment. It would stay in Israel. Poppy also explained that seventy-two was a multiple of eighteen. Each letter in the Hebrew alphabet had a numeric value. Here, eighteen represented the word *life*, the letters *Chet Yud*. Jewish people gave multiples of eighteen dollars for gifts and donations.

As he sat in the synagogue where Jews were praying, he felt a burning desire to somehow help his people. His father was Muslim, and Alan himself identified with the problems of the Muslims. He did not think that he himself was a violent person, but all he could recall hearing about was radical and extremist activities by Muslim activists. He remembered the World Trade Center bombing two years previously in New York perpetrated by Ramzi Yousef; Alan's understanding was that Yousef was trying to stop the United States from providing further aid to Israel. That, he thought, would never work. Alan had read about the recent history of the *intifada* and the fate of the Palestinians. He now was more determined than ever. Although he was so far away in the United States, he wondered how he as a kid could help the future of these people. They were not of Iranian descent, but they were Muslim. He wondered how he could help.

Back in high school, as the second intifada began, Alan grew impatient and felt a desire for action on behalf of Palestinians. He started to attend a mosque in Cambridge just over the Mass Avenue Bridge. It had been known as a conservative mosque, but a few congregants had been radicalized. Alan had met these gentlemen occasionally and heard them speak at meetings about the necessity to work together to fight the evils of the West. This was very difficult for Alan to understand, as his upbringing was one of privilege. As he studied the Quran and further understood its principles, he appreciated that he needed to live a double life as a teen. He would continue his education and become a physician, but he would also strive to help persecuted Muslims, whom he now saw from a different perspective. Maybe, he thought, radical action is necessary.

Alan continued to fight a constant inner battle. Whether it was religion, violence, or peace, there always seemed to be a duality. Part Jew, part Muslim—should he be a radical terrorist? Should he be helping humankind and strive to become a physician? These were his constant thoughts. He struggled continually, his mind constantly in chaos. Never to reach resolution, Alan lived in this ongoing strife. One day, he thought, this would end. But it would not.

Alan also was very confused about his father's interpretation of Islam. Peace could be interpreted many ways. As Alan matured, he developed sympathy for Muslims in Palestine and other parts of the world. *Islam*, he learned from fellow congregants in his mosque, came from the root word for "submission." So many radical Muslims thought that Christians and Jews needed to submit to Allah. With the ultimate desire of peace, jihad would forcibly submit non-Muslims to their way. Alan thus began in his early teenage years to develop a purpose for his life.

Alan was smart. Weston Country Prep admitted him at thirteen years of age with no problem. Ghaffar could not have paid the tuition if he had not worked there, but a special program was available for employees. Any dependents of employees who were admitted to Weston could attend and pay just 30 percent of the regular tuition. This was an opportunity of which few employees' children could take advantage. The admission standards were extremely exacting. After onerous exams and interviews with several admissions officers, the school accepted only the top candidates. No favors were taken for admission. The school was well funded by endowment, and no one could buy their child's admission into Weston. One in one hundred applicants were admitted. It was said that admission to Weston was a ticket to any college of one's choosing if a student stuck with the program.

Alan sailed through the academic requirements of Weston with top honors in science, math, and history. On the surface he was doing great, but he was unlike most of the class and did not fit in well. Ninety percent were WASPs (white Anglo-Saxon Protestants) from highly educated and well entrenched American families. Many of the surnames were well recognized in New England—Alden, Watson, Leister, Billington, Martin, and others that could be traced back many generations to the 1600s and 1700s. The rest were the new wave of wealthy Asian or Indian kids. The Chinese, who in the nineties were voluntarily coming to America, valued education. Alan stood out like a sore thumb; he did not consider himself Jewish, but he definitely was Semitic in appearance. He was olive skinned, and at thirteen he needed to shave every other day. Many times, despite being the standout student that he was, he held back in classes; he did not want to be the rock star in class and continue to intimidate his classmates. Although tall, he had not filled out yet. He was still skin and bones. He felt that he was certain to be the target of a few bullies only because of his differences and his smarts. Alan thought it was ironic that the kids whose families came from England to escape persecution (although he was sure they did not realize their own heritage) would be the first to be hurtful. He couldn't wait for the last bell on Fridays. He looked forward to his weekends with his father. It was only on these rare weekends that he got the opportunity to go to the mosque. Unbeknownst to his father, Alan often came back on Sunday afternoons by taxi and met with special groups to study certain portions of the Quran. During these study sessions, he made several friends and gained deep insight into the Quran that his father had never taught him. He was gaining a much better understanding of the radical movements that he read about in the paper and the reason for some of the violence in the Middle East. He wondered about freedoms that many of his Muslim brothers fought for in the Middle East.

Alan graduated at sixteen years of age and was admitted to Harvard on a full scholarship. He finally began to feel some freedom. For the first sixteen years of his life, he had lived with his mother and was watched pretty closely by his father at Weston Country Prep. Now he was more or less on his own at Harvard.

With his newfound freedom, Alan could finally head to the Cambridge mosque whenever he wished. He also was ready to grow a beard and start acting like a real Muslim. It was 1998, some five years after the first World Trade Center bombing in New York City. Alan did not think he would encounter many problems in a liberal school like Harvard with a full beard. He was right, for the most part. By the time classes started in early September, Alan's beard had grown in and he looked like he had aged four years. This was helpful since he was only sixteen years old, and he needed to look older, like the other freshmen. By November, his facial hair was really getting pretty scraggly. Many times, as he walked outside the campus either in Cambridge or took the T to Boston, he did garner some unusual looks. Once in a while he would hear some wise kid say something like, "Go back to Arab land, you terrorist sandnigga" or "Get ya bombs off this cah, you prick," dropping R's like most native Bostonians did.

He learned to deal with it. For the most part it was not a problem because there was plenty of hatred to go around in Boston. Everyone seemed to hate everyone else. With every century, new influxes of immigrants brought new people to prejudge and hate. That is the way it had always been, despite what they claimed, and would probably be that way for a long time. The Boston sports teams have always been the last to integrate. The Red Sox and the Celtics were perfect examples—almost all white for the longest time and last to integrate. That tells you a lot about not just the owners but the fans who supported the teams.

The Bruins fans even taunted black hockey players. A now-bygone large department store had cashiers write customers' races on personal checks in certain locations. Blacks living in Boston in the sixties called it the "Deep North." Hiring practices, temporary teachers in schools, and police brutality made for an ugly history. The practice of busing minority kids to school met with huge protests and major violence in the early seventies.

Alan did not have it so bad, and if he wanted to, he could have hidden in plain sight. He could have shaved his beard and dressed like a typical college student of the nineties. But he did not. He did well in college, studied hard, and majored in biology and English. He spent much of his time on Sundays at the Cambridge mosque trying to learn as much as he could about the relationships of the Muslim world and his own background. Alan was radicalized, but he never took a Muslim name. He felt that his first name was derived from a tribe of early Persians, the Alans. Since he did not use his father's last name, he did not want to further disrespect his father by changing his current name. He felt a strong tie to those who were oppressed. Not that he was ever oppressed or felt hurt in any way, but he understood that he might somehow raise others from their oppression. The oppression he felt was not so much self-imposed. It was influence from the outside, and he wanted to make a change. The problem he had in his own mind related to his career aspirations, how they related to the Quran, and how he could help Muslims who were living in oppression. He had for years wanted to become a physician. He had studied hard and was on that track. His grades in all the courses—advanced biology, chemistry, organic chemistry, physics, and calculus, which he had finished in high school—were all A's. He was even now doing a research project during his senior year with a professor at the Mass General Hospital on neural tissue regeneration. It was fascinating and gave him a huge interest in both research and medicine.

His dark skin and Muslim garb was not a problem; he dealt with it. But in September of his senior year at Harvard, everything changed. He was only nineteen years old when the world changed forever. Alan could not forget the cool, clear, crisp day in Boston. He began his walk to a morning English class, but everything stopped on the campus. An archway was crowded with students looking at a few screens. Replays of two jet airliners crashing into the New York Twin Towers played over and over again on someone's iPad. It was September 11, 2001. It did not take long for conclusions to be made. The attacks against the World Trade Center in New York and the Pentagon in Virginia—plus the downed jetliner in Shanksville, Pennsylvania, that had most likely been bound for DC—was proof enough that Al-Qaeda was attacking America. The United States was about to begin an assault against the Muslim world.

Meeting at the mosque had now probably put a target on Alans back. He would never have thought such an event would have happened. He was not prepared for this global change. He could have done many things to blend into American society but did not. Everywhere Alan went for weeks after 9/11, he was attacked verbally and often physically off campus. He became a prisoner on the Harvard campus. Even so, there were many rumblings among his classmates as he passed them in the quad and in the hallways. Things were not the same, and he needed to meet with his brothers at the mosque. They and their families were in worse situations. They worked in the community every day and took much more abuse and prejudice than he did. He continued to have thoughts of going underground or changing his appearance. He could shave his beard or shape it and not dress in the typical knee-length men's Muslim shirt. But he could not disavow his religion and beliefs; he was committed at this point to standing up to and defending the wrongs against all the Muslim people. Alan remained below the radar as much as possible throughout the remainder of the year. He took cabs to the mosque whenever he could and occasionally spent time with his father on Sunday afternoons. But mostly, after the morning prayer session, he returned to the Cambridge mosque and stayed there most of the day, studying and meeting with various groups, and then he returned by taxi to the campus instead of taking public transportation.

During those meetings both in his high school and college years, Alan became a changed person. He understood the persecution of the Arab Muslims and their sense of victimization by imperialism, colonialism, and racism. From all this developed "the resistance movement," including the major struggle against the West and Israel.

But in his mind it did not all fit with the history he had learned from his father and how the Arab nation in the middle of the first century conquered Persia and forced them into a Muslim society. The Palestinian situation was a much different situation, and the world had changed after hundreds of years. The Palestinians had embraced the resistance, and violence was an uncompromising way of life. He learned quickly of the celebration of a new holiday that began in Iran, Al Qud, the Arabic name for "Jerusalem." It was established to express solidarity with the Palestinian people and to oppose Zionism. In Tehran every year on the last Friday of the Muslim holy fasting month of Ramadan, crowds of Iranians set fire to effigies of Western leaders and burned Israeli and American flags. For the most part Alan believed that his Muslim brothers across the globe had been and were being persecuted. He had a mind to help them. He was not sure how he would, but he knew in time he would come to their aid.

Harvard accepted Alan into its medical school in September 2002. He was elated. He was happy to not have to leave his hometown since he had become very close to his Muslim brothers and their work in Boston toward the Palestinian Resistance. He would not have to be a newcomer in a new community in this strange new world where everyone suspected everyone else. Alan assumed that his career in medicine would somehow fit into this other program, though he was not sure just how yet.

The years flew by during Alan's medical training. He was a natural student and understood all the concepts taught in the basic science courses in the first two years of medical school. He heard things once and then really didn't need to study. Anatomy, pharmacology, microbiology, physiology, biochemistry—everything made perfect sense to him. He aced every written and practical exam and could not wait until his third and fourth years, when he would have time to rotate through clinical departments in the hospital. But he also knew that his time studying with his brothers at the mosque would be very limited. The third and fourth years of medical school would be grueling, and there would be limited time for outside activity other than studying.

The first two years of medical school were the toughest for most students. For Alan, however, they seemed to be simpler for him. He understood the subject matter as soon as he read it. All of it was falling into place for him. So, during these first two years, Alan used some of his extra time to study the conflicts in the Middle East and learned quite a lot about what was going on in Iraq and the West Bank. He decided that he had no time—as did his brothers—for what they called the political Islam movement and a future caliphate; it was too slow and had not worked. He and many others were at odds with the slow pace and wanted a militant Islam. To establish a global caliphate, they and many others thought now was better. They justified use of violence in a global caliphate. They thought and worried that the West could tear down the Islamic civilization. Now they believed it was the time for a militant Islam and war to eliminate Israel. The existence of the Jewish state directly defied Allah's will, according to many Muslims. But now, most of the activity had to be underground and through terror cells because of limited resources. Alan had to keep this all in mind as he continued his medical education.

As he did, he followed the news as best he could but could not spend enough of his time there to be actively involved in the goings on at the mosque or activities associated with any radical activities. He might have been if he were a different person or in a different job; right now, though, his thoughts were on completing his degree and seeing how he could help the resistance and all Muslims as a scientist and doctor.

Alan worked with one focus through all four years in medical school. He wanted to finish, get his medical degree, and continue his education in Boston before hopefully securing a neurology residency. All was going well and to plan. There was just one bump in the road. Most wouldn't call it a bump, but it diverted his attention. Alan had met a beautiful young woman at the Cambridge mosque during his undergraduate medical program. He had only seen her once or twice a month, but that was enough to lock her face into his memory. She worked as a part-time assistant to the Imam at the mosque where Alan would spend some of his time praying on weekends and meeting with like-minded men. Her name was Sabina, a beautiful name meaning "flower" in English. It took Alan weeks, but he finally came up with the courage to ask her out for a lunch date. The Imam had even encouraged him to ask her out. Sabina was quick to accept his invitation, and she was not embarrassed to tell Alan that she had been hoping that he would speak to her for quite a while. Alan told Sabina that he really wanted to spend some time with her, but he had limited time because of his busy schedule in medical school. They set a date for the following Saturday at one o'clock for a simple, light afternoon bite at a Harvard Square pasta and vegetarian establishment. Alan wondered why Sabina was always at the mosque on Sundays since the Imam had told him she worked on weekdays. He made a note to himself that he would have to ask her when they met.

Alan arrived early, and Sabina showed up a few minutes later at 1:00 on the dot. Her smile brightened up the already cloudless day. She was dressed modestly, wearing a hijab, allowing a full view of her face. Alan had only seen her in this attire at the mosque. The day was seasonally warm, and they decided to sit at one of the few outside tables. The restaurant was on a side street, so traffic noise was not an issue for a nice quiet chat. Alan and Sabina were both smiling and appeared very happy as they glanced at the menu. The two of them spoke little at first. Alan felt uncomfortable in social situations, and he placed his menu on the table.

"Sabina, do you drink alcoholic beverages?" Alan asked quietly.

"Well, to be honest, I do occasionally but I have never told my parents," she replied. "I think they would disown me. Do you?"

"Yes, I do, but not often or regularly. I was the product of a mixed marriage, and I sort of made my own decisions. My mom is Jewish, and my dad was Muslim. I found my way to Islam," Alan explained.

"Well, since we are speaking about our parents, mine are both from Iraq and came to the United States in 1980, when Saddam Hussein was gearing up for war against Iran and starting to use chemical weapons against his own people. My parents were both students. They immigrated to the United States and finished college. They then got jobs, married, had children, and here I am."

"I am glad you are here. It is nice to get to know you. I have very few friends here. I have lived here most of my life but have been a loner for some reason," Alan confessed.

"If we hang out together, you won't be a loner. We can take some walks, even go to a movie if this lunch works out. It will be nice to get to know you," Sabina said.

"Your offer sounds wonderful," Alan continued. "I have been very focused on my education for years now and really haven't socialized. I see an end in sight to the formal classwork, but things won't get easier. I have always done well and expect to get my medical degree in the spring."

"That is so exciting," Sabina said. "The Imam has told me about you and how you have worked so hard. Congratulations."

"I never really saw it as exciting, but it is. The next steps will be getting a residency, hopefully in Boston, and then moving forward in further training. I have always wanted to train in neurology," Alan added.

"Right now I am taking some courses at the community college," Sabina offered. "I don't have the money to attend full time, so I am slowly getting credits. I hope to eventually get enough credits so I can transfer to a full-time program and finally get my bachelor's degree and teaching certificate. I love children, and my dream is to teach young children."

"That is a great aspiration, and I hope you can do that," Alan replied. "Keep on working toward that goal. It sounds like wherever you live you can go to school and continue to gain credits. Are you planning to stay in this area?"

"I have nowhere to go at this time. My parents are here, in Revere, so they are close by. My brothers and sister are also in the area," she replied.

"I hope to stay here as well. It all depends on how the computer algorithm matches me to my choices of hospitals. I have requested certain residencies, but we will see what happens," Alan said.

"So, I am assuming you have a non-Muslim name since your mother was not a Muslim?" Sabina asked.

"Yes, true. And she took responsibility for raising me. My parents divorced when I was young. But my dad, who still teaches in Weston, always took me to his mosque every other weekend, and he tried to instill in me the key learnings from the Quran," Alan explained.

The waiter came by, and they each ordered salad platters, pitas, and ice tea for the table. Their conversation continued smoothly as if they had been long-time friends. Alan was not used to this, but for some reason he was expressive and his feelings just came flowing out. He told Sabina about his childhood, how he felt pulled between two opposite poles since his parents were from two different backgrounds. He suggested to Sabina that this might have been the beginning of some of his burdensome internal feelings. As Sabina responded empathetically, he wondered why he would speak like this on a first date. Is this any way to begin a relationship? Here he was at twenty-three years of age, graduating medical school, and he had almost no experience in dating. It felt good to finally speak with someone about his emotions after all these years. The first date might not have been the best time to unload, but Alan had a great time with Sabina and hoped she had as good a time as he did.

Their lunch ended in what seemed like minutes, but it had been two hours. Obviously, they had enjoyed their time together, and eating was not the most important aspect of the moment.

"So, will we see each other again?" Sabina asked. Alan breathed a sigh of relief.

"Every Sunday afternoon I usually come by the mosque," Alan teased. He hesitated a few seconds and then looked up from his drink of tea. "I would like to, if you want to get together. I really enjoyed our time." Alan glanced down at his watch.

"Do you realize we have been here two hours?" he added.

"Yes, it is great. Such a nice afternoon, and the hours just flowed in great conversation," she said, "I think that may mean something. Can we go for a walk?"

"No, I am sorry. The great time we spent means I have to study later into the night, and I now have to run, literally, to the hospital!" Alan said.

"I had a great time," Sabina said. "Maybe I will see you at the mosque."

"I did too. I will call you. I am leaving you this cash. I am sorry. Can you handle the check? I truly have to run, and I did have a great time. I will call you, Sabina," Alan said.

"Yes, I've got it. Bye, Alan." Sabina stood up, and Alan waved goodbye to his lunch date. He knew it was a huge sin to do anything else, as much as he would have liked to hold her hand or kiss her on the cheek before he left. But this was not possible now. He took off in a flash without looking back. The fourth year of medical school was a grind. As he ran off, he thought about how great this time was with Sabina but also how he regretted that he spent little time with his father, Ghaffar.

Ghaffar worked hard at his job as a physics teacher and eventually as head of the science department at Weston Country Preparatory School. He originally thought the school underutilized his talents, but with time, he found that was not true at all. Students and the school administrators loved his work. He marveled at the number of students passing through his classes who went on to great universities to further their education. Ghaffar could think of one in particular. The student followed up with graduate work in string theory at MIT, and his work was referenced around the world. That in and of itself made his teaching worthwhile. There were so many others—great teachers, surgeons, attorneys, and scientists—he had taught. He did not need his university setting and graduate students competing for his time and publications. His students' accomplishments rewarded him.

One of Ghaffar's biggest regrets was not spending enough time with Alan, his only son. Most of that time was imposed by the divorce, but he could have pushed for more time. Alan always seemed to be distant. Location was not the issue; they were always just a few miles apart. But something in Alan's personality did not allow for closeness. Alan had been a kind and peaceful person when younger. Now, when Ghaffar saw him on rare occurrences, he saw a hardened young man. Alan had an edge to him. Although Ghaffar knew Alan was preoccupied with his education and getting his medical degree as soon as possible, something just did not ring true for Ghaffar. Maybe it was his rearing by two disparate individuals. Maybe it was Alan's precociousness as a kid in school or his flat personality. He had finished high school at sixteen and college at twenty. His lack of maturity when entering college might have had something to do with his current state of being.

It was a sad day for Weston when, at the relatively young age of fifty-five, Ghaffar died. He had maintained his weight at two hundred pounds since he had started dating Leesa some twenty-five years earlier. He kept eating his healthy diet to stay in shape. Despite this, he collapsed one day during his lunchtime walk around the track. The basketball coach ran over to Ghaffar and administered CPR with the assistance of a student. The ambulance arrived about seven minutes later, and EMTs took over. He never regained consciousness and died before they reached the emergency room at Newton-Wellesley Hospital. It was a massive myocardial infarction. His lifestyle change had presumably not helped.

Leesa's move back to the DC area after Alan finished high school may not have been the best move for her or Alan. She lost total control of Alan as he went off to college, as most parents do. But now they were separated by four-hundred-plus miles. Alan couldn't drop in on a weekend if asked, not that he would have accepted. But she might have had some influence on his life. As it was, she had no clue of his comings and goings. The only thing she knew when he was in college was his interest in pursuing a career in medicine. She also knew that he became a deeply religious Muslim.

The years had not treated Leesa kindly. She had been a beautiful young woman, but she seemed to have aged more than her fifty years when the time came to bury her ex-husband. Living near her parents probably didn't help at all. They were still alive and in their early eighties, and they were an extra burden on their only child. They needed constant attention. Having no siblings was about the only thing that Leesa and Ghaffar had in common, and they carried on that tradition in the next generation, leaving Alan to fend for himself.

Leesa still needed to work, and shift work even as a head nurse was difficult. Furthermore, the commute into Georgetown from Bethesda became more difficult with every passing year. It was no wonder she carried herself with stooped shoulders, no makeup, and salt-and-very-little-pepper hair, overdue for a makeover.

Alan had seen his mother probably once a year for the last seven years, so the change in her appearance was gradual and he did not take notice. But anyone else familiar with Leesa just seven or eight years earlier would have been shocked at the change. Ghaffar and Leesa did not share any friends after their divorce, so there was no chance that she would see anyone at the funeral who would know her.

As required by Muslim tradition, the funeral was held the next day. Leesa flew up from Washington. She had remained in contact with Ghaffar. Their divorce was as amicable as any could have been. The two had managed to raise their son without many major issues, and Alan turned out to be, in their eyes, a good kid. He was the brightest of the bright and finishing his final year at Harvard Medical School in Boston. The other attendees at the funeral would be congregants of Ghaffar's mosque, many of the faculty and students from the school, and neighbors in Ghaffar's Boston suburban town of Framingham, where he had moved years ago. The service was held at the mosque and cemetery, conveniently located in Wayland, Massachusetts, not too far from Framingham, Boston, Weston, and all the towns in between. As per Muslim tradition, no females attended the burial ceremony. Leesa was not aware of this restriction but went along with the rule nonetheless.

Leesa and Alan stayed at Ghaffar's house in Framingham Center, near the state university. They observed the typical Muslim mourning period of three days at his home, but Alan was in the final days of his last year at medical school. He stayed at the home for a couple of hours in the morning and came back in the evening. Since Leesa was not a Muslim, the mourning by Ghaffar's Muslim friends and fellow parishioners was restricted to the times that Alan was present. Alan was very saddened by his father's untimely death. He wanted his father to see him graduate from medical school in two months' time. And in time, he wanted his father to understand his new core values and his long-term goals as a devoted Muslim.

The house was open to visitors, which was not a comfortable experience for Leesa. She was upset for her son at having lost his father, but at this point she felt like a house sitter and dishwasher as mourners brought food and came to visit Alan.

Alan arrived on the last day of public mourning at nine in the evening and received about ten mourners. It exhausted him. By the time the group had comforted him, prayed, and partaken in some food, it was ten thirty. They all left by eleven. As the door closed, Leesa went down the stairs to greet her son and clean up for the last time. She would then close up the house in the morning and return to Washington. Ghaffar's debts were not certain, so the status of the house would remain in limbo until the will went through the probate process.

"Alan, I know it has been a horrible week for you," Leesa began. "Losing your father will hurt for a long time, and you will never forget him. He will always be a piece of you."

"Mother, whatever you say now won't help," Alan replied. "Neither of you have been in my life very much for the past eight years. I am not the same person I was at sixteen when I went to college, and Dad did not know me very well even though we lived in the same city. We were on totally different planes. I love you both, although it is difficult to tell you."

"That is the most I've heard you say in years," Leesa declared.

"Well, I have been busy building my own life, and before that deciding who I am and what type of life I would live. I am going to bed. Have a good trip back. Good night, and thank you for being here for me and Dad," he concluded.

Alan stepped forward and around the kitchen island and hugged his mother. It was, as she tried to recall, the first time in probably five years that he had showed any reaction or love toward her. He then turned and jogged up the stairs two at a time. Leesa sat on one of the barstools at the island and broke down. She didn't even know if it was a true hug of tenderness from her son or something he felt he had to do. As tears streamed down her face, she also could not recall the last time she had let herself have an emotional reaction. It was not a cathartic response. She was lost. She had long since lost a friend and husband, and now her son had basically told her he was not anything like he used to be. Who was he? She thought she had given him a nourishing home for the first sixteen years of his life. Was it the lack of a father figure in the home? He had Ghaffar in the same town and saw him every two weekends. *Did I not give him direction?* she wondered. *Should he have gone to religious school? Well, it is too late now. He is twenty-four now and will be a doctor in two months. I guess what will be will be.* She prayed that she could be at his graduation in June.

Leesa turned to the dining area to clear the platters of unconsumed food. It was all going in the garbage disposal. Another hour's work and the place would be clean and ready to close up in the morning.

Alan's last months in medical school couldn't have been more difficult. As much as he wanted to spend some extra time with Sabina, he couldn't. His last rotation was ob-gyn, and it was grueling. It was not intellectually demanding, but it was the long hours and the unpredictability of the next page from the labor and delivery department. Now was the home stretch in a long run to his degree. It was also not good timing when Alan's father had died suddenly that day while walking at school. Alan grieved alone for the man who introduced him to his faith and was his spiritual guide as a young boy.

So it was no wonder he had no time to see Sabina. Furthermore, he had not been to the mosque in several weeks. A week after Ghaffar's death, Sabina finally called Alan. She had not wanted to be aggressive.

"Alan, this is Sabina," her message began. "I have not heard from you or seen you for several weeks. Please call me. I hope nothing is wrong." She sounded quite upset and had thought about leaving the message a week ago, having asked other parishioners in the Cambridge mosque if they had seen Alan. No one had, but she was never sure about the truth. She knew many were radicalized, and truth was never easy to come by there.

His father had prayed at a suburban mosque, but word about Ghaffar's death had not gotten out to the greater Boston area. Alan called Sabina the next morning after he got off from work.

"Sabina, it is Alan. I'm so sorry for not calling you," he said. "My father died last week. This has been a terrible few weeks. I should have called you even before that."

"Alan, I am so sorry. I had no idea that your father was sick or close to death," Sabina said.

"He was not. He died unexpectedly of a massive heart attack. He is with Allah now," Alan replied. "Let us get together again soon. I have some good news on top of this bad news. Since we last talked, I learned that I will stay in Boston for my next year of training."

"That is wonderful to hear. I hope we can get to know each other better," Sabina said. "I have been working hard with the Imam on several papers he is writing on radical responses, and the time seems to go very quickly."

"Yes, let us talk again later. It has been a very hectic two weeks with my father's passing, and I am falling behind on my clinical work."

"I will text you in a couple of days. Please answer me," Sabina said.

"I will," Alan replied.

The following Sunday afternoon Alan spent one hour at the Cambridge mosque and met with the radical Imam. This Imam, who was now well published, had become an inspiration for terror activities. As such, his ideology had begun to draw many people to his mosque who believed in his radical ideas. It was likely that this mosque would in time be a threat to national security.

It was not unusual for Alan and others to meet with the elderly Imam shortly after the midday prayer. This group had, as most outsiders knew, become a radical Islamic group, and members complained that they were often watched by or followed by government types. This day seemed different, however. The Imam wanted to spend some one-on-one time with Alan. Alan had let everyone know that he would be in the Boston area for probably one or two more years. After that, his postgraduate medical education could take him anywhere in the country.

When they met, the Imam complimented Alan, telling him he had become a very intelligent and special person during the many years he had known him. He had grown from a teenager to a young man who now grasped the seriousness of the plight of Muslims worldwide. The Imam told Alan that he wanted to keep in contact with him since he could be a very important person in developing key strategies for jihad. There were plans for an American caliphate, and this mosque would be integral in the planning. Also, the Imam told Alan that he had many contacts in the Middle East and would share them with Alan if he were to travel there in the future. They spoke of Alan's lifetime goals and how he could use his education to further the goals of the jihad. The Imam turned the conversation toward militant jihad and reminded Alan that it was useful to consider that the funding for such activities would be available, and he continued to remind Alan that bright young men like him could be aided and funded to carry out important missions. Alan felt enthusiastic after their meeting and promised to continue to study hard. He thanked the Imam and also promised to return to pray as often as he could. He told him that he would see Sabina, so he would come to the mosque often. With that, he hugged the Imam and left with a smile on his face.

Alan had consolidated his view of radical Islam many times in recent years. The Ayatollah Ali Khamenei issued his fatwa in 2012, indicating that all Jewish people worldwide must be destroyed. Further, because Israel was a primary danger to Iran because of its nuclear capability, Iran justified its position for destroying the State of Israel. With these recent words in mind, Alan's lifelong thinking and learnings about Muslims and particularly Palestinian people were coming into focus. A new fatwa by the Grand Mufti of Jerusalem confirmed that he was on the right track. The Mufti issued a statement saying that if Muslims were caught selling land or homes to Jews, they would be killed. The fatwa clarified that Jews were enemies of Muslims. He further said it would be a betrayal of Allah to make any such transaction. Of course the fatwa was not new, as it was just the same as the position of Hamas.

Alan revealed details to his colleagues of his long and slow romance of Sabina. In point of fact, it had been two years of on-again, off-again dating mostly, hindered by his heavy schedule of intense training in internal medicine and followed by laboratory work in a world-renowned genetics research group at Brigham and Women's Hospital. Alan had a "love at first sight" feeling when he first met Sabina, but it turns out that Sabina did not. How could Alan understand these things or know his true feelings? He focused on his studies and spent his free time on Muslim radicalism. It was difficult to put Sabina into a box. But as Alan matured and his desires grew, he tried to make more time for himself and for her. In Alan's year of postgraduate training, which was focused in the laboratory, he spent more time with Sabina. Halfway through the year, Alan took her to the Cambridge cafe where they had their first date. He had taken the afternoon off to spend the day with her.

It did not take Alan long to get to the point he wanted to make this beautiful day. He came straight out and asked her.

"Sabina, will you be my wife and life partner?"

She was shocked but also overcome with joy. She thought he would never ask her to marry him.

"Alan, I would be so blessed to spend my life with you," she said. "Yes, yes. After these past several months, I know you are dedicated to me. I will be your wife. I love you with all my heart."

"Sabina, I know I have not been very attentive to you or listened to all your needs. But please believe me—I will. You are the love of my life, and I want you with me wherever our lives take us," Alan stressed.

"Of course. That is what I want, and I hope you will want a family as well," she said.

"Yes. We can work on that. But you must know that we may not be in Boston," he told her. "My next step of training is a three-year neurology residency. It could be here, or it could be in California. Anywhere in America."

"Yes, your work is of top priority. We can always travel back here to see my family," Sabina said.

"It won't be easy, but you will make new friends wherever we go. You are so sweet and loveable." Alan concluded, "And I may even get my residency right here. Let's celebrate. We will be married. That's number one for today. Everything else is secondary. I do not understand what has to be done for the wedding. I guess we have to set a date. But before that you and I will go to a jeweler downtown to pick out your engagement ring."

"Aren't you supposed to do that?" Sabina asked.

"Maybe," Alan replied. "But I want your hands there with me. How can I buy the best-shaped diamond for you without having your beautiful hands with me?"

Tears of joy streamed down both of Sabina's cheeks. She could never remember a time in her life when she was any happier. Alan hugged her tightly as she beamed.

"One last thing: after we tell your parents, I will leave all the difficult stuff like the wedding planning to you and your mother. Is that fair?" Alan joked.

"Ha!" Sabina responded. "You're not going to get out of it that easily. Now let's get out of here and go downtown like you promised."

They got up from the table and headed to the T to cross the river into Boston.

It was not long after he had asked Sabina to marry him that Alan heard about his next move. Johns Hopkins Hospital had accepted him into their neurology residency program. This was one of his top choices. So many top doctors were at Hopkins, plus there were many opportunities beyond a residency that could lead to long-term commitment to the city. Further, the Imam in Cambridge had told him he had connections to a mosque in Baltimore that would be useful for Alan. Alan called Sabina immediately at the mosque to tell her the news.

"Sabina, I now know where we will be going in July," Alan said.

"Well, tell me already!" she shouted.

"Baltimore, the Johns Hopkins Hospital," Alan responded.

"Are you happy?" Sabina asked.

"Oh, yes. This is one of the best hospitals that could have selected me. I am thrilled." Alan added, "I hope you are all right with this."

"Of course. This is your career, Alan. It is not a world away from here, and I want the best for us," she said.

"I am so happy for us. Thank you. Let us celebrate later tonight. I must finish my lab work so we can plan our last month here in Boston and our move to Baltimore. I love you," Alan said.

"Goodbye." Sabina hung up her phone.

Sabina was thrilled to be sharing the rest of her life with Alan. She told her Imam in Cambridge the news, and he was very happy for her and said that the mosque in Baltimore would be a great place for her to continue her work with him. He would place a call to the Imam there. She was pleased to hear that as well since she could continue her work with and forge a better relationship between the two mosques.

When Alan asked her to marry him, she was not imagining a move. Now she was getting married and embarking on an adventure to a place she'd never been. She was moving to Maryland with Alan as he continued his career. In her whole life, she had never traveled in the country any farther than New Hampshire and Maine. Now a whole new world would be opened up to her. She had never even contemplated living anywhere outside Boston. Meeting Alan has been such a life-changing event. Baltimore was known to those in the know as Charm City. It had undergone a major renaissance in the last ten years, and the downtown harbor area was the place to be. That would have to wait for a bit, however. The new staff needed to stay close by in housing just off Broadway across from the hospital. Beyond Alan's three-year commitment to the neurology discipline, Hopkins, and the city of Baltimore, if things went well he hoped to continue his training in the neurovirology division.

Before any move to Maryland could be made, the marriage that had been planned by Sabina and her mother was to take place. It was all arranged for the middle of May. The couple had been engaged for several months before the wedding. Even though Alan's father had died in April, sufficient time had passed according to Muslim custom for a wedding celebration to occur.

Sabina wore the beautiful diamond ring that they had bought together months earlier. She dressed in a traditional, stark white, ornately beaded, high-neck hijab.

The wedding was a simple ceremony with family and just a few friends in attendance. Alan did not even see fit to invite his mother. This was a Muslim wedding and totally foreign to his mother, with whom he had little if any relationship. After the ceremony, the small group convened for a traditional meal.

The next six weeks flew past. There was just three days' time for a quick escape "honeymoon" in New York City. Alan had little free time as he finished his research activities before starting his residency. New York opened Sabina's eyes to a new world. Boston was a large city, but she had imagined nothing like the crowds as they exited Penn Station, the hustle and bustle of the sidewalks, the incessant horns, and the towering skyscrapers of the city.

The not-so-distant past of 9/11 continued to hang over New Yorkers as the couple walked out of Penn Station. Several people looked askance at them, and several policemen in and outside the station seemed to study them closely. Alan took Sabina's hand and got to the taxi line as quickly as they could. They were not going to walk now with bags in hand. Who knows? The police might have thought they were carrying weapons or bombs. In just a few minutes, they grabbed a car to the Plaza Hotel on Central Park South. After checking in to the most iconic hotel in New York City, Alan and Sabina both looked into each other's eyes when they finally made it to their room. After all the commotion, they felt relaxed after a hectic and sometimes intimidating trip to this city. Although Alan had seen and been the object of prejudice, Sabina had more or less been isolated by her family. Alan turned to her and said, "I will protect you for the rest of my life. That is my duty. I love you. Do not let a few looks or taunts by crazy bigots ruin our short honeymoon."

"I won't, Alan. I love you with all my heart," she said. She embraced him, and he hugged her tightly.

They both took off their lightweight jackets and then embraced again and kissed passionately. Alan started to unbutton her blouse as she pulled her midcalf skirt down to the floor and kicked off her shoes. Sabina took off her hajib and finished the job on her blouse while Alan took off his shirt, shoes, and pants. They then both dove onto the luxurious queen-sized bed. As Alan removed Sabina's bra and panties, he marveled at the silky smoothness of her skin all over her body. Her whole body was sensuous to the touch. Alan had been with Sabina before, but today seemed different. There were no distractions. Sabina took down Alan's underpants, and his erection was incomparable to any she had seen on him before. And she had never seen any other man. She grabbed his penis and put it in her mouth. In the meantime, Alan was working his magic with several of his fingers on her clitoris and in her vagina. He heard her moaning as he was rocking in her mouth. With that noise, he knew he could not last much longer. He gently pulled out of her mouth and gently entered her vagina, missionary style. She let out a pleasing sigh when he entered her, and they rocked back and forth for at most two minutes when Alan could not wait any longer. They both came at the same time, something that would be an ongoing positive feature of their marriage.

Alan and Sabina planned to do what most visitors to New York City planned that evening: dinner and a play. The play was an easy choice, and the Plaza Hotel could always get tickets to the best shows. They were on their way to see *Wicked*, the number-one show on Broadway. But where to go for dinner was another matter. Alan thought they might want to try the Jewish deli scene just for the experience, but Sabina was not interested in that whatsoever.

After another lovemaking session in the late afternoon, they showered together and got dressed for the evening. They headed down the elevator and crossed the lobby, where they asked the concierge for recommendations near the theater for dinner. He suggested Orso. It had a nice menu of fish, chicken, and steak and was near the theaters. The restaurant had been there for close to ten years, so they must be doing something right, he said. Alan and Sabina agreed on a 6:15 reservation. They stepped out to the front, and the doorman whistled for a cab to get them downtown.

That evening and the next two days flew by for Alan and Sabina. Alan could not remember a time when he had nothing on his mind other than the present time, Sabina, and himself. Nothing else mattered in the world. As he looked back on his life many times during these three days in New York City, he smiled and felt happy inside. At no other time in his life had he felt like he did these days. He hoped that Sabina felt the same way. She had lived a more sheltered life than him and probably had other pleasurable days and experiences. He knew she did not have the difficulties Alan had as a youth or the troubles he had of being caught between the two diverse cultures of his parents. When the long weekend was over, they headed back to Boston on the train. Sabina fell asleep with her head on his shoulder as they zipped through the Connecticut landscape, which no longer had much of the old tobacco farms. It was now a landscape of homes and strip malls sprouting from the soil of the New Haven suburbs. It had been rich ground for cigar wrapper tobacco, grown in one of the state's fertile areas irrigated by the Quinnipiac River. The Amtrak train headed into Rhode Island and finally into South Station in Boston, and Sabina and Alan arrived home. This would be home for just a few weeks until they made their move to Baltimore and began their life together.

After returning that night from New York, they relaxed in Alan's apartment, and then planning for the move began. He had just a few experiments left on his project that he was going to complete in the next two weeks. That would give the new couple a solid week to ten days to move to Baltimore. Since it was only a one-day drive from Boston, they would have lots of time to get oriented and enjoy themselves in their new city before Alan would be working a grind of a schedule as a first-year resident. Sabina even talked about finding a job at the Baltimore mosque, similar to what she was doing in Boston. Alan did not say anything but was concerned about his new wife making her way in a new and strange city, especially in the political climate as it existed.

"Maybe something like that would be available," Alan said. "There will be a lot of new people to meet in our same situation, moving from all over the country. I think it might be fun for you to take a little time off and make some friends in our new home."

"You are right. What am I thinking?" Sabina agreed "I should stay around the home and see what is going on in our new city. There will be plenty of time to do new things or build a career. Maybe I should take some more college courses."

"Let us just see how things go. If something jumps up in your face, look at it," Alan responded.

The rest of their conversation went on and on about timelines and packing clothes and their wedding gifts. They would pick up anything they needed upon arrival in Baltimore. They had one car, Sabina's old blue Volvo wagon, and that would do the trick for now. The car was ten years old and in great mechanical condition, but it definitely needed another set of tires. Alan planned to buy a new set before their trip to Baltimore. After an hour or so of charting their course, they had their game plan and were ready for their trip at the end of June. The excitement on Sabina's face could be read from across the room. That expression didn't leave her face for weeks.

The next two weeks flew by as Alan finished up his lab work and summarized his experiments for his mentor. He knew that the extra year of work in the lab would pay off not only now in experience but in the future as he would try to procure grant money for his academic career. An academic career would be just the mechanism Alan would require to have the freedom to move with impunity around the country and world to accomplish goals that were just starting to mature in his mind.

Once in Baltimore, the newlyweds shopped to fill up their small apartment off Broadway near the hospital. Alan did not pay much attention to what Sabina was buying. The hospital had supplied most of the furniture they needed. Sabina and Alan shopped for everything else that goes with everyday living, and that kept Sabina busy while Alan's mind drifted to larger issues. He paid close attention to his wife, of course, and but she was not aware of what laid deep in the mind of this brilliant physician scientist's brain.

July 1 could not come fast enough for Alan. He began his residency in neurology on July 1, 2007, at the ripe old age of twenty-five. Alan was younger by far than any of the other previous residents who had started the program at Hopkins. Most of his contemporaries had still been in medical school at his age. The days passed quickly, and being at one of the top institutions in the world, Alan had an opportunity to see and learn from many unusual cases. Patients who could not be diagnosed or treated elsewhere in the world were often flown to Hopkins. Furthermore, the rich and famous wanted to be seen by the best, so they would come this facility. The hospital's reputation preceded it.

The weeks turned into months and the months into years, and after two years Alan knew he wanted to continue in the field of neurology. When he had some precious time off, Alan found a mosque in Baltimore, where he connected with the local Imam. In fact, Sabina told Alan she had first found the mosque weeks earlier in alignment with her goal of finding a job. It was on the other side of town and unfortunately not in an area where Alan would want Sabina to travel by herself. During Alan's meetings at the mosque with the Imam and fellow worshippers, he learned of a close connection to his Cambridge mosque. After several discussions and a call from his former Imam, it was clear that they were aligned politically and had similar aspirations. Alan brought some new ideas and insights to the group that he had yet to put on the table. He agreed to allow Sabina to volunteer at the Baltimore mosque during the daytime. However, Sabina had been working there a couple of days a week for a full year and a half already without Alan's knowledge.

Alan met with the chairman of neurology and the chief of neurovirology at the end of the second year of his residency. They told him that he was doing incredibly well and would be appointed chief resident for his final year of residency. This was a huge feather in his cap, and Alan was extremely proud of his accomplishment. He spoke with the chief of neurovirology, indicating his desire to work in that lab as a fellow for a year or two after his residency. The chief told him that they receive many applications for these positions each year, and he would be in the pool of applicants like everyone else. But Alan might have an inside track given his laboratory experience and excellent clinical credentials. There would be two openings in the upcoming year and possibly a third depending on job opportunities for the current fellows.

Just after he heard about his chief residency appointment, Alan took Sabina down to the Inner Harbor for lunch on his day off. They then walked around the pavilion and crossed the street into a high-rise area.

"Where are we going?" asked Sabina.

"I wanted to show you a condominium that I think we deserve!" responded Alan.

They walked into a model on the first floor of a building with a huge sign that read "Harbor Moon and Marina." It was right across the street from the Inner Harbor, and boat slips were already in place labeled for the community.

"We don't have and can't afford a boat, Alan," Sabina said.

"We don't have to buy a slip," he said. "That's extra. We are just looking at a place to live. Let's just look. We've been basically living in a dormitory for two years. I think it is time to move up and out."

"I agree, but I may have to work a real job. I am just volunteering," she said.

They walked into the office and were greeted immediately by a nicely dressed, middle-aged woman who could not wait to show them the plans for the tower and the condos for sale.

"Good afternoon. I am Jan Gates, manager of sales for Harbor Moon. Welcome to the newest and greatest living accommodations in the city of Baltimore," she said. "Whom do I have the pleasure of meeting?"

"Hello, Jan. I am Alan Mazer, and this is my wife Sabina," Alan answered, giving no indication of his medical profession.

"Well, welcome again. Let me show you the scale here on the floor of our building. The structure is totally complete. We are now finishing each unit to each owner's specifications. Please take a few steps over here. On this table you can see our location relative to the Inner Harbor. Let me ask you first—are you from Baltimore?"

"We are living here in the city in an apartment," Alan responded.

"We would like to someday relocate," Sabina added and understood immediately the way this was being played by Alan.

"As you know, Baltimore is a very unusual city with its assorted neighborhoods. But in this building and others nearby, we expect this to be a very cosmopolitan area," Jan explained. "We expect the people moving in here to be a very mixed group from around the country and world. I am sure that you must know that, having lived in Baltimore—how long have you been here?"

"We have been here for two years now but plan to be here for many more," Alan added. "I guess you assumed we were not from Baltimore."

"No, no assumptions in this business."

"We are from Massachusetts, near Boston," Sabina said.

"Wonderful!" Jan exclaimed. "As you know there is great shopping, restaurants, and museums right nearby, across the street from the Harbor Moon complex. The Orioles' and Ravens' stadiums are just a few blocks from here. If you have guests coming to town, there are plenty of hotels nearby as well. You can jump in a water taxi and get to so many places. The museums and national aquarium are just a short ride away. Are you boaters?"

"No, no time for that," Alan replied.

"Well, that is true for so many young couples, but as time goes on, you never know. You are right across from the harbor, and in time, you could have your own sailboat or motor craft and head right out to Chesapeake Bay." Jan continued, "A separate benefit of our complex is our own marina. You could own your own boat slip in the future. Or if not, find a friend who has one!"

"These amenities are all great," Alan said. "Jan, I think we would like to see a couple of models before going much further."

"Of course. Tell me, what you are you looking for—two, three, or four bedrooms?"

"I think we need at least two bedrooms and an office area," said Sabina.

"I agree," said Alan.

Sabina smiled, and they followed Jan hand in hand to the elevator. The ten-story building was L-shaped, and most of the units on one side of the L were completed and occupied. The first and second floors of the other side of the L were not yet occupied and held the gymnasium and some model units on the second floor. They rode the elevator there, and Jan first took them into a large unit that overlooked Light Street and the harbor.

"This is one of the larger units," Jan explained. "I am just showing you this so you have an idea of what is at the top of the scale in terms of square footage. This unit is the same size as we go up all the floors and increases in price as you get to the ninth floor. The tenth floor has the much larger penthouse-type units. This is a four-bedroom unit with twenty-four hundred square feet. From there, we go down in square footage. The base price on this is $679,000. This fully outfitted apartment comes with all the appliances and your choices of finishing touches. And, by the way, you should know that unlike most of Baltimore, this area of the city is very cosmopolitan and the up-and-coming place to live."

"I think we need to look at smaller units, like we spoke about earlier—maybe the two bedrooms plus a den," Alan said.

"Of course. I just wanted to show you the largest model on the lower level," Jan said. "This real estate can only grow in value over time given the limited space in this section of town. The next unit is a three bedroom. It has one room that has a limited side view of the harbor; the other windows from the other bedrooms look out upon the courtyards, pool, and greenery areas. Very lovely. Let's walk into this unit. It has two full bathrooms. The dining room and living room are one gigantic room leading out to a patio. This unit is twenty-one hundred square feet."

"What is the base price of this unit?" Sabina asked.

"There really is no base price. It includes everything—all your finishing, the builder includes everything, and you get your choice. This model at the second- to fourth-floor level is $549,000. The cost per square foot is a little less than the larger model on the same floor. There are more refinements in the building in the larger model, but not many," Jan summarized.

"This is getting closer to our affordability level," Alan said. "What's the other model you had in mind?"

"There is one more—a two bedroom and a den. The den has no window," Jan said.

"Well, let's see that one as well while we are here," Sabina said, "but it doesn't sound like the den is a great place to put a desk."

They moved down the hall to the next unit. Both bedrooms with windows had nice views of the pool, and the porch had room for two small chairs and a table. It was not a very large unit.

"So what is the square footage for this unit?" asked Alan.

"This is 1,730 square feet," Jan indicated.

"Who would want such a small unit?" Sabina wondered aloud.

"This has been very popular with many of our older clients who now have two homes, one here for the summer and another in a warmer location for the winter," said Jan.

"Jan, thank you for your time. Can we please have your card and a brochure? We have just started to look at homes, but this looks like something of high interest," Alan said.

Jan handed her card and glossy printed materials to the couple. They took all the paperwork and gave their names to Jan. Heading out the door, they both looked back at the towers and wondered to themselves how they might like life at the harbor. Alan was thinking it would be a great refuge from the hospital environment. He could be alone with his thoughts and peer upon the waters while contemplating the rush of ideas that often come to him. Here, he would be inspired and could take his thoughts and let them incubate undisturbed.

Sabina had different thoughts, of a family. The two of them had hinted to each other that it was time. Alan's career was on a good track, and she was ready to be a mother. She stood and thought about that extra bedroom and knew in her heart that Alan was thinking it would be for the growing family. If she had only known or had seen any hints of Alan's dual personality or the twisted thoughts permeating Alan's mind, she would probably run.

Alan was extremely pleased to be given the opportunity to be the chief resident in his final year of the program in neurology at Hopkins. It would be extremely taxing to be on his game and responsible for all the residents as they made their way through the program. He would have to advocate for and not just train the new crop of physicians entering the program. It would be about putting his stamp on their education but also about being the best he could be as a physician at the same time. Besides his teaching and organizational roles, he would continue to have a huge patient load. Alan wondered how he would have any time to live his Muslim life. He was just developing a close relationship with the Imam in Baltimore and was developing unique and radical ideas. It puzzled him how difficult it was to get into his inner circle but then assumed it might be part of a greater plan. He would be patient, as he had worked hard in the past to get to this place.

Alan's third year as chief resident started to fly by. He and Sabina got to enjoy an occasional day off and always spent their time doing things around the city. One place Sabina loved was the Baltimore Zoo. It was usually not crowded with tourists, so Alan and Sabina took casual walks and lunched on hillsides at the park. They often took time to visit the exhibits as well. One day, after Alan opened a bottle of wine, which he allowed himself on occasion, he offered some to Sabina. She also would drink alcohol at times.

"Alan, I don't think I should have any wine today," Sabina said.

"Are you not feeling well?" Alan asked.

"I am feeling just fine. I think I may be having a baby," she blurted out.

Alan shouted with excitement. "Why haven't you said anything before today?"

"I am only three weeks late, that's why. But you know I am very regular," she answered.

"Let's pack up our stuff. There's a pharmacy over on Northern Avenue. I want you to get a pregnancy test. Come on," Alan said excitedly.

"I have waited three weeks. Come on. We can have a nice lunch, have a walk, and then go home for the 'big test,'" Sabina said.

"Yes. Let us have a pretest celebration. I will drink to a positive test," Alan joked.

"No joking. That is bad luck. Don't even talk about it," Sabina said.

"Okay, you're not pregnant. You sounded like my grandmother from Potomac for a moment there," Alan said.

"That's funny." Sabina noted, "You barely ever mention your family. Someday you must tell me about them."

"I will, but not today. I am in a good mood," Alan responded.

Alan went to Sunday midmorning prayer at the mosque on one of his off days in January. Sabina was over four months pregnant and doing very well. She was continuing her volunteer work at a local shelter supported by the mosque, helping in the kitchen a few days a week and also working at the mosque. It was enough to keep her busy but was wearing on her body as she got into her second trimester. After the midmorning prayer, Alan met with the Imam. He had kept him abreast of his heavy load at the hospital and the reason for his lack of participation at meetings. Alan explained that he hoped to stay in Baltimore for the rest of his career and that he had recently applied for a fellowship that he hoped would allow him to continue his education at the Johns Hopkins School of Medicine and Hospital. Further, he told the Imam of the good family news—Sabina was four months pregnant. He wanted to raise his family in Baltimore, work closely with the Imam and his mosque, and develop plans that would further the jihad. He also had hoped to buy a new condominium in the downtown area and was hoping to scrape together the down payment. The Imam knew what an asset Alan was to the community and the struggle in general, so he told Alan that resources would be available for him and his family and to not worry. He wanted Alan to work with him and his congregants in the future. Anything that he could do to help him would be a pleasure. Alan was extremely grateful and thanked the Imam. He left his office and then attended their meeting for the first time in many months. It was a good feeling to be among friends—real friends.

Alan's final year in his residency program continued to go extremely well, and it was just one month later, in February, that Alan learned he would stay on as a fellow in the division of neurovirology, one of Alan's dreams from years ago. He had the opportunity to work with many skilled clinicians in the department of neurology, and he was even recognized as one of them. Now he would train and work in one of the best labs in the world. Even though Alan had spent over a year in the lab of a top scientist in Boston, it was only a tease. He did well in the neurology program and was thrilled to continue working there as a fellow. As an undergrad he had heard about the famous neurovirology and immunology division, exploring and unearthing infections of the brain and epidemics around the globe. The chief of this lab, known worldwide as the Father of Neurovirology, had established the group. Staying in Baltimore and working in this department would more than make up for the fact that he used to be able to walk to Fenway Park from his lab and the hospital just off Brookline and Longwood Avenues in Boston. Although he might miss the Red Sox and the shouts of the fans over the left field wall, he wouldn't miss his treatment by many of the Bostonians. That prejudice remained seared deep in his memory. Alan did think that prejudice was one trigger for his radical thinking.

He continued to be a devoted physician and always asked the right questions. He earned his stripes and did well as a young fellow. Given his background as a scientist, Alan had the intellect to solve clinical problems and knew he had the acumen for a research track as well. He then applied to the National Institutes of Health for a grant to study a little-known viral infection in Egypt and Sudan. It was an arbovirus, one carried by mosquitoes and birds, but at this time it was not causing a significant problem in humans. No one knew for sure what virus caused the local problem, but slowly Usutu virus was firing up. Usutu had been discovered years before in Africa but was now slowly winding its way across the globe. It had not caused many problems but was popping up in Europe and elsewhere. It had the potential to heat up quickly, just like other mosquito-borne viruses, like West Nile virus had a few years back. A major outbreak was possible if mosquito control in the affected areas was not taken seriously and monitored carefully.

Alan was forewarned that applying for a grant was no guarantee that he would be funded, especially with recent cuts in the Federal National Institutes of Health budget. But he was always quite sure of himself and seemed to not be worried. He was not the type to be envious of others if he were not to receive a grant. But others were an immediate problem; they were his competition. Other faculty members in the neurovirology group were also applying for funding from the same source. The timing of the funding was also critical. If he were to do any research and not just see patients and teach, a grant was a requirement. With no grant, there would be no money, no research, and no permanent faculty position. He had big ambitions and could not accomplish them as a clinician. He needed the resources of the university and his research. He was given only a temporary faculty-level appointment at Hopkins for the purpose of applying for the grant, but that would all go away if he did not get the award. Alan submitted the grant on March 1.

Alan worked hard all year. By October of the second year of his fellowship, the Virology Study Section of the National Institute of Neurologic and Communicative Disorders and Stroke reviewed his proposal and gave his grant a high priority. They were highly critical of the young scientist; his proposal was weak in certain areas, and the goals were unlikely to be completed in its three-year award period. But during the time between when his proposal had been submitted and the committee reviewed the grant, three children in Aswan, Egypt, developed severe encephalopathy after apparent infection with a mosquito-borne virus. His timing could not have been better. The committee reviewed the grant again and gave it a higher priority than it had in its study section meeting. Alan received his first grant. He was now guaranteed a continued faculty position at the university. He thought he could breathe easier.

Government grants were not the only source of funding for faculty. Alan learned quickly that the biotechnology and pharmaceutical industries had deep pockets for both clinical and basic research. As he learned his way around this world, he started to speak with some of his colleagues about the best way to attract money from these sources. He started by going on the lecture circuit. Unlike the old days, when faculty would present their findings to their friends at other institutions, it was now reasonable to give presentations at biotechnology companies and foundations. Such events could spark interest in one's research and gain monetary support.

Alan had just finished giving a Friday afternoon seminar to the research department at Immunoviratherapeutics Inc. in McClean, Virginia, a suburb of Washington, DC. They had invited him to one of the company's monthly meetings in which the organization tried to engage outside investigators and hear about their ongoing research. Alan had just begun his work on arboviruses in the Middle East. He was a young investigator, now an assistant professor, and he was hoping to get more information from the company and make new connections that could help his career. The company had no ongoing programs on mosquito-borne or tick-borne viruses, but it was possible that they would delve into this arena in the future, Alan reasoned. These viruses always seemed to pop up and give rise to major problems in tropical and subtropical areas around the globe. They were the focus of his research during his fellowship, and this was a local company that would be worth wooing.

It was a small crowd of twenty-five to thirty people, but most seemed quite interested in his presentation. Or it could have been the Friday free beer and chips and the end of the workweek that brought these folks in to hear him. A few people lingered after his presentation, and one in particular asked several questions. Ashraf Khaleed asked if he could help Alan carry his computer and briefcase out to the car, as he was leaving now as well. Alan accepted his offer. At his car, Ashraf told Alan that he recognized him.

"Dr. Mazer, I believe I have seen you before. My name is Ashraf Khaleed. I live in Falls Church," Ashraf said. "I have worked here at Immunoviratherapeutics on developing point mutations in viral vaccine candidates for several years. I attend on occasion the Islamic Center of Inner Baltimore. I have relatives in Baltimore, and I think I have seen you there. Am I mistaken?" asked Ashraf.

"You are correct," Alan said. "It probably surprises you that you have seen me at the mosque, with a name like Mazer. But, yes, I am a practicing Muslim and have been since I was a teenager. I attend several mosques in the area. It is nice to make your acquaintance and to know that we are brothers and have a common interest," observed Alan.

"Dr. Mazer," he replied, "I am happy that we can discuss virology and other topics along with the Quran."

"Ashraf, I would like to invite you to visit my lab anytime you wish. I am just building up my research group, and you never know when there might be a place for a solid worker with experience in the field. Or just someone to talk over new ideas with."

Ashraf smiled and was extremely excited that he had the courage to approach Dr. Mazer after the presentation.

"Dr. Mazer, I will definitely take you up on your offer," Ashraf proclaimed. "I am in Baltimore often, and it would be an honor to meet with you and your staff. It has been a grind sometimes at the company. But do not get me wrong—I enjoy my work here."

"Ashraf, just give me a call a day ahead of time and we will get together. I have to run to beat at least some of the northbound rush hour. Thanks again. It was a pleasure to meet you."

ALAN'S CAREER EXPLODES
2012

Alan was just launching his academic career. He was the newly appointed assistant professor at the prestigious Johns Hopkins University School of Medicine. A young man who was a product of a mixed Iranian-Jewish marriage, had grown up with little supervision, and had to be strongly self-motivated now found himself at the upper echelon of the academic world. The fact that Alan represented two totally diverse selves did not seem to interfere with his life. He now began to use his medical and scientific acumen to not only help patients but also develop radical terrorist strategies to inflict serious harm. It was rather astonishing that this did not seem to faze Alan. His plans had not yet been fully conceived, but they were incubating. He had a personality defect for sure but not a clinical split personality. At all times, he believed he was using his intellect and training for the betterment of society.

The ending of his fellowship and the beginning of a faculty role brought on more pressures than he could imagine. One grant was hardly enough to run a lab, buy equipment, and hire an assistant. Alan found himself in his office more than he wished, writing proposals to government and private granting agencies to fund his projects. This was the game that had to be played; however, he hoped it would get easier in time as he improved his skills.

Alan also knew he had at least two other jobs. He now was a family man, or close to it. Sabina was due to give birth in August, and as a surprise for both of them, two children were on the way; twins were in the offing. She was a very happy woman, especially knowing that her family would be growing in size, but Sabina was not enjoying the additional forty pounds in the middle of a hot and humid Baltimore summer. Her Boston-based mother planned to help her for several weeks to get settled into a routine with the two babies. She couldn't wait.

On top of all that, the mosque was having regular meetings to discuss its activities, including military and violent jihad. The Imam was well connected and was now part of a Muslim group building an American caliphate. Sabina played a role in helping to set up the some of the meetings in Baltimore, but that could not go on much longer with two babies on the way. Groups of Imams, including Alan's former Imam from Cambridge, were organized across the country and met periodically with leaders of ISIS, the Muslim Brotherhood, and others to review secret potential plans for paramilitary and terrorist attacks on the West. Alan was brought into the loop on this with the local Imam because of his intellect and unusual insight on what might be accomplished locally. Alan did not approve of the suicides and bombs and run tactics, but as a relatively new person in the group he did not indicate his displeasure. The local mosque had wanted Alan to participate and had recently loaned him a large sum so that he could buy a unit in the downtown condo complex in Baltimore. Sabina and he were so happy in their new surroundings at the Inner Harbor location. The last thing Alan wanted was to spoil any relationship he had with the mosque and his benefactors.

Alan returned home after a long day. The day was made worse for every Muslim by both the actions and thoughts of everyone around them who thought they were guilty of what was now known as the holiday highway attacks. Everyone was overwhelmed after the extremely tense and grueling day. No one would soon forget the dead and injured on the highways around the capitol. Hopkins received its fair share of those victims and patients, many of whom did not survive. The final fatality count was not yet in, but it was already over one hundred.

The day was not yet over for Alan and Sabina. The terrible events had been traumatic for Sabina. A short walk around the Inner Harbor brought more taunts and even finger pointing on this sad day, even in her late pregnant stage. She understood why people would be angry, but as an individual, she had nothing to do with the event. Yet everyone jumped to conclusions that jihadists had attacked America again. Of course, they were correct in their assumptions. She hurried back to the condominium as fast she could and stayed sequestered there the remainder of the day. That quick walk may have triggered the beginning of labor—premature labor. She was not due to deliver her babies for five or six weeks, and the contractions were far apart so maybe these were Braxton Hicks contractions, she figured. She had just exercised and hoped they would stop after drinking some water and resting. The contractions continued. In fact, they continued regularly for several hours, between eight and twelve minutes apart. When Alan got home, her contractions had been going on for about five hours. She was not in much pain, but he knew it was time to go to the hospital. With twins on board and it being six to seven weeks early, it was best for her to be monitored in a labor and delivery unit. It was not unusual for multiple births to occur early, around thirty-six weeks' gestation. This was a little early.

As soon as Alan changed his clothes, he told Sabina that it was best they go to the hospital. She grabbed her prepacked bag, and they took the elevator back to the garage where Alan had just parked his car. It was a quiet evening and a very easy drive back to the hospital. Alan took advantage of the valet parking attendants who were still on duty, dropping the car at the front door. After the bombings that morning, the attendants were not at all happy about taking the car from two dark-skinned Muslim people. Alan flashed his Hopkins ID, and they did not hesitate to help Sabina out of the passenger seat. Alan accompanied Sabina to the labor and delivery desk. In a matter of ten minutes, she was in a room and being monitored. As far as Alan could tell, both the babies' heartbeats were rapid, as they should be, and Sabina's contractions were just as frequent as they had been in the condo. He was feeling a little better about the situation. Her doctor was due to see her in about forty-five minutes. He kissed Sabina on the forehead and started out of the room for a short walk down the hallway.

He ended up in the waiting room, where the talking heads on CNN were reviewing the truck-bombing events and blaming everyone from Iran to Saudi Arabia. The fatality count was rising; it stood at 323 with over 700 injured from the massive explosions in and around the trucks. Alan knew that many more would succumb to their injuries. This was obviously the worst attack on America since 9/11. The trucks had been commandeered and stolen at truck stops on each of their routes in the early morning hours. The drivers were probably killed in the cabs; remains of the drivers were found at some of the explosion sites. Preliminary investigations indicated that the trucks were then loaded with tons of explosives or jet fuel, crashed, and set off at the same time on the different highways.

It was not clear now what would happen around the globe, but the world had changed again. For several years since 9/11, the US intelligence agencies had prevented many attacks. There had been just sporadic lone-wolf attacks by either affiliated or unaffiliated terrorists. This was different. This was a coordinated attack, and ISIS had now taken responsibility. So the question posed to the nation and its leaders was, What happens now? What is the response? Does the government send troops to country X or country Y? Was this an attack from within? What do we do with our own citizenry? This attack on US soil killed hundreds of innocents and showed others that the economy of a whole area of the country could be paralyzed by blowing up several dozen stolen trucks.

It was now about ten o'clock. Through the haze of the day, Alan sat in the waiting room by himself, now exhausted on one hand and elated on the other, waiting for Sabina to progress in her labor. The president of the United States addressed the country from the Oval Office. President John Adams O'Malley, a young, first-term Democrat from Massachusetts, was being tested for the first time in his administration.

Elected in 2012 on a campaign of bringing the "world together," he was now under pressure to respond to the worst attack on US soil since 9/11. It had been only thirteen hours since the first explosions.

He began his speech. "My fellow Americans, tomorrow will be an Independence Day we will never forget. July 3, 2012, will not be remembered as your usual getaway day for summer vacations. Today we were attacked on our own soil. We mark 236 years of greatness in America tomorrow. And as your president, I will not let this attack bring a stop to the continued success of our country. Those who attack us do so for a simple reason: We are a strong nation that enjoys freedoms and rights not seen anywhere else in the world. I am sitting before you tonight asking for your prayers—prayers for all those who have died or were maimed by the attacks today on the United States of America. Yes, we were attacked, and whether this attack was initiated by just outside terrorists or with the help of some of our own citizenry, this is a warning: you will all pay dearly. I implemented government emergency responses immediately after the attack, but that is not enough. We have tightened our border, but that is not enough. We asked before that if you 'see something, say something,' but that is not enough.

"You all know that I was elected to bring us all together for a world of peace and harmony, but I am fearful that, for all, that is not enough. I cannot stand by and see our nation and people destroyed by those who want to bring us down to their level of savagery. If that is what you want, then we will take you down. It makes no difference if we are Democrat or Republican. You will see the measure of our full force. There will be a quick and devastating response; we hope that will be enough. Celebrate the Fourth of July in the knowledge that your country will have a swift response against those who have attacked us.

"Again, pray for the fallen, for our first responders, and for our armed forces, who will be on the battlefront. Thank you. Good night, and God bless America."

It was a short statement from the president, the president of peace. But the message was clear: action was due shortly. Alan's head ached from the confusion and consternation of the day. He was not happy with this new American caliphate and jihad. He had suggested to his Imam on more than one occasion that attacks should be targeted to make a point. Large-scale attacks would only drum up more hatred for the Muslim people and would result in counterattacks. Alan's ideas involved more surgical attacks initially. He had refused to say anything when the larger group met, but he would speak up next time. Alan had an idea to eventually utilize biological weapons to target certain populations, but again they would be specifically targeted. The Imam liked Alan's ideas but told him that such plans are good for the long term; for now, the military jihadists could not wait to act. Alan had explained that he already had plans in place for the next summer at the Olympics—targeted plans. Today's attack seemed like an insane assault.

Alan would have two children coming into the world in a matter of hours. All his thoughts were about having a better place for them. He looked up again at the television screen: "breaking news." This time it really was breaking news, already. To his amazement, he saw live coverage of surface-to-air missiles launched from the US carrier strike group stationed in the Gulf of Hormuz into small cities in Iran such as Bandar Abbas, Bostanu, Kong, and others near the coast. What Alan could not see were the long-range missiles being shot toward Tehran. There was no television coverage of Tehran. These missiles were headed not toward population centers but to the nuclear facilities that were purportedly for enrichment of reactor-grade uranium for nuclear power. In fact, US intelligence suggested that highly enriched uranium was being produced for nuclear warheads at these targets.

Alan knew there was no way Iran was involved in the day's bombing in the DC area, and now retaliation was coming down on one of the only countries with nuclear capabilities in the region. This response could possibly lead to a global catastrophe and another world war given the strong ties Iran had with Russia, China, and Syria—nothing like the goal of any of the Muslim radicals he had studied. Why was the United States bombing Iran? Alan knew the United States did not have its intelligence on this correct. There was no strategic interest in these small coastal towns. No nuclear development was ongoing in these locations. This tit for tat was a mistake. Alan knew this knee-jerk reaction had to be wrong. The terrorist attack that day was coordinated by the American caliphate. There might have been lots of outside funding, but Iran was not the source.

The day's events and thoughts about what was yet to come exhausted Alan. He had nodded off and was awoken with a start by a nurse.

"Dr. Mazer," the nurse said, waking him with a light touch on his shoulder.

"Yes, what time is it?" he asked, as he looked at the clock on the wall. He looked at his watch as well and could not believe he had been in this chair for over ninety minutes. "Never mind."

"Please come back to the labor and delivery room," she implored.

Alan got up and followed her quickly back to Sabina's room.

"Dr. Mazer, I know we have not met. I am Dr. Cohen, one of the OBs in the practice that Sabina uses. It looks like one of the twins decided to fix its placenta right near the opening of the cervix. I am sure you know this condition—placenta previa."

"So Dr. Cohen, somewhere in the back of my mind I think this calls for a C-section. These babies are not coming out. Am I correct?" Alan said.

"You remember your OB rotation well," said Cohen. "We need to prep Sabina for surgery and get your twins out as soon as possible. No more stress of labor for mom or babies. Do you want to gown up?"

"I would just as soon stay in the waiting room," he answered. Alan then turned to his wife. "Sabina, I know you are in good hands." He crossed over to the head of the bed and gave her a hug and kiss. "I will see you and our big family in a little while. I love you."

Alan left the room while the nurses and Dr. Cohen began to wheel Sabina down the hall to the operating room.

Thirty minutes later, the nurse came back to get Alan.

"Congratulations, Doctor. You are now the proud father of two born-on-the-Fourth-of-July babies, real true-blooded Americans. Come on back. We have both babies and Sabina in a room now for a few minutes," she said.

"Thank you!" Alan jumped up in excitement. "Is everyone all right?"

"Let's go down to the room," she said.

They walked about fifty feet to a recovery area, where Sabina lay in bed comfortably. She smiled weakly. She was still under light anesthesia and had undergone an epidural block as well.

"You look great," Alan said. "I love you."

"Me too," Sabina said weakly and smiled.

Dr. Cohen walked in and shook Alan's hand.

"Congratulations, Dr. Mazer. You are the father of two healthy but premature children, about thirty-four weeks' gestation. Your son seems just fine, a little larger than your daughter. Their lungs might be a bit underdeveloped, so we have them both in the neonatal intensive care unit. We need to watch for apnea. We will keep a close eye for jaundice and place them under the bili lights if they have any. I think everything will be fine," said Dr. Cohen.

"Thank you for your quick response, Doctor. I cannot thank you enough," said Alan.

"My pleasure. Congratulations again," said Dr. Cohen as he left the room and hurried off to what was probably another delivery.

Alan turned to Sabina and gave her a big, light hug around her neck.

"We have two wonderful children. I am going to call your mother and tell her the news," he said. "We won't have her come down until they are discharged."

"Please call. I know it is late, but I am sure she will want to know," she said.

"I will call her right now. Get some rest, Sabina," Alan said as he kissed her on the forehead.

Raising twins was a lot easier with Sabina's mother spending the first eight weeks in Baltimore after the babies were discharged from the hospital. Little Najah had to stay in the intensive care unit two weeks longer than Aamir, but she came home just one week later. Alan enjoyed being a father, but he also had the independence of his job. Alan had planned his calendar and international travel to coincide with the children's infancy. He worked overtime in his own lab and office during the first several weeks after the kids came home. The timing was perfect in terms of his ability to write papers and finish a grant proposal. He then flew off to an international scientific meeting.

Alan was on his way to a meeting in France. He enjoyed the interactions with colleagues around the world and taking the stage to present findings from his research. But Alan really did miss the time away from his young children, Aamir and Najah, and Sabina. Now as a faculty member he had fewer clinical responsibilities after his two-year fellowship. But he was waiting on his additional funding. More money would allow him to grow his lab and give him more independence to travel to research meetings, present his findings, and also meet with new collaborators.

As a fellow, Alan had submitted several clinical case reports, but only one was accepted as an oral presentation at the International Neurology Conference in Paris. That was of no major consequence to Alan, as he was using this international neurology meeting for many other purposes. Because he was early in his career, it would be an opportunity to introduce himself to many important scientists in the international neurovirology arena. Alan also had meetings scheduled with his Egyptian and other potential Middle Eastern collaborators on his encephalitis project and another project on a new measles virus vaccine.

After the second day of the meeting, the schedule was light, and Alan's case report presentation went well. The next day was the conclusion of the general meeting. This was the day Alan had been waiting for, when he had convened his two other meetings. The first was with collaborators from Egypt for his possible project in Aswan. The long-range work in Aswan and work with these collaborators depended on additional funding from partners in Egypt. The National Institutes of Health had already funded key elements of the project, but Alan wanted to build a large lab in Aswan to work on mosquito-borne viruses. The second meeting, for his long-range planning, was a more important one on measles vaccines and autism. Alan had heard about large numbers of children, more than could be explained by chance alone, in the Middle East as well as London and Paris developing autism or autism spectrum disorders following receipt of the MMR vaccine. This had not been the first report of such an association. Furthermore, this association had been reported many years before and then disproved. He was certain that it was nonsense. Yet the controversy continued, and despite the downplaying of the original report, anti-vaccine groups continued to wave the original data and new anecdotal reports in the faces of their pediatricians.

Given Alan's credentials, and his department affiliation, it was possible for him to convene a meeting of those physicians who had reported these newly published but uncontrolled studies. The plan was to pull these doctors together to discuss their experiences and determine if there were common threads that needed to be shared with the scientific community and public. Alan would push this hard. Alan did not believe there was an association between the measles virus vaccination and development of autism, but this was a cog in the machine of his long-range plans.

The pediatric infectious disease expert from Pakistan, Dr. Mahmoud Asir, had been following approximately fifteen hundred children in his clinic for over ten years since implementing a measles eradication program just outside Karachi. The number of measles cases had been reduced dramatically over the years, but he received increasing anecdotal reports over the same period of autistic disorders in the population. Dr. Asir did not have a matched controlled group, and the follow-up was not complete or well documented. His surveillance of the pediatric practices in his community showed a slight increase in the percentage of children with autistic spectrum disorders.

The presentations from London, Saudi Arabia, and Paris groups showed similar trends but nothing significant. And the population studies were not at all the size of the Pakistani group, giving pause regarding the significance of the findings. Dr. Mazer concluded the meeting by suggesting that the four groups publish their data in a paper that recommended that more work be done. Dr. Asir and the rest of the group were very grateful that Alan had pulled them all together at this meeting. Dr. Asir was especially thankful, as he might now get more recognition beyond his homeland. After the meeting concluded, Alan asked Dr. Asir if he had some extra time to meet with him before he departed for home. He said he did, of course, and they set a time for dinner.

Alan thought that these papers by themselves were nothing but a continuation of the anecdotal stories that others had reported in the past. There was really nothing to them. The increased surveillance for autistic disorders following vaccination and changes in the definitions of disorders were certainly the reasons for the reports.

Alan dozed off in his hotel room in the late afternoon after the meeting. He had nothing on his schedule for several hours, not until dinner at 8:00 p.m. with Dr. Asir, when he wanted to discuss how they could work together on generating data on the measles vaccine and autistic disorders. In a fog, Alan awoke a few hours later after a well-deserved rest. The television had been tuned to CNN International. He dialed his brain in to the top stories for a few minutes. No new Middle East conflicts—was that good?

For dinner, Alan and Dr. Asir met at a quiet restaurant far from the convention site, on the left bank. Alan began by introducing himself properly.

"Dr. Asir, Mahmoud, I wanted to meet with you alone. I had been given your name by others in the States before I called the meeting today."

Dr. Asir began to back his chair away to leave, the harsh noise of the chair's feet on the floor breaking the peace of the dining area.

"No, wait. I am your friend and am with you," asserted Alan. "I am a Muslim. Despite my appearance, my well-kept beard, and my name, my father emigrated from Iran in the seventies," explained Alan. "Although raised by my non-Muslim mother from the age of five, I decided to study the Quran and become Muslim."

Dr. Asir slowly pulled his chair back to the table. "All right, Alan. Go on," Dr. Asir said.

"First, I imagine you have seen the news today. The world has changed again," Alan said.

"Yes. Do you know anything about the attacks in Washington in July?" Dr. Asir asked. "Was Iran behind these? I heard ISIS claimed responsibility."

"I am sure ISIS was behind the attacks. I know enough to know that Iran had little or nothing to do with the bombings in the States. I am well connected with the American caliphate, a group of Imams and mosques whose goal is to bring jihad to America and the West," Alan responded.

"I am fearful that a major war will begin," Dr. Asir stated. "Iran has many friends in the world. The United States does as well. This goes beyond a Muslim conflict against the West."

"I am afraid you are correct; political movements have not helped our cause, which is why we are developing a global caliphate with a militant Islam. I cannot see now how a world war will help us. It will only wipe out most of our population if they use nuclear arms," Alan said. "If a war can be somehow thwarted and there is a calming, then maybe we should discuss ways we can work together."

Alan continued, "I am a scientist and clinician just as you, but I see an opportunity here to fight back against the wrongdoings of the West. It is only the beginning of a larger plan I have developed with just a few collaborators. I think you can be a major aide on the public relations and scientific side."

Dr. Asir exhaled. "When we first sat down, you really frightened me. I thought you were CIA or something like that."

Alan continued, "I am sorry for the misunderstanding. Let me continue. The whole measles vaccine story is one I have been thinking about for years, even before my formal training. There is so much paranoia surrounding its use and complications. I think we know as physicians overall that children need to be vaccinated. What I am thinking is that a little more bad press could cause even more paranoia and make the population of US and European children even more susceptible. But that's only the beginning. I am working with a company that is developing a new vaccine, and I have some thoughts on what we might be able to do with their product."

Dr. Asir smiled. "Pakistan and our people have a long-term relationship with the United States, but there does not seem to be a common opinion on what it can do about the ongoing fighting in Afghanistan. Without that, I think a wake-up call will help, and I will assist on my end."

"Good," Alan responded. "I would like you to draft that paper on the measles vaccine data we met about earlier in the day. Then you should circulate the draft to the other collaborators. Maybe in a year's time you and the other authors can submit the manuscript for publication. In eighteen months or so, we will have more people worried about what's going on in your population of kids. It might be a real phenomenon. I will be happy to review the paper for you. However, as for authorship, just keep the participating clinical sites as authors. I do not want my name on the paper, as I am not an active participant."

"Understood," replied Dr. Asir.

They both sat back, relaxed, and ordered a nice meal, realizing what the real collaboration was all about.

Dr. Alan Mazer looked impatiently at his watch as he stood up and left to do his grand rounds at a little after nine in the morning. He was not in the mood for listening to questions from egocentric fellows and residents who were only trying to get noticed by a few of the full professors in the audience. Mazer had been at Hopkins for most of his postgraduate medical training, and as an assistant professor in neurology, he had little patience for these shenanigans. He had picked up a few important nuggets from the lecture but was certain that the inane questions he was hearing now were not going to give him a greater understanding of current therapies for multiple sclerosis. He was thankful that he had sat toward the end of a row in the auditorium and only had to disturb two colleagues as he ducked out of the hall.

Mazer headed back to his office after grand rounds. He was attending this month, which meant a heavy load of clinical responsibility at the hospital. His reading, grant and paper writing, as well as the oversight of his lab staff and fellow always seemed to suffer in the months he attended each year. But that was part of the job. And he was looking forward to the end of the month, just six days away, when he would be winging his way to the Middle East—Saudi Arabia, in particular—to engage in another project.

Sabina checked in with Alan by phone. She was running on empty after chasing Aamir and Najah around the condo, feeding them constantly, and changing diapers every couple of hours. Alan had little time to hear her complaints as he had patients to evaluate, a lab to oversee, and papers and grants to write. On top of that, he could not speak with her about the other things that he was up to and planning. Sabina knew that he had a trip planned in a week and that she would have no backup for two weeks. But then again, she thought this might be a good time to get some work done with the Imam and others at the mosque and leave the kids at the daycare center for a few hours.

THE COLLABORATION
2015

"And this has been a very interesting show tonight, if I do say so myself," Gerri Nesmith summarized. "In the first hour we had the good fortune of having on our show virologist and neurologist Dr. Alan Mazer from one of our nation's top institutions, the Johns Hopkins University School of Medicine, as well a United States representative from Washington State, Jane Jefferson. Further, an activist in the cause against vaccination joined our show. We will take a few calls after the commercial break, but I wanted to summarize my thoughts before we go further."

Nesmith continued, "Dr. Mazer certainly represented the case for continuing administering measles vaccines to our children. He told us how millions of kids have died from measles around the world and still do today. Plus, without control, there will be thousands of hospitalizations and unnecessary sicknesses, as well as lost time from work for parents and caregivers. He talked about the need for a threshold of immune children so that we have a 'herd' immunity protecting the few unvaccinated children. He made a strong case, and honestly he positively scared me and probably the audience. On the other hand, our mother from the anti-vax group kept up her insistence that the measles vaccine was associated with autism and autism spectrum disorders around the world. She admitted that some of the earlier data from England may have been falsified, but more data coming out of everywhere from Pakistan to Paris and everywhere in between showed some evidence of vaccination problems. The good Dr. Mazer said such data was not from well-controlled studies and was not reliable.

"Our legislative representative, Ms. Jefferson, had a whole different perspective. She has to deal with the safety of the whole community from both perspectives. She needs to protect her community and understands both sides. She must rely in the end on what is good for the majority of her citizens.

"Is the measles vaccine helpful or harmful? Is determining this not the federal government's responsibility—that is, the FDA's? Do we trust the FDA and its consultants to make the correct decisions? When do we step back and say that an old decision might not be correct? Is infection with measles and the chances of pneumonia, brain disease, or death more desirable than the possible link to autism? All food for thought, and I'll take your calls after the break. We may need to have these guests back on a future panel."

Ashraf Khaleed walked out of the mosque in Baltimore on a beautiful late Sunday afternoon in June. Surprised to see Dr. Mazer also leaving from afternoon prayer, Ashraf hailed him as he was walking to his car.

"Dr. Mazer!" Ashraf called out.

"Oh, hello, Ashraf," said Alan.

"Nice to see you. I did not see you at prayer," said Ashraf.

"There were so many people there, so it was easy to get lost in the crowd. Where are you walking? I can give you a ride," Alan said.

"I am headed over to the Inner Harbor for an early supper. Would you like to join me?" asked Ashraf.

"Well, that's a great idea. I live over that way. My treat. Hop in," said Alan.

Alan drove over to his condo complex and parked in his garage.

They then walked over to one of the Inner Harbor pavilions to find a restaurant. The place was packed with tourists and pre-Oriole game fans. The better restaurants were in Little Italy anyway, so they continued their walk about a mile and went to a favorite, Sabbatino's. They declined alcohol, and both ordered ice tea. It had only been two years since they had met at Alan's original lecture at the company, but they had kept in contact occasionally about the progress of the measles vaccine work. Further, they had seen each other at the Baltimore mosque once in a while.

As they ate their meals, Alan started up a conversation.

"We have not spoken in much detail about my interests and yours, but I think we might have some common ground beyond science," said Alan.

"I am not sure what you mean," Ashraf said. "Why don't you explain?"

"I know you were shocked when you saw me when we first met and I told you I was a Muslim. And now that you see me at your mosque, which you know is radical—you are a pretty sharp guy. You might think, *Why is Dr. Mazer going here?*" Alan said.

"The thought crossed my mind," Ashraf conceded.

"So why don't we have a frank discussion," Alan began. "I am interested, as you might be keen to learn, in militant Islam. It has been a long learning process for me. This began in my early teen years when my father took me to his mosque and continued in my college years when I went out on my own to a radical mosque. And I take it very seriously. I want it done properly, but I also want it done with immediate action against the West and the State of Israel. The political solution has not worked. I am telling you this now because I think that, from what I have seen and heard at this mosque, you are probably of the same mind."

"Yes, I am," Ashraf said. "I am surprised to hear you be so direct. But yes. I never expected you to come out like this. But since we all pray together, there is no reason not to. Correct?"

"Exactly. I hope we can trust each other. We need to recruit others who are like-minded within the mosque. But meanwhile, I have some major efforts and ideas that I think you can help initiate," said Alan.

"Me? Okay, I am listening. I honestly thought you were going to ask me if I wanted to work with you in your lab." Ashraf chuckled.

"Well, that is still on the table," said Alan. "This is all about the measles vaccine that is being tested by your company right now. I know it is in preliminary trials right now, but last time we had a conversation—and it was confidential—you mentioned that one of the mutants had a problem. There were some neuroinvasive qualities in the animal models. It caused neurological problems. Is that correct?"

"Yes."

"Well, eventually, for my own work I would like to do some study of these in animals. I think I could probably get a grant from the company to do some of that work. But I have an idea for our work. This mutant went almost all the way to trials. It acted in culture like the virus strain that is in trials now. Everything is the same, correct?" asked Alan.

"Yes, that is my understanding. But I am not privy to all the data," Ashraf responded.

"I am proposing that if and when this vaccine is approved for marketing in a few years, we have a job to do. This may not be a perfect bioweapon, but the mutant virus has a neurovirulence attached to it. You told me it caused problems in two models, mice and primates," Alan said.

"Yes," Ashraf confirmed.

"What we should do is store away several vials of this mutant virus. You have it; you made it. And when the time comes to produce it for the market, do what you have to do to get it into production," said Alan. "Then what could happen, if we are lucky, is this mutant virus would affect many children. It is a long shot, but we can try."

"That will not be so easy. There are so many controls, plus I am in research and that is manufacturing," Ashraf responded.

"Well, it sounds like you might have a few years to wiggle your way into a position that gets you into manufacturing," Alan suggested. "It is now 2016. You have been a great asset to the company. I suggest you ask your boss for a move to a new part of the business—a transfer. Tell him you want to learn a new part of the organization. It fits with a career move, does it not?"

The waiter came by, asked if everything was all right, and poured more iced tea for them.

"This is a lot to take in—your positions, your ideas, what I need to do. But I think this is all doable. This is a long-range plan. In the meantime, what else are you doing?" asked Ashraf, "And what can I be doing now?"

"For now, you should just do your job. Do not do or say anything out of the ordinary. Do not raise suspicion. I will take measles vaccination to a new level. On one hand, some of my international colleagues, especially my Muslim colleagues, will provide more evidence that the measles vaccination might be associated with development of autism spectrum disorders. On the other hand, when we are closer to the approval of the vaccine, I will tell the country the importance of being vaccinated. I am working with my overseas contacts on another bioweapon against Israel. I have a laboratory in Egypt," Alan said. "Let's just leave it at that for now. I cannot get into any more specifics. Let's enjoy our dinner and the rest of the weekend."

"I did not understand, Alan. Thank you for pulling me into your confidence and allowing me to help you. I can do this. I am committed to the fight," said Ashraf.

"This is why you are here; this is why I am here, why *we* are here. Let us work together," Alan concluded.

After that, they relaxed and finished their meal. Alan was pleased with how things had gone that afternoon. The meeting at the mosque had not been a random event. Alan had been checking Ashraf's attendance, noting that he visited just about every other Sunday so he could see his mother in Baltimore. He was certain Ashraf would be a good lieutenant on whom he could count. And of course, he was where he needed him—in the middle of the action, in the Immunoviratherapeutics labs where he needed him to work Alan's gambit.

It did not take long for things to come together for Alan. His meeting with Dr. Asir from Pakistan had paid off in spades. Dr. Asir did more than draft a manuscript linking the measles vaccination to development of autism and autistic disorders. After attending the group meeting and consulting with Alan, he pulled together an international social network program. His brother knew the ins and outs of social networking. He was a marketing expert and at the forefront of utilization of this technology. He had been involved in launching and marketing major electronic products in Southeast Asia and knew how to create a big buzz. Dr. Asir suggested linking a few children's negative experiences to autism in his uncontrolled observation trial. He also pulled data from the UK study, which had already been proven wrong, showing a link between the measles vaccine and autism. From this misinformation, the two brothers developed a multipronged explosive attack on the measles vaccination. Within a matter of weeks, antivaxxers around the globe started to see the information on multiple social media platforms—Facebook, Instagram, Twitter, Pinterest, YouTube, Snapchat, Reddit, Renren (in China), and others. These people began to copy the information and start their own blogs and sites. The campaign against the measles vaccine was at an all-time high within eighteen months of the first post by the Pakistani brothers. As a result, measles virus infections increased all over the globe, most notably in Europe and in the States. In the past, most measles cases were imported into the States by immigrants or travelers, but this was no longer the situation. Now many children were never vaccinated. Also, those who had received their first injection were not being brought back for their booster injections. A huge pool of children was at risk. With all these at-risk children, Alan set out to get the word out on the importance of vaccination. The stage was set to vaccinate children with the mutant neurovirulent measles virus vaccine that Ashraf would place into production at the appropriate time.

In a few months, Alan opened his email to his daily download and tracking of neurological disorders related to viral diseases, including measles virus. To his surprise and joy, he saw that one of the first papers on the list was "The role of measles virus vaccination in autism spectrum disorders: A multicenter observational study" in the *International Journal of Medical Neurovirology*, authored by Dr. Asir from Pakistan; the groups from London and Paris; as well as contributors from Jordan and Egypt—all groups that had attended his conference in Paris in 2012. The paper took Dr. Asir two years to publish, but here it was, in black and white for the world to read. Dr. Asir came through and got it done. Alan had seen the initial draft of the paper twelve months previously but had thought it would never get published. He read through the published paper. The data were just as reported at the meeting, not significant. Dr. Asir actually got this observational data published. It was a third-ranked journal and very weak data. Additionally, Dr. Asir's brother knew how to get the press. The paper's results got released again on several websites and social media sites, causing a repeat of the uproar that had started several months earlier with the same information. It was not great science, but that was not Dr. Asir's goal. It would help Alan's aims. The only downside for Alan was that his name was in a footnote thanking him for his help in convening the group in Paris. This reduced his credibility when speaking on the importance of vaccination.

The anti-vaxxers would use this as a justification to legislate freedom from vaccination. The paper and existence of all the "measles naive" children who had not been vaccinated would only help Alan in his long-term goals when the new Immunoviratherapeutics vaccine was released.

A BUZZ AT THE OLYMPICS
2013

Since the highway bombings in July 2012, the State Department and Homeland Security had issued travel warnings for countries in the Middle East, including Egypt. The States' bombing of Iran followed by blustering back and forth among the powers of the world for several months had put the world on edge. After the bombings, rapid-fire warnings were issued by Iran, Russia, and China aimed at the US military's movements that were seen from reconnaissance satellites showing Russian troops and equipment flown in and amassed on the northern borders of Iran. A Russian navy carrier fleet was headed toward the same area in the Caspian Sea. It was clear at this point that Russia was ready to defend whatever there was to defend in Iran, suggesting that the surgical US strikes may not have knocked out the nuclear enrichment facilities. Regardless, further work by US intelligence agencies determined that they might have acted too quickly. Most of the funding for the highway bombing attacks had certainly not come from Iran, but rather from an international ISIS group from

Iraq and Syria. Then finally, President O'Malley met in a trilateral summit in Johannesburg, South Africa, with the president of Russia, Iran's strongest ally, and the president of Iran, Hassan Rouhani. At this meeting O'Malley made an open apology to the people of Iran, much to the consternation and amazement of his political allies. In addition, he promised funding to aid in reparations for the destruction ravaged upon the communities. He left the meeting like a dog with its tail between its legs, but they averted war. To the world, the United States and O'Malley left with a huge black eye. But O'Malley had been elected on a peace platform, and this was as close to his platform as possible—an apology and averting a global crisis.

Alan needed to get to Egypt despite the stern travel warnings from the State Department. There was no time like the present, especially since the virus he was studying in Egypt seemed to be an active seasonal virus. He needed to get something set up now as this first grant was funded for only three years. Results were imperative, at least for this perspective. He hoped this would be one of many international trips to study viral diseases affecting humanity.

Alan reclined as far as he could in his coach seat as he began his long journey to Egypt. This was not the way he had hoped to fly, but in a couple of years he would achieve status and be upgraded to business or first class. He had some miles on United already, so he was hoping to keep flying the same airline.

Flying from the Washington and Baltimore area to Cairo required a stop, so it was unfortunately easier to go to the Dulles airport in Virginia and then to Baltimore-Washington International Airport. It took a solid eighty minutes of travel time on the ground versus twenty minutes in the car to BWI, but it was worth it. Flying out of Dulles required only one stop instead of two, and the total flight time was significantly less. Plus, Dulles's passport control and customs department had significantly more staffing. Alan had learned a lot of these little pointers from his colleagues in the department who had traveled around the world on many missions. He was new at this game, but even though his ego was huge, he took their advice—anything for more comfort and to get ahead.

Unfortunately, the flight to Frankfurt was full, and there was no room to spread out. He hoped the next flight to Cairo would not be as jammed. He was glad he had selected a window seat so as to not be disturbed en route by anyone who might need to get up to use the restroom during the overnight transit. This strategy would have worked well, but during President Day Weekend many families take vacations. The cabin was filled with kids who were screaming or fighting with siblings throughout the whole flight. He thought, *How can this be happening, and why did I leave on this flight on this week? Do families really want to go to Europe in the middle of the winter?* As he pondered, he thought that there must have been some great deals. Alan decided at that point that he needed to be cognizant of school calendars and that maybe it was time to use a travel agent instead of the internet to book flights. An agent might have some insight on the best days to travel. Maybe the weekend of a school vacation is not one of them. *I will learn,* Alan reflected, *but what is done is done.*

Alan contemplated taking an Ambien to put him out, but he wanted to be in control; he put on his noise-canceling headset, which did not, however, cancel out whining kids. He tried his best to rest for a few hours before landing in Germany. Upon landing in Frankfurt, the transfer to his Cairo flight was made without fanfare and relatively easy. He even had time to sit down in the huge duty-free area and have a strong coffee and a couple of brötchens with butter before catching his next flight. His Cairo flight turned out to be quite empty. The political unrest in Egypt had kept tourism at a painful low for the country, and few families or business travelers from the United States were on their way on a Saturday morning from Germany to Cairo. An uneventful flight to Cairo ensued and ended Alan's air travels. He landed in Cairo and, with some anxiety, took a cab to his hotel in the center of the city.

The news reports fed to the United States for months had been unsettling. After Mubarak resigned under pressure, the Islamic Brotherhood eventually took control of Parliament. The Brotherhood's Mohammed Morsi was an overwhelming choice for president. However, within less than a year, the honeymoon was over. Morsi revoked decrees, took back powers, and changed military leadership. This all was coming to a head now, so Alan wanted to get to Aswan soon, away from Cairo, and get on with his work. He wondered how it was possible that he was funded to do this work in a country that was about to explode at the seams. He had many plans and was collaborating with scientists in the States as well. Delays and politics would be a problem on many levels for Alan. He had hoped his anxiety about the unrest in Egypt would be relieved somewhat on Sunday. He decided to stay put in his hotel the rest of the day. Before getting to work, however, he had scheduled one full day of relaxation and sightseeing before heading down to Aswan.

Alan boarded a tour bus on Sunday morning with just a few other Americans for a day trip to the plains of Giza. He was hopeful this would not be his only visit to the sights of Cairo, as he was always interested in the history and wonder of the pyramids. After what seemed like an interminable two hours of sights around Cairo, in which he had little or no interest, they finally arrived at the Great Pyramid complex. He was in awe of the three huge pyramids and felt they were a wonder to behold. Unfortunately, there would be too little time on this trip to really explore the area. Alan was satisfied, however, to be there in person and to be at gazing and wondering about these magnificent structures. Besides the well-known Giza complex, there were so many others that he would not get to see, and of course, without permission from the Supreme Council of Antiquities, there was no chance to actually enter the certain chambers of pyramids themselves. This, for now, would be enough. Alan boarded the bus having snapped several photos, and they were on their way to the Great Sphinx, another grand and probably the most well-known monument on the plain. So many sights seemed to fly by that Alan would need to go back and study a map to learn what he had missed on his bus ride. His appetite for Egyptian history not fulfilled, he only hoped for more visits in the very near future.

On the way back to his hotel from the tour agency bus stop, Alan could not help but notice an ornate and wondrous mosque. The mosaic work was magnificent. People began to stream into this place of worship. It was about four o'clock in the afternoon when Alan heard the call to prayer as most of the city seemed to grind to a halt. Alan did not pray as often as he should and kept his Muslim background a secret. He felt the urge to cross the street, enter the mosque, and partake in the afternoon prayer. Several things were on his mind: he did not look like a religious Muslim, a major war had just been averted, and he was an obvious Westerner. But he went anyway. Being in Egypt, it seemed the right thing to do. Although his name was Alan Mazer, his heritage was Muslim, and he felt good about entering the mosque for the afternoon prayer. He hoped his father would have felt good about it as well.

The next day Alan began his trip to Aswan via a short flight on Egypt Air from Cairo to investigate the outbreak of an acute viral disease for which he had just received his first grant. Boarding the plane, Alan felt a sense of calm; he thought he was leaving a potential war zone. He had seen no violence but could sense nervousness and rumblings as he passed people on the street. He saw military personnel on the streets with their machine guns at the ready and was sure that trouble could be just a misstep away.

He was proud of his accomplishment and needed to take advantage of this research opportunity. He had given himself a solid three weeks to get things started in Egypt. Upon Alan's arrival at the small airport in Aswan, the dean met him. Dr. Baas Shafquat was the dean of the newly established medical school in Aswan. The two of them had communicated earlier in the year, and this was going to possibly be a great opportunity for each of them. Alan, with his resources and talent, would attempt to establish a virology research lab in the new department of microbiology. Dr. Shafquat, with his connections throughout southern Egypt, would try to raise capital for the program. It would be a first for the fledgling school with a small faculty and student enrollment.

Dr. Shafquat was an internist and did not have the specialized training in neurology or an understanding of viral diseases of the nervous system that Alan brought to Aswan. Dr. Shafquat knew what an opportunity this was for potentially treating important outbreaks but also for putting a new university on the map. On the other hand, Alan thought this was not only a perfect location for his research but also an outpost for his work and objectives in the Middle East.

After a quick drive around the scarce campus and buildings under construction, Dr. Shafquat showed Alan the soon-to-be-opened infectious disease laboratory that he thought Alan might want to use in his virus work. They stopped the four-wheel-drive vehicle and got out to take a look. The building was just about completed, with the exception of a few interior lab benches and equipment that would be needed to make the laboratories functional. Dr. Shafquat pointed down the hallway to a large corner room.

"Alan, my friend, you are the first scientist to have any real funding and opportunity for studying infectious disease here in Aswan," Dr. Shafquat said. "So, with that, here is the corner lab overlooking the rest of the campus. I wish you the best of luck in your studies!"

"Dr. Shafquat, I cannot thank you enough for putting me in such a nice space, and I see we already have some equipment plugged in and running," Alan responded gladly. "How did you manage that?"

"We have some wealthy donors who have heard about your intellect and potential," responded Dr. Shafquat.

"Well, this is unbelievable. I will be back here as soon as I can in March to get going on our project. It is important to determine what virus is infecting our population here and causing these neurological disorders," Alan declared. "And, in the meantime, I would like to meet with some of your benefactors during my stay here to thank them and talk about the future."

Alan was very pleased with his new Aswan laboratory. Moreover, he was eager to get back to Egypt and already thinking about his next trip in the spring. At that time, he wanted to make additional connections and to actually start his project. He planned to identify this virus or pathogen, if not a virus, that was infecting children in the southernmost part of the country. But tonight, the dean told Alan, he had to first meet several prominent local businessmen. They were, as Dr. Shafquat indicated, of a similar mindset. Furthermore, they were interested in funding his work to help Alan identify the agent striking some of their weakest and youngest in the community. The dean continued to tell Alan that many people had heard of him through the Imams in Cambridge and Baltimore and would be honored to meet with him. Dr. Shafquat had arranged another dinner for when Alan was next scheduled to arrive in March.

At the dinner, Alan spoke briefly and thanked them all for their interest. He had met each of them individually just before dinner, when they had some tea and appetizers. This was a great opportunity to understand each of the men's political and religious backgrounds. Alan would plan to approach each of the appropriate persons very carefully later on in the week to talk about plans and thoughts about militant Islam and future support of Islamic fundamentalist groups around the world.

As Alan took time to meet with several of the rich and powerful industrial and corporate leaders of southern Egypt during the next several evenings, most were shocked to learn that he was first a Muslim and second a radical Muslim. Some might have been clued in since he wanted to meet with them in private after touring the new medical school and laboratory with him and the dean earlier in the week. These rich leaders all whispered after meeting with Alan that it was somewhat ironic that such a brilliant American medical scientist had gone down this path. But, then again, they became quite interested in his father's background and sought to understand Alan's upbringing during a time of great upheaval. Alan was not particularly looking for more resources for his laboratory at the time. He told each of the individuals, whom he had scouted out well in advance regarding their politics and ideals, that he needed support for radical Islamic attacks on Israel and Western states. Alan had the methods but not necessarily the means and money to carry out biological attacks on these states. He was hoping he could use his laboratory here as one focus for his research under the cover of his grants.

Alan was very convincing regarding his thoughts and mechanisms for continuing a violent jihad. He brought to the table his knowledge of biological entities and how to convert them to dangerous weapons. Finally, Alan felt that the West would be surprised and defenseless with what he had in store for it. The meetings went well, and he ended that part of the week feeling good about himself and the support the effort would receive.

After a week in the lab, hiring a technician, and meeting with a half dozen or so influential and rich radical Muslim leaders, Alan felt that he had made excellent headway. He had gained the trust of all those he met, sharing plans with them of ongoing vaccine programs that he had initiated with a Pakistani collaborator. Things were looking good, and he felt confident as he headed back to the States.

As he started the trip back to Baltimore, Alan was once again looking forward to time with his family. He missed Sabina and his twins, Aamir and Najah. He wasn't big on child care but certainly loved to play with them on the floor as they grew rapidly into toddlers. Sabina continued to work in the mosque and took her children with her. The mosque expanded and even had a child care facility. Alan, now back at Hopkins, had his patient care duties once again as well as his grant- and manuscript-writing responsibilities. He was not excited. He was bored. He realized how he loved field work.

It was mid-March, and Alan was champing at the bit to return to Egypt. Additional cases of febrile infections were being reported, and some children and adults with neurological symptoms were showing up in rare instances in several locations in the Middle East and North Africa. He was certain this could be related to a mosquito-borne virus earlier suspected in Aswan and for which the NIH had granted him money to study. Further, he had hired a technician to set up his laboratory and had ordered and shipped supplies and equipment so that, when he arrived, he could be ready for any virus isolation studies necessary from patient samples. It was time to go back immediately. Sabina discussed the timing with Alan, but to no avail. Alan left for Egypt.

Alan heard his name called over the airport intercom as he waited for his departure at 5:00 p.m. for Frankfurt on his way to Cairo. It was his follow-up trip investigating the outbreak of possible Usutu virus in Egypt and elsewhere in the Middle East. When he heard his name paged, it usually meant trouble—that a patient was critical. But he knew this was good. He felt he was on his way to his first upgrade. Alan hustled over to the United desk. With a big smile on his face, he approached the agent.

"I am Dr. Mazer. I was just paged," said Alan.

"Dr. Mazer, I was wondering if I could interest you in a first-class ticket—"

"Absolutely!" Alan interrupted.

"Please let me finish, Doctor. We are overbooked. I can get you on the 8:00 p.m. to Munich with a connection to Cairo that gets you in a little later the next day. You will be going first class to Munich and business class to Cairo," she concluded.

"I like those plans. Let's do it. Thank you," Alan responded.

After picking up his new boarding passes, Alan headed to the United first-class lounge. He now had three hours before boarding. He downed a full glass of water and had a beer, taking after his father. After about fifteen minutes, he had some snacks and some warm appetizers, read all the newspapers in the lounge, and watched people as they came and went. He even had a piece of pie, as well as some cake, for dessert, although he would be served a full meal on board. After two hours, he headed over to the regular boarding area and waited there. He was just bored at this time. He watched people in the lounge for that last hour before his flight. The flight took off without a glitch and with no whining kids, along with first-class reclining seats. It was a relaxing trip.

Alan was looking forward to a little holiday before heading to Aswan. He had planned to spend a few days at Giza and had even made connections with the Council of Antiquities to enter into certain restricted areas of the Great Pyramid, before the morning hordes of visitors arrived. But when he landed in Munich, he read an urgent text message from Dr. Shafquat. Two children had just been seen in the emergency department in a hospital in Aswan. One was complaining of symptoms that were reminiscent of encephalitis, while the other presented with a fever and mild facial paralysis. Alan thought these could be unrelated, but it was unusual to have two children at the same ER at the same time with possible viral neurological symptoms. Given the importance of identifying the agent responsible for causing previously reported cases, Alan needed to hustle down to Aswan. He wrote a quick email of apology to the director of the Supreme Council of Antiquities and closed his phone. As Alan sat in the first-class lounge waiting for his connection to Cairo, he started to plan the virology workup for the two patients. Alan thought it was a long shot, and he was not confident in his ability to isolate a virus from patients once symptoms had set in. It was usually too late at that time. He had worked with many experts in this field, and it was very difficult and a discouraging area of investigation. Even so, the technician he had hired on his first trip to Aswan had the virology lab operational. He had first done a thorough cleaning of every piece of equipment and washed down all the floors and benches. The incubators for cell cultures were calibrated and set to the appropriate temperature and atmosphere. Cultures of various cell types were obtained from the American Type Culture Collection (ATCC) in Virginia.

Alan had arranged on his first trip to have cell lines from the ATCC sent on his arrival to his new lab. They would then be stored in liquid nitrogen at −186 degrees Celsius. When the lab was operational, the technician would thaw the cells and grow them in the required growth media. They would be expanded and maintained in the incubators. Alan ordered several standard human and animal cell lines used for isolating viruses. These included HeLa cells, a cell line derived from the cervix of a woman named Henrietta Lacks who had cervical cancer; BHK, a baby hamster kidney cell line; primary human lung fibroblasts; and Vero cells, a monkey kidney cell line. These cells had a good chance to grow a fresh isolate of a virus from human specimens. He also ordered a cell line derived from the mosquito *Aedes albopictus*. Alan thought he would want to try to grow any isolates found in a mosquito-cell line. This might be a way to speed up the identification process. He needed all these cells growing when he arrived and hoped he had hired the right man for the job. Finally, Alan ordered a few strains of mice for the vivarium. He would inject them and then try to isolate virus from them. In many cases, this was the only way to isolate a virus.

He also brought with him a panel of antiserum. These were sera known to react against certain viruses. If he isolated a virus, he could then determine whether any of these sera would react with or neutralize the virus he discovered. These experiments would go a long way in helping him determine what was causing the local outbreak in Egypt.

The attending emergency room physician ordered a spinal tap on both girls who were admitted to the Aswan hospital. Fortunately, he had been one of the few doctors who had toured the new facility with

Dr. Shafquat in March when Alan had first visited Aswan. The dean had asked for anyone with available time to accompany him on the tour of the new labs. He stressed the importance of having such an important researcher from the Johns Hopkins Hospital. As luck would have it, this young doctor kept tucked away some of the knowledge that Alan had passed along that day. The emergency room doctor made sure he kept the possibility of a viral etiology for the neurological symptoms in mind in his differential diagnoses for these girls. That possibility led him to store some cerebrospinal fluid for Alan's lab to use in looking for a virus. He also stored whole blood samples for Alan and told the lab to send them immediately to the new virology lab. The tech, Nabhan, at the lab was surprised to receive the specimens. But having worked in a clinical and research lab previously, he knew exactly what he needed to do. Nabhan took each specimen and immediately divided it in half, freezing a portion for future use and keeping the other half in the refrigerator. At this point he could not guess how Alan would want to try to isolate a virus from the clinical specimens.

Alan arrived in Aswan as quickly as he could. He took a reasonably new taxi to the brand new hospital. It was just two days after the girls had been admitted to the hospital with high fevers, chills, and muscle and neck aches. As much as he needed to speak with Nabhan and get things moving in the lab, Alan wanted to first examine the two patients. He got to the pediatric floor with some direction and was disheartened to learn that the young girl with encephalitis had died in the early morning hours. He called down to pathology and asked that they take extra slides of tissue from various areas of the brain. Alan was interested in doing immunofluorescence and in situ hybridization studies for virus detection. After reviewing the chart of the girl with facial paralysis, he walked down the hall to see her. She was a ten-year-old who presented with a moderate palsy or weakness on one side of her face. This palsy was not unlike many others Alan had seen, such as a problem with the seventh cranial nerve or Bell's palsy. A number of agents could have caused this, he thought, and this was nothing unusual. In any case, he was going to attempt to isolate virus from her bodily fluids. Alan asked to make sure that her vision and hearing were monitored regularly, as many viral infections caused hearing and visual abnormalities.

Alan jogged down the hall and hit the down elevator button. He told the nurse at the station that he would be back to see the girl in a couple of hours. The nurse smiled at him as he entered the elevator. Alan headed to his new laboratory, where he was happy to see Nabhan busy at work without supervision. He decided that he must have made a good choice.

"Good afternoon, Nabhan," Alan said loudly over all the laboratory noise. "It is good to see you once again."

"Dr. Mazer, I heard you were coming," Nabhan replied. "Nice to have you here. I have many things to report."

"I am sure you do, as do I. We have, as I think you know, two clinical specimens," Alan conveyed.

"Yes. I received them two days ago and split them into two. One half I kept refrigerated, and one half I placed at negative seventy degrees," Nabhan answered.

"Perfect. And which of the ATCC cell lines do you have up and running, ready for infection?" Alan queried.

"All of them. I got very lucky. Everything came out of the freeze nicely," Nabhan said with a huge grin on his face.

"That's great. What I'd like you to do is just use the BHK and Vero cells to try to isolate virus from these samples. I also want to inject a portion into one- to two-day-old suckling mice. How are we doing on the animal front?"

"We have two or three pregnant Balb/cJ mice that should be ready in a day or two," Nabhan responded enthusiastically.

"Okay, then, that will give us three chances to find an infectious agent in samples from these two patients. Unfortunately, I have some sad news. You did work before in a large lab in Cairo and didn't know where the samples came from. This is a much smaller facility. There still is confidentiality here, but I am sorry to tell you that one of the children that these samples came from died today," Alan summarized.

Nabhan asked, "Dr. Mazer, I am ready to undertake all these different methods of viral isolations from patient materials, but I do have a question or two."

"Yes, please, go ahead," replied Alan. "We need to be on the same page, so please don't be afraid to ask anything."

"Well, in my experience and based on what we have ordered for the lab, we need not have all these cell lines up and running or animal facilities to detect viruses. We now have nucleotide hybridization detection techniques, PCR, and panels of known antigens. We could look at the clinical specimens for viral nucleic acid or antibody in the serum to determine with which agent the patients are infected," Nabhan said.

"Yes, we can do that. You are absolutely right," Alan said. "But in this lab we will do all the above. Plus, we want to also culture the live virus as well," he added. "We will wish to determine if the virus we are finding here is any different from previous isolates that have been found."

"Is that for a vaccine?"

"Yes, exactly," said Alan.

"Aha. That makes sense to me. Thank you. I am on it. This will be an exciting place to work. I hope that I can meet your expectations," said Nabhan.

"I am sure you will," Alan replied, and he turned toward his new office.

"We will continue our work and try to find what agent was responsible for this devastation, Doctor," Nabhan said.

"Thank you, Nabhan. Let us get to work," Alan concluded.

And that they did. It did not take long for Alan and Nabhan to isolate and identify virus from these two patients. They confirmed that a viral infection had caused the disorders. The caretakers of the girl who had developed an acute inflammation of the brain, encephalitis, had taken a sample of cerebrospinal fluid from which virus was isolated. The virus was then grown in the lab on several cell lines and further characterized. Alan and Nabhan grew the highest levels of the Usutu virus in the BHK cell line, a long-standing cell line derived from baby hamster kidney cells. The virus grew to very high levels, 10 to 100 million infectious particles per milliliter of culture fluid. Using this virus, Alan decided to proceed with animal experimentation to see if he could detect any neurological effects when it was injected into newborn or adult mice. As expected, in this model, the newborn animals did not survive infection; when low doses of this agent were injected, the animals died within seven days. The adult mice, at four weeks of age, were also infected. He expected these animals to survive and not to show any signs of disease. This is what most investigators had seen with similar viruses in this same model. Alan was shocked when he started seeing untoward effects in a few days. The animals were dragging their hind limbs and appeared to be on their way to complete paralysis. This virus was neurotropic in nature. He isolated their brains and found a pathology reminiscent of a chronic viral infection. The immune systems of the mice had been overwhelmed and incapable of combatting this infection.

Alan and his lab had now performed the initial groundbreaking work in Egypt that determined that Usutu virus had caused the neurological disorders in Aswan. Further, this strain of Usutu was neurovirulent. Alan would continue his work but would not go to the World Health Organization for any funding. He had plenty of resources in southern Egypt. The Usutu virus was widely recognized as the next great threat to Southern Europe, the Middle East, and Africa. Further, it infected a number of bird species and was transmitted to humans by mosquito bites. This was not easy to contain without excellent mosquito control techniques or vaccine intervention. At this time no vaccine was available, and it was similar to the West Nile Virus and other mosquito-borne viruses. It did not take him long to isolate Usutu virus from several patients admitted to the Aswan hospital with early signs of infections that could lead to encephalitis.

Now an even greater problem became layered atop the explosive new epidemic in the area. Several years previously, the International Olympic Committee had awarded the summer games to the Kingdom of Jordan, to be held in Amman. This wealthy country had been planning, investing, and building a huge complex for the Olympics. The athletes and many of the world's population would come to the area in three years in September. These would be the first Olympics in the Middle East, and it was a huge risk for the country in terms of both security and infrastructure. Even though the virus was circulating and there was the potential for infection of athletes and visitors from around the world, the WHO gave its blessing to the Olympics. Much of the scientific community was outraged. There was a possibility that the virus would be a significant risk for the athletes and visitors during the Olympics. Further, worldwide spread of the virus was also possible as individuals became infected and then traveled back home. If a person were sick on the way home and then a mosquito took a blood meal, the cycle could start anew in the person's home country. In addition, that country would now have a new species of mosquitoes infected with the virus and a potential new vector for the infection. But Jordan's government said that it would control the mosquito population, and that allayed fears.

The entire world was watching and preparing for the Olympics and attacks on the Jordanian venue. Like magicians and their sleight-of-hand maneuvers, multiple breeds of terrorists were watching and planning for attacks on venues and locations all over the globe.

Now that he had found this neurovirulent strain of Usutu, Alan thought long and hard about how he could use this virus as his first agent to hit Western and Israeli targets. He was not alone. He was just part of small cell in Baltimore, not really linked to a global network as far as he could tell. He was on his own right now in Egypt, an individual not truly aligned with the likes of ISIL, ISIS, Hamas, or Al-Qaeda. He had his supporters around the world, many in Egypt, and he had developed a group of people who were working with him on the measles project. But other than Dr. Asir from Pakistan, who was working on his long-term measles virus project, most were not aware of his bigger plans.

Most of Alan's work had been with other viruses, and he was working on a parallel plan with measles in the States. Maybe this was too much at one time? There was a lot at stake. With his Muslim supporters in Egypt, Alan felt good about his position in the lab and hospital in Aswan, and he could operate out of that location. He needed to split his time though. He had a job and grants to write and a lab in Baltimore. At times he felt like a whirling dervish.

With the Olympics coming up in the next few years in Jordan, Alan's mind was quickly turning. He thought he had found his first bioweapon with the neurovirulent Usutu virus. But he didn't know how he could best deliver a mosquito-borne virus to a foreign country. How could he target this? Jordan planned on controlling the mosquito population. How could he get this into a controlled area? So many questions. Was this the correct venue? Should he try to deliver the virus to Israel? As an American, he could easily enter Jordan or Israel, but how could he get infected mosquitos or eggs into the land of milk and honey? Both Israel and the Jordan Olympics were good targets, but the logistics of each were mind-boggling.

Alan kept on searching for the best ways to deliver millions of infected female mosquitos or eggs to Israel or Jordan. It was frustrating. Females are the only mosquitos that take blood meals and can infect humans. Could he send the mosquitos surreptitiously to Israel on flights into Ben Gurion Airport near Tel Aviv? If so, how could they be released? And if released, where? Once released, mosquitos had a range of, at most, one to two miles. Releasing them at the airport terminal wouldn't be any good, he thought. Even on the runway, what good would that do? Closer to the terminal or in a terminal was a better release point. A larger percentage would survive and would either take blood meals (infect humans or birds) or lay eggs in a puddle somewhere. In any case, the potential spread of virus could be started, and no one would be the wiser.

Or was it possible to have several people drive and release mosquitos at various locations across the Israeli border? This was starting to sound like his best option. He would need to think of a method to cool down the mosquitoes and hide them in vehicles such that they could be transported from Egypt into Israel without causing suspicion.

The more Alan thought through this problem, the more he shifted his thinking. The Olympics in Jordan were three years away. Maybe it would be a better venue to attack specific Western elements, including the Israeli delegation. Entering Israel with biological supplies from the Egyptian border, or any border, would be a lot more difficult than entering Jordan. And he could enter Jordan now and start working with colleagues to increase the Usutu virus burden in the area. Plans formulated in his mind. He needed to enter Jordan and get this strain of Usutu concentrated near the upcoming Olympic venues. A direct entrance from Egypt might not be wise. He was concerned about his movements from one Muslim country to the next. He was not sure at this time who was watching whom, and there was much concern in the

States about citizens' traveling to countries in the Middle East and the possibility of their becoming radicalized. For all Alan knew, he was already on the radar of the US and Israeli secret agencies.

He did not have any contacts or virology collaborators in Jordan. At every turn, Alan came upon difficulties concerning a mechanism to distribute the mosquitoes or virus into target sites. He turned to the scientific literature to see who in Jordan might be able to help him. He went to the library, being very cautious about having his searches traced, and used the computers in the medical school library. In the literature, he found a series of articles by an ecology professor who had been publishing for the last twenty years from the university in Irbid, Irbid National University. This was a major Jordanian university in the north of the country. Professor Fareed Al-Razi, head of the science department, had been studying for many years the ecology and interaction of mosquito populations and blackbirds in Jordan. Not only was this professor studying the interaction of mosquitoes and bird populations in Jordan, Alan also determined that the professor had recently become quite the radical Muslim activist. He had appeared on many local television and radio shows discussing his negative opinions on US involvement in the Middle East. At a public university, this might have been a disadvantage in obtaining further funding for his work. But the professor pushed on and was not going to give in at his age. Alan called the professor while he was in Egypt. Evidence of his paranoia, he called from a burner cell phone that he had purchased at a local shop. He connected with the professor and explained his situation and work, saying that he was investigating an interesting virus-bird interaction in Egypt and would like to meet him in person. Professor Al-Razi was an established teacher and scientist but just in his small university, so he was extremely flattered that a scientist from Johns Hopkins was so close by and wanted to meet with him. He answered affirmatively.

Jordan was an interesting location in that it sat at the intersection of three continents—Africa, Europe, and Asia. This made it a place where several species of migratory birds interacted. Birds carry several mosquito-borne viruses, and because of its unique location, it was possible that Jordan could be a central worldwide depot for the mosquito-bird interactions. Mosquitoes just had to infect a few birds, and then these birds would fly to another land. Professor Al-Razi studied these birds and mosquito interactions for years. And he also happened to be a radicalized Muslim, just like Alan. When the two had communicated, it was not really clear to the professor what Alan had on his mind, but he certainly was in awe of this bright young scientist. No one from this esteemed institution had ever visited Irbid National University. Alan told the professor that he would not be able to meet him on this trip but would contact him soon by email so that, hopefully, they could get together in the next month or two.

Alan winged his way home again to the States after another fruitful trip to his Egyptian lab. Upon each return, his children always seemed to have reached more milestones in his absence. This time they had taken their first steps while he was twirling test tubes in Aswan. It sounded like he had missed out on too many events and told himself and Sabina that he would try to limit his trips to the Middle East if he could. Sabina appeared more distant with every return trip, but they still shared a loving relationship, and the flame in the bedroom still burned bright despite the distractions of family and work.

Syria was in the news and now needed huge numbers of physicians to treat the ravages of the chemical-weapons attacks on its citizens. With civil unrest ongoing now for years, Syria's citizens were devastated. Alan wanted to take leave for four weeks from his Hopkins position to help. Leave was not a problem. However, Sabina was furious about his desire to go. His children barely knew him, she argued. Alan finally convinced her of the medical need, and she relented. She told him he should do what he thought his conscience guided him to do. He thanked her, but Alan knew what she really believed. In any case, he had his own mission, and the medical leave was a guise.

Alan gladly took on a new role with Doctors Without Borders, requesting that he be deployed on the southern border of Syria, near Jordan. He was a mastermind of deceit. Although most of the major problems were happening in the city of Saraqeb, where citizens had been hit with chemical weapons including sarin gas, medical attention was greatly needed in cities and rural sites in the south. That's exactly what

Alan wanted. He was posted outside As-Salkhad. It got him closer to Jordan, where he hoped to travel after his four weeks of medical work with DWB. After settling in, he quickly went to the administration area and sent out a note to Professor Al-Razi, using the DWB computers. He told the professor that he planned to be in Jordan in about four weeks' time and would telephone upon his arrival in Irbid.

The clinic assigned Alan a room in the clinic to see any patient who walked through the door. It mattered not what a doctor's specialty training had been. With Alan's arrival, there were two doctors on staff. Now the general practitioner had a neurologist in the "group" in case he had a question. The other physician was a recently retired fifty-five-year-old GP. Alan figured he must have married into money or been born into wealth. He couldn't figure out how a GP could retire at such a young age otherwise.

Upon entering his office at seven in the morning, he found a queue of at least twenty people. They all had papers in hand. Alan hoped that what was written on the papers was in English and they had some command of the English language because all he could say was a few words plus "Where does it hurt?" in Arabic. And he was hoping that the patients in Syria could understand the Arabic he spoke in Egypt. The first patient to walk in his door was a boy about ten years old with a woman Alan presumed was his mother. Alan said hello in Arabic, and the boy greeted him, saying hello in English. Alan was relieved. *At least the children speak English,* he said to himself.

"What can I do for you? How are you feeling?" Alan asked.

The mother stared at Alan without saying a word and did not appear to understand anything he was saying.

"My mouth hurts," he said.

"What is your name? I am Dr. Alan," Alan said.

"I am Aabis. It hurts when I swallow," Aabis said.

"Okay, let me look in your mouth and your ears. This won't hurt, okay?"

Aabis gagged a bit when the tongue depressor went into his mouth.

Alan took a flashlight and looked into the boy's throat and then around his oral cavity. He then took an otoscope and looked in both ears. Alan listened to his chest and heart.

"Aabis, I think you have a mild infection. It should clear up in a few days. I will have the nurse in the other room give you a medicine for your nose. This should help you. Please come back to see me in three days if you are not feeling better," Alan continued. "Give this piece of paper to the nurse. She will give you the medicine."

"Thank you, Dr. Alan. I will," Aabis said. Aabis took his mother's hand, and they walked out of the room to get his medicine. The mother nodded on the way out as her way of thanking Alan.

The remainder of the day was filled with mostly similar, easy-to-diagnose cases. The major problem was communication. Children had been taught English in Syrian elementary schools only for the past ten or fifteen years. But they were taught only basic English skills for a few years and then switched to the French language. The nurse had a good command of English and Arabic, so, for many patients, Alan would have to ask for her help in translating the problems and examination results. This slowed the process. Over the first week, Alan gained some command of basic interactive and medical Arabic for examinations, and work sped up a bit in the clinic.

Alan found this work quite boring. He knew he was helping people in medical need, but it was an interminable four weeks. He also knew in his heart that, in the end, his other work would be of even greater help.

For those four weeks, Alan painstakingly set broken bones and took care of acute infections; he faced nothing more challenging than providing some seriously late prenatal care. After finishing his Doctors Without Borders work, Alan started his road trip to Jordan. He had hired an armed guard and a driver from As-Salkhad, the large city nearby. With them, he did not expect any trouble on the journey. The driver and guard had all the paperwork necessary to cross the border. Alan's plan all along was to return from his mission with Doctors Without Borders through Amman, Jordan. He had to make just one stop in Irbid to visit a colleague. These were his valid reasons for visiting Jordan, and his paperwork was in order.

The crossing of the Jordanian border at Al-Ramtha was fueled with anxiety. The border guards slowly examined every piece of paperwork and whatever personal belongings Alan had in his possession. It took twenty-five minutes with the car turned off before the Jordanian border guards allowed passage. Explaining why the armed guard was present took most of the time, but they did let him pass as well. Upon leaving the post, the driver was finally able to turn on the air conditioning, and their clothing started to dry out. With traffic, the car approached Irbid within an hour. Alan had arranged for a two-day stay in downtown Irbid, at the Irbid Plaza. It was not supposed to be anything like the Plaza Hotel in New York—just a run-of-the-mill hotel. That was all he wanted after staying out in Syria for four weeks. He wanted a long, hot shower and a good meal. He was to meet with the professor the next morning, take a ride to Amman, and go back to the United States in two days. He had been out of contact with Sabina except by email for four weeks and was hoping to call her from the hotel in the morning.

Alan had made reservations at a local restaurant just a few blocks away, a five-star cafe serving local Jordanian food. He took a booth inside at the back of the establishment and ordered an iced tea. He was tired and hot and not interested in alcohol. After a few sips of bottled water, the waiter brought him his drink and a menu in English to inspect. Alan had a light meal comprising bites each of tabbouleh, hummus, falafel, warak enab, and kousa mahshi.

The next morning after breakfast, Alan called Professor Al-Razi from the hotel lobby phone. He was in his office at nine o'clock and excited to take Alan's call.

"Dr. Mazer," replied Al-Razi, "so nice to speak with you. I am so happy that you are in my city. I take it you are comfortable and well?"

"Oh, yes, thank you, professor," said Alan. "And it's nice to speak with you also. I am staying at the Irbid Plaza. I do not think it is too far from the university."

"No, it is not. If you are free now, I can pick you up. Is that good?" queried the professor.

"Excellent. I have so many things to discuss and questions for you. Thank you," Alan responded.

"Yes. Let me pick you up at ten," said the professor.

"Great. Thank you again."

The professor arrived at the hotel promptly at 10:00. Alan was waiting outside as an older Ford SUV arrived at the front door. He had been surprised to see so many American-made cars in Jordan until learning that Ford and other companies did have a presence in the country. An older gentleman dressed very conservatively in a sports jacket and bow tie exited the vehicle and called to Alan.

"Dr. Mazer?" inquired Al-Razi.

"Yes, it is I. Professor?" responded Alan.

"Yes, indeed. Please, come with me. Let us return to the university. It is such a pleasure to meet you, Dr. Mazer," said the professor.

The two men chatted on the brief trip to the campus, speaking mostly about family, the countryside, weather, and the like. The reason for Alan's visit and interest in meeting Professor Al-Razi was not broached. Such topics could wait for later in the day.

As Professor Al-Razi parked his vehicle in front of the Biological and Epidemiological Sciences Building, translated in English under the Arabic language sign, he asked, "So, Dr. Mazer, I really am very curious. You are a famous research doctor from Johns Hopkins and have now done some volunteer work in Syria. Very nice. I cannot imagine what you need to see me about."

"You understate your significance as a scientist," Alan said. "You have published many interesting and important works for years on the migration of birds in Jordan and the interaction of the mosquito population with these birds."

As the two scientists walked to Professor Al-Razi's office they continued their conversation.

"Yes, it makes up most of my life's work," he said, "but I am still not quite sure of what you would want from me."

"Well, let's talk candidly if we could," Alan said. "I would like first to talk about my politics and religion and then about my science."

"Fine. I didn't expect that," the professor answered.

"I am Muslim, despite my last name. And I was radicalized in my teens. My father immigrated from Iran, and even though I was raised by my mother and kept her last name, I am Muslim," Alan said. "All through my schooling in Boston and now in Baltimore, I have been working with Imams who are associated with the American caliphate whose goal is to help establish a global caliphate. I am, despite my work as a physician, an active jihadist."

"I would not have ever guessed," said Professor Al-Razi. "How can you be so open with me?"

"I know from the press that you have similar leanings, and I have seen you on television talking about the United States," Alan responded. "So now might be a good time to discuss how we can use our science to move our agenda forward."

"Let us talk," Al-Razi said.

"As you know, the Olympic Games are coming to Jordan soon. In the last year I isolated a virus from children in Egypt that infected their brains and caused very serious disease. Since that time, I have found the molecular area of the virus that gives it the ability to infect the brain and have grown a supervirus. This is a virus, the Usutu virus, that is carried and transmitted to humans by mosquitoes," Alan summarized.

"That is why we are talking—so we can utilize some of my knowledge of bird migration to get the virus into certain locations," the professor said.

Al-Razi entered his office first and sat in a well-worn leather chair. The professor directed Alan to sit across from him on another old seat, at a pockmarked table strewn with many papers, and they continued their discussion.

"Well, if it were that easy," Alan said. "But it is not. I cannot rely on the natural process to infect people. The odds are not in our favor. It would take years to get a large number of mosquitoes in the area infected. I am hoping to somehow import infected mosquito eggs to Jordan."

"Uh, yes," the professor murmured.

"I have thought this through so many ways. First, I was going to drive mosquito eggs in my car or take them on a flight right into Israel," Alan recounted, "but such plans would never work. So I thought we could set up a collaboration. It is possible we could ship you frozen infected mosquito eggs from our labs in Aswan. You are a renowned mosquito researcher. There would be no question there."

"I do not think there would be an issue, no," he answered. "We have controlled freezers to keep the eggs at correct temperatures."

"And the next step would be the most difficult. You or a trusted colleague would need to thaw the eggs in small bodies of water ten days before the start of the Olympics within a few hundred feet of the sites at the Olympic Village," Alan said.

"That would be something that we need to really work on, but I think it can be done," the professor responded.

"If this works, within a matter of a week, hundreds of athletes from around the world will be infected, many will have severe neurological disease, and many will die," Alan continued. "I am hoping our intelligence can get information on where the US and Israeli delegations will be residing. Those will be the locations for most of the egg drops."

"As you are speaking, I am realizing that we need to get specific workers involved, people who will have access to the village before the start of the Olympics," the professor said. "I am hoping I have access to someone who is trusted and yet can get clearance for these types of jobs."

"An excellent idea, professor. And we have plenty of time to implement this idea," said Alan. "Now that we agree on a plan, let me head back to my hotel and plan my journey back to the United States. I have been gone a long time and miss my family. I thank you for seeing me and hope to speak with you again soon."

"Let me drive you back to your hotel," said the professor.

"I think that is a good idea," Alan said. "The fewer people who see me here with you, the better."

They left, and in a matter of ten minutes Alan was back at his hotel planning his flights back to Baltimore. He also did not forget to call home, but he did forget the seven hour time difference. It was about six in the morning in Baltimore. Despite that difference, Sabina and the children were thrilled to hear Alan's voice. It had been a week since he had last called from Syria, and the connection had not been great. She was happy to hear that his trip home was starting the next day. She wondered at first what he was doing in Jordan, but Alan explained that the best connections given his location were from Amman. Sabina was glad this trip was ending.

In the year following Alan's meeting with the professor, he continued his work on vaccine development and antiviral therapies with several drug companies in Aswan, the Middle East, and Northern African areas. He was well funded for the clinical studies and was free to interact with groups of scientists and "interested parties" in these areas. After two years of work that yielded poor results on the treatment front, Alan had learned a lot. Once symptoms of disease started, it was too late to treat children or adults who had been infected with this mosquito-borne virus. Usutu virus was not something people would want to get into their bloodstreams and by chance into their brains. From his ongoing attendance of meetings and surveying of reports and the scientific literature, he determined that the US military was working on and administering vaccines to prevent troops from getting infected with this virus before being sent overseas. He knew that, in the end, this virus would eventually affect large populations of people across the world. The development of a treatment was lagging, and no one knew if the vaccine in use would be effective.

Alan was becoming quite the accomplished expert on arboviruses, those pesky mosquito-borne viruses. At the start, he did not know how or if he could target them to broad or specific populations. That had been frustrating. But now he was in Egypt and Jordan, a stone's throw away from Israel. And, from there, he thought, there must be a way to target the Jewish population. But his meeting the previous year with Professor Al-Razi in Jordan could not have come at a better time. There was no way yet to spread the virus to Western countries, but an attack on Western athletes with the Usutu virus at the Olympic Games was now possible given the professor's genius and contacts in Jordan. Such a demonstration would show the world the intellectual strength and purpose of the military jihad. At this point, Alan knew that all his planning, from the fellowship to the grant writing to the Doctors Without Borders, all the way to his meeting with and recruiting Professor Al-Razi, would pay huge dividends for the Muslim world.

It had taken years of planning, but the time had come for the Olympics to finally open in the Middle East. Billions of dollars had been poured into infrastructure development and athlete training for this event. Very little investment had gone into ancillary activities that would soon create a buzz around the Olympics.

The opening ceremony began with a flame lighting like none that had been seen before. The Olympic flame was brought into the stadium on camelback by one of the first four Jordanian athletes to ever participate in the Olympics, in the 1980 Russian games. The crowd erupted in cheers. After the flame was lit, an Arabian-themed dancing celebration began. Horses strutted across the field, stood up on their hindquarters, and looked to the sky for a second as jets whisked across the clear nighttime desert sky to the delight of the huge crowd. After the steeds galloped off the turf, the Jordanian athletes paraded to the cheers of their countrymen and all the other athletes filed into the stadium in a long process.

During this march of the athletes, a buzz was in the air, not only because of the excitement but also because of a few wayward mosquitoes. Professor Al-Razi had plenty of contacts in the construction and landscaping crew, to whom the professor and his network paid a hefty sum. Under cover, millions of Usutu-infected mosquito eggs had been placed strategically in puddles around the Israeli- and American-athlete living quarters. The puddles of water were close to sprinkler systems around the Olympic venues that watered the foliage in the desert community, so they did not dry out. And now, ten days or so after the eggs had been placed in the water, mosquitoes began biting the athletes in the Village, and a few were now buzzing and biting in the stadium. Dr. Mazer's presence was known all over the Olympics, even though he was back in Baltimore, at work on another important virus—measles.

About five days into the Olympics, many of the Israeli and American athletes started to fall ill; a few others did as well. The Village medical center, overrun with athlete patients, started to send some of them to the emergency departments in Amman hospitals. Most patients presented with high fever and headache; some had neck pain, and others had some motor-coordination difficulties. Doctors there noticed that, compared to other representative countries, a higher percentage of the Israeli and US athletes were affected by these conditions. One in three of the Israeli athletes were hospitalized. Five died. Seven Americans died, and twenty were hospitalized. Many athletes from other delegations were sickened and died as well, but not in the huge numbers seen in the Israeli and US delegations. The news coverage of the sickness dwarfed that of the athletic competition. Calls from around the world came in to stop the Olympics. A few of the spectators also succumbed to the illness, but none of them died. Investigations started immediately. The Jordanians looked into the food, water, and all supplies, especially those provided to those hardest hit. The news media immediately suggested a targeted terrorist event, given that mostly Americans and Israelis had been affected.

The doctors felt that an infectious disease agent was the culprit but did not yet have a diagnosis. It would take some time to determine the exact cause. It looked like a virus, but it was not typical. Some of the patients remembered being bitten by mosquitoes, so that was a beginning to the trail of the investigation. Serum samples from several patients with symptoms and from matched controls without symptoms were sent to the laboratory of the World Health Organization in Geneva. This lab could test for antibodies to a number of mosquito-borne viruses. It was hoped that there would be a quick answer so that if anyone else presented with symptoms, doctors would have a handle on treatment.

The doctors did not have to wait long before the results were in; a different source gave them the answer. A video was posted on Twitter: ISIS claimed responsibility for an attack on the Olympics. They claimed to have swarmed the area with Usutu-infected mosquitoes, with a neurovirulent strain of the virus that could readily infect the brain and cause a quick demise. They said they had purposely planted mosquito eggs near the Israeli and US Olympic Village locations just days before the start of the Olympics. Doctors could tell that these guys knew their stuff. The Olympic Village campus was spread out. Mosquito range is only about a mile, so when these mosquito eggs hatched, the infected female mosquitoes had honed in on just the people close by, infecting them.

The news media went berserk. The scenarios espoused were outrageous, but they filled airtime—anything from "global war" to war against a variety of Middle East targets to "spray Jordan with DDT" and finally to "quarantine everyone." This was a well-coordinated attack for which the world was not prepared. It appeared as though ISIS was now a biotechnology machine, not just warriors launching long-range missiles or paying off young men and women to blow themselves up with TNT strapped to their bodies. ISIS had come a long way with its superior communication technology, but no one had expected anything like this. How could they have developed into such an enemy in such a short time? The onslaught of talking heads rehashing the same news for three days was almost worse than the original attack on the Olympians. The media provoked more anxiety, and anxiety spread faster than any virus. There was no prepared response to a mosquito or to an expansive enemy. Who would have thought that ornithologists would be the lead guests on CNN, Fox, and MSNBC after a terrorist attack? The bird migration had already occurred, so the spread of the virus was not a certainty, as the Jordanian air space may have had plenty of infected mosquitoes but most of the birds that could have spread the nasty virus around the globe had already left the scene. Fortunately, the Olympics had been held in late summer because of the extreme heat in Jordan.

The West had no real confident response to allay the fears of their citizens. This had truly been a terror event, an invisible threat, but one with huge consequences. Biotechnology companies did all they could to grab funds from their governments to quickly develop vaccines and treatments in the hopes of countering a future pandemic of Usutu virus in their countries. But in all honesty, the leaders did not know if this was just the first shot, so to speak, or if others were coming from ISIS or other terrorist organizations. What other surprises were being incubated? Needless to say, this was not an easy time in the world, and developing new drones or similar weapons or nuclear warheads was not an answer to microscopic threats.

Mossad, the Israeli national intelligence agency, investigated the Olympic illnesses and deaths of the athletes as soon as they were reported. Even before ISIS had tweeted their video, the central office in Tel Aviv had already given undercover Mossad agents in Jordan intelligence about possible individuals involved in the attack.

Professor Fareed Al-Razi watched with amazement the news on his television screen as the Olympic Games progressed. After just several days, the broadcasters began to announce even more sicknesses of athletes. He knew what had occurred, but he could not believe that Dr. Mazer's virus had been as potent as he suggested. The professor also could not understand how the mosquito population that he had provided was so efficient in transmitting the virus.

Just a week into the Olympics, when Jordan should have been celebrating its great accomplishments and its new venues and bringing the world together, a great exodus began. The Olympics continued, although many delegations did not stay. No crowds of people stayed to watch the Olympics, as most everyone left in fear for their lives. They thought that, despite security measures, something else might be forthcoming. If this could happen, maybe something else could too.

Al-Razi heard a knock on his door at home around dinnertime—nothing unusual in his neighborhood. But the knock itself was unusual. When he opened the door, two men stormed in, taped his mouth shut, put a black sackcloth over his head, and tied it shut. They sat him down on a chair in his living room.

"Professor, we will not hurt you," said one of the men in perfect local dialect. "In a few hours when the sun sets, we will be taking a trip. Then we will be asking you some questions. If you can answer our questions truthfully, then there should not be any problems. Just nod your head if you understand."

Al-Razi nodded.

"Good. Then we will sit here with you and leave in a while," he said.

The two men gestured to each other; one stayed in the living room with Al-Razi while the other stayed on lookout in the front hallway. They were Israeli Mossad agents. The central Mossad office had determined that only one Jordanian national who had worked with mosquitoes was also a radical Muslim. That person was Fareed Al-Razi. But he did not work with viruses. These two agents needed to connect the dots.

After dark, at 9:00 p.m., the two agents took Al-Razi outside. They locked his house and walked to the back of their panel truck. He stepped into the truck without resistance. Once he was inside, they injected him with a dose of a sedative that would keep him asleep for several hours. They placed him in a small compartment, a false back of the truck, and placed a panel covering over that section of the truck. They were on their way to Israel to interrogate the professor for his role in the murder of the Israeli and other Olympic athletes.

Mossad had no information on who had provided the deadly Usutu virus to ISIS. Alan Mazer was sitting comfortably back in Baltimore.

He had been wise enough to not request additional funding for his work on this virus after his initial studies in Aswan. Alan received plenty of money from local benefactors in Egypt. He applied for his first grant not having any idea what virus had caused the early problems in the Middle East. No electronic records existed with Alan's name associated with Usutu virus. And he purposely had not published anything on this virus. In addition, the new virology lab in Aswan was not yet on Israel's tracking system. Alan did not talk about his work in the States. This project had only been a vehicle to get Alan a faculty position when he first started at Hopkins.

The border crossing at the Jordan River went easily for the Mossad agents. Their Jordanian identity papers made for easy passage from Jordan to the Israeli crossing. After passing through the checkpoint, the Mossad agents sped quickly to an outpost just north of Tel Aviv.

They arrived at the outpost in the middle of the early morning and walked a still sleepy professor to a windowless room. There, the agents donned masks and then pulled off the cover and tape they had earlier placed on Al-Razi's head and mouth.

"This should go very easily if you cooperate," said the first agent.

"I don't know what you are talking about," the professor said.

"This is lie number one. You will not get many lies before the torture begins. Let me set some rules," said the second agent. "First, we know you are a radical Muslim. Two, we know you are the only mosquito and bird expert in Jordan. Three, we know that you contacted people to put mosquito eggs in the Olympic Village. That we know. We need more information. We know you know nothing about viruses. So as you sit here now, we will find out how Usutu virus infected and killed our Israeli brothers and sisters, Americans, and others at the Olympic Games."

"I don't have any idea what you are talking about," Al-Razi said.

"That is lie number two. Do you know baseball? Baseball is now becoming popular in Israel. Three strikes and you are out," said the second agent.

"When did you get the infected mosquito eggs to place in the Olympics?" the first agent asked.

"I did not get any infected mosquito eggs," he persisted.

Agent two left the room for a few minutes and then returned. The two agents made him sit against a wall with his head covered once again. They then put his back against the wall with his knees halfway up. If he slipped at all, they put him back on the wall. His leg muscles burned, and he cried in pain. They kept on lifting him up into the same position every time he slid down.

"Are you ready to talk now, professor?" said the second agent.

"I would talk, but I have nothing to say," he cried.

Finally, after at least thirty minutes of wall sitting, they pulled him from the floor and placed him on a backless stool with his head still covered and his hands now tied behind his back.

"Professor, this will be your last chance before things get pretty bad for you," said the second agent, and with that he slapped Al-Razi hard across his nose. "Where did the mosquitoes come from?"

"I don't know, from the water?"

"You are being a wise guy now, and that is not smart for an older man. You might not live through our questions," said agent two.

"If you are smart, you will answer now," said the first agent.

"What was the question again?"

"You know the question," said the second agent, and he slapped him hard on the jaw. "Where did the mosquito eggs come from?"

"They came from Ethiopia," he groaned.

"And how do we know this is true?" asked the first agent.

"I guess you must believe me," he said.

"We do not," said agent two.

The two agents undressed the professor, with the exception of his blindfold, and restrained his legs and arms with zip ties to a cot in the corner of the room. They then set the air conditioner to ten degrees Celsius and left the room. Two hours later, the agents came back to a man who looked beaten. They put their masks on and took his off. He looked ready to tell everything he knew about anything they would ask.

"Okay, professor, are you ready to tell us the truth? Did those mosquito eggs come from Ethiopia or some other location? And who gave them to you?" said the second Mossad agent.

"The eggs came from Ethiopia," he said.

"Are you sure?" said the agent.

"Yes, yes. Please can I have a blanket?" Al-Razi begged.

"Just a few more questions. Who gave you the eggs to place at the Olympics?" asked agent one.

"A Chinese doctor. I do not know his name. That is all I know. Please can I have a blanket?"

The first Mossad agent gave him one blanket that covered his legs, barely.

"How can you not know his name?" asked the second agent. "He brought you the mosquito eggs—millions, I guess?"

"Yes, millions. They came to me by courier from Syria, frozen. ISIS commanders told me what to do and I obeyed," said the professor.

The Mossad agents untied the professor and threw his clothes to him. They turned off the air conditioning, left the room, and locked the door. They had received lots of information. They already knew that Al-Razi was a key man in the plan. They knew he was lying. The source of the virus was not yet clear, but Al-Razi would be questioned further. For now he was going into a lock-up, and Israeli intelligence would investigate scientists worldwide studying Usutu virus.

NARI'S TRAVELS
2018

Nari Lee hated the Southwest Airlines 6:00 a.m. flight. It meant not only getting up at the crack of dawn but also, upon arrival, renting a car at BWI, another royal pain in the ass. This rental location was not as bad as the one in Providence, where the mile-long moving walkway took her to the rental area, but she lived there. She didn't need to get a car. At BWI a slow bus took her two miles to the rental car facility. She literally jumped off the bus, took the long walk over to the elevator, and went to the Hertz area. She paid more for Hertz, no longer the largest company, but walked right to her car in a slot with her designated name in the "Gold Lane." As do most "nonsmoking" rental cars, this one smelled like smoke, but by then Nari had no time to switch out cars. She exited the rental car facility and found the best route to Sinai Hospital on the north side of Baltimore to meet with an important client.

Nari Lee approached the front desk at Sinai Hospital. She was glad to see Sergeant Williams at his post. She knew him, and he recognized her face. She had come to Sinai to see one person, Dr. Jim Gregory, head of Pediatric Infectious Diseases.

"Dr. Lee, I am seeing you quite often recently. You should probably get an employee identification tag." Sergeant Williams chuckled to himself and peered down at the diminutive Dr. Lee from his high stool behind the desk. Nari Lee was a nicely dressed woman in her early thirties. She stood out from the crowd, not just because of her Asian appearance in this setting but because there was something about her demeanor and posture that demonstrated a strong air of confidence. She waited patiently for Williams to call Dr. Gregory's assistant to get approval for her pass into the hospital.

Nari smiled back at Williams. She had several stops to make in Baltimore and Washington during the day, as she wanted to provide some new data to physicians in her area on a new vaccine her company was investigating. Nari was not a sales representative; she was a scientist, an immunologist. Her role with the company was not to sell drugs. In fact, hers was a relatively new type of role for the biotechnology industry. This was an educational role. She and her peers delivered important information, what a newscaster might call real "breaking news," on the company's new products. No promises were made, and these products were not yet on the market, but her information would give doctors who were the leaders in the community a sense of what could be available for their patients.

Williams handed Nari a badge and sent her on her way. She had about ten minutes before her meeting, so she stopped for a quick coffee at the hospital cafeteria. Starbucks and Dunkin' Donuts had yet to find their way into this hospital lobby. After reviewing her calendar and notes for the upcoming meetings for the day, she noticed that it was getting quite close to her appointment time. She tossed the mud-like coffee in a garbage can near the elevator and made her way toward Dr. Gregory's office in Pediatric Infectious Diseases.

Dr. Gregory's assistant, Ann, led Nari toward his office. As Ann turned and walked toward the office door, Dr. Gregory cracked it open. "Please come in, Nari. It is good to see you again; you are getting to be a regular here. Come in. Come in."

Dr. Gregory was probably in his midfifties and had been at Sinai

Hospital for fifteen or sixteen years. He liked the environment. He had tried private practice for several years, but his love was always infectious diseases. When it came to infections, all he saw in his group private practice were a lot of runny noses, influenza in the winter, and the occasional strep throat. Getting on a hospital staff again gave him the opportunity to see children with many problems. It challenged him. And now, after all these years, he ran his own division within the Department of Pediatrics. Dr. Gregory had increased his staff over the last several years and even conducted clinical studies of investigational medications. This had not been done prior to his running the division. He knew that he would not compete with Hopkins, but that was not his goal. He had his own niche. And just having industry representatives such as Nari seeing him was a step in the right direction.

"Good morning, Dr. Gregory," Nari said. "I usually come here to download lots of new data from our company's research department, but not today. This is just a quick stop. I wanted to personally invite you to a meeting this spring, close by in DC. The Society for Prevention of Childhood Infections holds its major fundraiser in the first week of April every year. Immunoviratherapeutics, being intimately involved in this area of research, supports this society. This year they have planned an afternoon golf event at Congressional Country Club."

"Now you are speaking my language, Nari," Dr. Gregory said. "You know I love the game, if I could only get to play."

"That is exactly why I thought of you. We have sponsored a foursome. I will be playing, and I am inviting you and will bring along another two doctors from my region. A fantastic dinner will follow the golf. And as a huge bonus, Jerry Seinfeld will be the after-dinner entertainment," Nari said.

"This is wonderful. You can count me in. Thank you so much for the invite, and I honestly look forward to our next scientific chat about the ongoing measles vaccine work at your company," said Dr. Gregory.

"Bank on it. I have a trip planned back to the area in the next month or two. Plus, you know I will bend your ear on the course in April," Nari said. "I am off to Hopkins and Maryland with some other invitations. See you soon, Dr. Gregory."

Nari turned and waved goodbye to Ann as she left the office.

Nari headed south on the highway to Hopkins in hopes of dropping in on Dr. Alan Mazer. She knew full well he was not a golfer but had attended the dinner in years past. She just wanted a little face time with him if possible as she extended the dinner invitation. As chance would have it, Dr. Mazer was just leaving his office when Nari came upon him. He did not recognize her, even though they had met at least three times there and at other venues. She reintroduced herself and handed him the envelope as she explained the contents. Alan said he would be happy to attend the meeting in April and then continued down the hall without a thank-you. Nari did not think he really got it. This was a special event. She doubted he knew that the tables cost $10,000 each. Yes, they were all donations and the money all went to a good cause to support research, but she would have expected even this man to have come up with a thank-you.

Nari then stopped at the University of Maryland School of Medicine across town. There a team of scientists were studying unusual, newly discovered viruses from Africa. Nari handed an invitation to the chairman of microbiology. He was currently not working with the company, but Nari thought that since he was also a pediatrician, they might have future mutual interests. And she also knew he had played on the Harvard golf team some twenty years earlier. It would not be bad to have him in her group, she thought.

That was it for Baltimore. Nari then headed south back toward Washington and the home office in McLean. She had plenty of time to fill in the rest of the foursome, and completing the table with home office personnel would not be a problem. This was an event that everyone wanted to attend.

The next morning Nari headed back to Providence. She needed to focus on Boston and New York physicians in the next few weeks before planning any further trips back to the mid-Atlantic region. The schedule was grueling, and given that the company soon would have two products, her plan was to speak with upper management about getting some help. To this point, her pleas for new hires had always fallen on deaf ears.

Nari spent the next three weeks running around Boston, upstate

New York in brutal weather, and then New York City, trying to prep many physicians she knew and others she was trying to get to know about the company's up-and-coming measles vaccine. The problem she had was that she could not say much. She had no new data to speak about. The vaccine was not yet approved for sales and marketing. It was not legal to promote something that wasn't approved, and that was not her job. She was the scientific face of the company. All she had to speak about was an early safety, a phase 1 study with the measles vaccine and the MPV vaccine that continued to do well. The company had completed the large, pivotal study, but the study had not yet been published. It was due out in the press in the next few weeks, and Nari could not wait to speak about it. She kept telling herself that these visits were important; they were setting the groundwork for when the data would be available and for FDA approval.

After a grueling month, Nari decided she needed to take a week off. She decided to fly to see her parents in California. It had been a long time, and she longed for some time away from the grind. She had accumulated so many frequent flier miles on multiple airlines and had a status that allowed her to easily get a free flight in a winter month. Nari called her mom and dad, and they were happy to have her visit. So Nari's arrival was not a surprise visit, but in all honesty, she felt like it was when she walked in the door. She had sensed such a closeness to her mother and father when she grew up. She was an only child, and they gave all of themselves to her every day of their lives. She did not have that same feeling when visiting now. They were not cold to her at all, but their child now was their new visitor. It just seemed like her parents were so involved in their company and had little interest in her. Her parents were heading up a new software company focusing on artificial intelligence. Nari was happy to see that they were so engaged in their work but, honestly, not to this extent. Nari thought, *I am the person who you raised and loved. What happened to that love? At what stage do you say, "I can delegate this and spend time with my only daughter"?* Her parents had made it in America. They had raised a successful daughter and had a fortune but did not want to stop. Nari felt abandoned and had no friends left in the Palo Alto area. She went back to the East after three days, feeling much worse than when she had arrived.

When she returned home to Providence, she said to herself, "I think I am really home at last." After spending fifteen years in the area, it had finally sunk in: she belonged on the East Coast. Nari turned on her computer and immediately planned her trip to her favorite place, the Baltimore-Washington area, and the home office.

The next Monday, she took the first flight out of Green Airport to Baltimore. Nari had emailed Dr. Gregory at Sinai Hospital late in the prior week and had set up an early-morning meeting. She was sure that the first part of the day would go as scheduled unless flight delays or road conditions would mess it up.

"Dr. Lee, so nice to see you again," said Sergeant Williams at the Sinai Hospital security desk.

"Good morning to you, Sarge," Nari replied. "I am glad you remember me. I am here to see Dr. Gregory. I have a 9:00 appointment."

"Who else," he said. "Just sign in as always, and I will print out your badge and then ring Ann to tell her you are here."

"Thanks, Sarge. Just let me know when I can proceed up," she said.

Sarge waved her ahead, and Nari headed down the hall.

"Hello, Dr. Lee," said Ann. "I am glad to see you so soon after you last quick visit. Dr. Gregory is in his office. Would you like some coffee?"

"Yes, please. Thank you," Nari answered.

"Good morning, Nari," said Dr. Gregory.

"Good morning to you. Great to see you," said Nari. "Have you been practicing your golf swing at all? We have just a few weeks to go."

"I am sure that's why you're here. Of course. Let's face it—we will be counting on your ball. What do you really have for us today?"

Nari thanked Ann when she brought in the coffee. "Dr. Gregory, we have some very interesting data I would like to share with you on our new measles virus vaccine. The abstract for the study, which is just published, will be presented next week at the International Infectious Disease Conference in San Francisco," Nari said proudly. "It is very exciting, and we feel that it could, in time, even replace the current standard vaccine."

"Wow, slow down, Nari. And please, first, after all these years it is time you start calling me Jim. Second, we have been using the standard measles vaccine, or MMR (the measles, mumps, rubella trivalent vaccine), for years. It is effective. The measles strain used, the Enders's attenuated Edmonston strain, would be hard to beat. And as you know, the group down the road at Hopkins has been studying measles all over the world for thirty-plus years. I tend to listen to their recommendations. And to be clear, your vaccine is just for measles. I don't want to have to stick my children with another needle for the other vaccines."

"Dr.—I mean, Jim—I would agree. We know how well the standard vaccine has done over the years," Nari began. "We have made two simple genetic changes in the proteins of the virus that stick to the cell, the H and F proteins. These are simple but significant changes to the measles strain. I cannot reveal too many details. Suffice it to say that the immune response to the fusion protein or F-protein of the virus is stronger, and that will help block infection for a longer duration. Our product was just tested in over five thousand children, and they required only one injection instead of two for the same level of protection. And fewer local reactions were reported. We look extremely promising. More data will be released after the presentation next week. Plus, the manuscript will hopefully be published in a top-tier journal. I am hoping for the *New England Journal of Medicine*. I cannot promise anything, but we are hopeful for a decision by the Food and Drug Administration by year's end."

Dr. Gregory responded, "Well, that does add a nice twist to the story, and something to think about. With that additional information, that could be important in preventing outbreaks of measles in school-age children. Not requiring an additional injection in toddlers or at five to six years of age would be a big advantage. Now, I remember your first product at Immunoviratherapeutics. I didn't have much hope for your company's MPV vaccine. The medical world recognized the significance of the virus. It caused fifteen thousand to twenty-five thousand premature babies to be hospitalized. But RSV got all the press and concern. You guys developed a vaccine, and all of a sudden MPV infections in preemies were all but gone. Your strategy of vaccinating mothers with high-risk pregnancies did reduce hospitalizations. I was sure this would fail, just like the RSV vaccines in young children, but it surprised me. What a great product you developed. You must have some very bright people working there."

"I can agree with that," Nari replied, "and let me add, our people are also working on making the measles vaccine trivalent so you hopefully would not be sticking the kids with an extra shot."

"Well, that would be a godsend and another great update. Thanks again for visiting today," Jim said.

"If you have any ideas for further projects you want to consider with MPV, now is the time to start developing them for next season. We need to get them in process by late spring so we can review them," Nari said. "We have an interest in older children, so think about that, and possible maternal vaccination studies."

"Interesting ideas. Thanks for you insights, Nari," he said with a grin.

"My pleasure. I am now heading down to Hopkins and then on to Georgetown and Children's in DC. I think the traffic on 95 will be less than torture now that it is past nine o'clock. All the best," replied Nari.

Nari headed toward the elevator with a huge smile on her face. She was usually charming, but having good data made her interactions with her docs easy, and they were interested in listening to what she had to say. Plus, it gave her an opportunity to get back to see them again. Face time was so important with the opinion leaders. If she had nothing to show them, why would they want to see her? Yes, Nari's was a pretty face to look at, but Jim Gregory was not like other doctors; his opinion was going to be swayed by data, not by the looks and charm of a visiting medical specialist from a biotechnology company. She dropped her badge off with Sarge and waved to him, as he was busy with three people in a queue to visit patients in the hospital. It was going to be a good day, a good week, and hopefully a good year for Nari and for Immunoviratherapeutics Inc.

After visiting Jim, Nari headed southbound on I-83 to the Hopkins medical campus in inner-city Baltimore. She had a quick meeting scheduled with Alan Mazer, who had finally agreed to meet with her again and take part in the company's speaker's bureau. It was great to have top-notch academicians speaking on behalf of the company. These speakers would give seminars on the disease and how various products might treat or prevent it. Nari knew that Dr. Mazer had collaborated with the research group on measles virus mutants for some time, so she wondered why he had been so unwilling to sit down with her for any length of time since she was the scientific representative for the company. Finally, he had agreed to see her, and she did not want to press him. Her plan was to drop off a CD and thumb drive containing a draft slide presentation on the new measles vaccine that they hoped to market the next spring. She also wanted to ask just a question or two about his research to gain some credibility. She had to hit him over the head with a hammer to make him understand that she was a bona fide scientist with a PhD and a PharmD and a scientific representative for the company who could really be a conduit for him to assist him in obtaining funding for projects.

Dr. Mazer apologized as he entered his office about ten minutes late. "Good morning, Dr. Lee. I am Alan Mazer," he said, again not recalling that he had met Nari many times before. "I am sorry for being late. I am attending this month and have a large patient load. My last patient got me tied up."

"I understand, Dr. Mazer, and thank you for taking time for seeing me today," said Nari.

"What can I do for you? I know that you have tried to see me several times," Alan added.

"First, I understand you have agreed to join our speaker's bureau when we launch our new measles virus vaccine. Thank you. I have some material for you," Nari explained.

"Okay, let me have it," Alan said quite gruffly. He placed the folder on his desk and eyed Nari up and down.

"Of course, but let me explain briefly. This is still in draft mode. I have both a thumb drive and a CD, whatever is most convenient for you. Both are the same PowerPoint presentation, with suggested notations. Again, these are drafts and have to be approved by the FDA for presentations in educational seminars," Nari further clarified, "so for now, do not use these slides in any presentation as representing Immunoviratherapeutics."

"Understood, ma'am."

"Dr. Mazer, since I cover this geographic area as the scientific liaison for the company, you should feel free to contact me for any work you wish to do with any of the marketed products. I know you have ongoing work with the research team in the pipeline, but I am your go-to person for anything you need," Nari added.

"Got it. I will keep that in mind. Please, can I have a couple of your cards?" Alan asked.

"Of course. By the way, how are things going with work on the mutant virus? I heard you had done some work on that with Ashraf?" Nari inquired.

"Yes, I am always interested in how viruses can invade the nervous system. But I have nothing yet. I will keep you in mind for any further work with the new vaccine when it comes out. Thanks for coming by. Got to run now, Nari," Alan said as he whisked her out of his office and turned the other way down the hall.

Nari left Hopkins quickly. She was happy to see Dr. Mazer but surprised by the quick exit. His reaction was unusual. She understood that people were busy and she oftentimes only got a quick hello and goodbye, but this was different. Nari was quick to note that as soon as she had mentioned the work on the mutant virus, he clammed up. This was not a secret; the company had funded the work. She kept that in her notes so she would remember to not bring it up again. She wanted to develop positive long-term relationships and try to have fruitful conversations with her docs if possible.

Nari made quick stops at both Georgetown and Children's hospitals. Her meeting with the chief of pediatrics at Georgetown was suddenly canceled for what she learned was a fundraising meeting for a new research building. If she had only known it was in Florida, she would have flown down there with her golf clubs. Alumni held a golf event to raise money for the new building, a common occurrence in the biopharma industry. Meetings were double- and triple-booked, and the pharmaceutical specialists were usually the last to know. They were bumped off the schedule. That could be exhausting and frustrating when one took the time to fly somewhere to see someone. This happened all the time, even when she went overseas, and that really was discouraging. But, she thought, it happened, and maybe this doc owed her now.

Her last stop was Children's Hospital in DC, and this visit went much better. Nari was bringing in one investigator from a Northern Virginia site on the vaccine study to present data from the earlier phase 2 study. The investigator did a great job, and most of the pediatric infectious disease staff attended the meeting. Nari guaranteed the attendance by providing a wide selection of sandwiches and salads from a local favorite restaurant. After an hour and a half, she headed to the home office in McLean. It was always a good idea to get face time with the boss and top management. It couldn't hurt her career path.

9

COMPANY MILESTONES
APRIL 2018

Immunoviratherapeutics Inc. once held its annual meeting in the company cafeteria. Today, the annual meeting convened at the JW Marriott in downtown Washington, DC. The meeting was moved there as the company had grown and had increased revenues, local shareholders, and huge expectations. All employees who owned stock were obviously allowed to attend, but thankfully most did not. They knew that it was mostly a formal business meeting, and everyone had work to do. Further, the president and board would frown on a room full of staff members. However, a few attended because the president had asked them to submit nominees for new board members from the floor. Ashraf Khaleed, having been one of the original one hundred employees, was one of those in attendance. He did not appear happy, however, as he sat waiting for the meeting to start. He studied the proxy and noted what he thought were exorbitant salaries of each of the officers of the company. Ashraf also could not believe what he saw when he turned to the stock ownership and option page. Colonel Arnold Ickerson, the founder, CEO, and chairman of the board, owned almost 5 percent of the company and was being awarded another 150,000 options this calendar year. In the current market, the colonel was worth north of $75 million on paper. Others were also worth multiple millions, and Ashraf couldn't get over how long he had worked, what he had done for the company, and how little of the company he owned.

A few members of the senior sales team also attended the meeting, as did Nari Lee. Ashraf glared at Nari as she passed him to take her seat toward the front of the room. She did not notice him. Nari had been hired before the launch of the MPV vaccine and turned out to be a strong employee. She lectured all over the country and helped bring aboard many product advocates, many who were originally naysayers for such a product. She was well rewarded for her work and had a lot of exposure within and outside the company. Her work, many said, was responsible in part for the successful launch of the first vaccine. Ashraf was despondent. He had helped develop the vaccine and had received very little credit for his work. He was to be the fourth author on an upcoming scientific paper, yet to be published because of disclosure issues, the lawyers said. And, here she was walking proudly toward the front row of the meeting room as if she owned the place, Ashraf thought. He wondered if she would have some special role in this meeting.

Ashraf nominated the new board member on cue, as requested. Another laboratory worker seconded the nomination. They both did their jobs admirably, and the chairman thanked them both.

It turned out that Nari did not have a role at the meeting. The new board member was approved. Other business of the board meeting was conducted without any issue, and the meeting was concluded in less than thirty minutes.

Ashraf sat in his seat for a few moments and watched some interactions among the upper-level management, board members, sales team, and of course Dr. Nari Lee. He was burning inside. Ashraf got up from his chair, did an about face, and left the hall without addressing anyone. He did not think he could have approached the group at the front, but on his way out of the hotel, he had regrets. He thought, *What is wrong with me? I had every right to say hello to my coworkers. I helped get them here. I am a fool.* Depressed, Ashraf turned the corner and handed the ticket for his car to the garage attendant. It would be a long drive to McLean irrespective of traffic.

Back at the meeting, Colonel Arnold Ickerson, the CEO, bellowed, "I am now opening the meeting to the floor for any questions by our shareholders," in his loud, military commander's voice. "Yes, I see one hand over there on the right. Please identify yourself for the minutes before asking your question."

"Of course. I am Harriet Jamison. I am wondering why the company is working on an old virus like measles. There is already an effective vaccine. Can one of you explain where we are going with this, please? Thank you."

"I can handle this, but my chief of research can jump in if I fumble the ball," Arnold began. "That's a very insightful question. There is a good product out there. But I want to give a little background on the measles virus first, and the problem. Not that many years ago measles was considered one of the 'great neglected diseases of humankind.' Millions of children died every year from the indirect consequences of measles, secondary infections, and the immune suppression it caused. Then, thanks to concerted research and vaccine delivery to developing nations, measles cases were reduced significantly. In the States, measles was virtually eliminated. There was an occasional imported case from an immigrant, but that was it, and there was no spread since almost every child was vaccinated. Then—pardon my French—the proverbial shit hit the fan in the late nineties and early part of the twenty-first century. A paper published out of the UK suggested that autism and disorders on the spectrum could be related to measles vaccination. The effect was felt in the developed world. Moms would not give their babies the measles vaccine. Well, guess what? Measles has raised its ugly head again, and it's a big problem. The vaccine in use requires two doses for effective protection. And, if successful, our product, MVoneshot, will require just one injection, so I think we will have unique advantage. As for autism and the author of that paper, I will bet my ownership in my company that the scientist will be found guilty of everything from scientific fraud to hoax and everything in between. I hope that answers your question, madam."

"Yes, thank you, Dr. Ickerson."

"That concludes our meeting. Thank you all for attending. I look forward to a successful year, and I hope to see you at our next annual meeting," said Arnold.

The timing could have been better for the annual meeting, but that was not important in the overall scheme of things for the company. At four o'clock that same afternoon, the Food and Drug Administration sent a fax to the head of regulatory affairs at Immunoviratherapeutics. MVoneshot had received FDA approval. The news excited Arnold and the rest of the company. The team knew now was the time to get the engines started. Arnold had hoped to receive the news earlier so his team could have been making product and getting ready for the vaccine "season" earlier. But, good news was good news. Arnold issued this statement after the close of the US markets: "Food and Drug Administration approved today the first new measles virus vaccine requiring just one injection for complete effectiveness. MVoneshot, developed by Immunoviratherapeutics, is safe and effective for children from age 1 to 13 years of age. Measles virus has in the past caused millions of deaths worldwide and thousands of hospitalizations in the United States. One in one thousand children dies from measles infections. It is important to remain vigilant and continue protecting our children by providing safe and effective vaccination. We at IVTP will continue to work to develop other safe and effective vaccines for your children and you." The rest of the press release went on with standard verbiage and safe harbor statements. In after-hours trading, IVTP was quite active and went up fifteen dollars per share.

April in Washington, DC, had to be the best time of the year. The cherry trees on the Tidal Basin were just about to burst with color, and buses loaded with children were visiting the monuments as school trips overtook the National Mall. Many professional organizations planned their national meetings for springtime in Washington. Also, the Society for Prevention of Childhood Infections was hosting its annual national fundraising event at the Congressional Country Club in Bethesda,

Maryland. Scores of physicians and scientists and donors from all over the country had converged on the fairways and greens, not so much to show their abilities, which were lacking, but to enjoy the day. And it was a brilliant day. No one got lost, no one was injured, and everyone claimed to have finished eighteen holes. Immunoviratherapeutics claimed the golfing prize, with Nari Lee's foursome winning the low score. Most importantly, Jerry Seinfeld was hilarious, and he donated his services. The auctions of donated art, fine wine, and other gifts brought in over $500,000. Altogether, the society netted over $1 million.

Later on in the year, Ashraf Khaleed worked carefully at the biohazard hood monitoring the robotic arm of a machine that was dispensing small amounts of the measles virus vaccine stock or seed into plastic vials. This was not the actual MVoneshot vaccine but the inoculum used to eventually make the vaccine. It had taken many years to come to this step for this vaccine. Ashraf had worked for Immunoviratherapeutics for seven years. In days gone by, he would do this by hand, using a plastic pipette and carefully filling each tube. Contamination by bacteria or fungus was rare in the past, but now with robotics and the elimination of humans, it was almost impossible to have contaminants introduced.

He worked tirelessly on any project given him. He was now in a GMP (Good Manufacturing Practices) production facility, one used for all steps of commercial production. As required in a GMP facility, every procedure used was validated, and everything was run according to a strict set of standard operating procedures. Further, only certain trained personnel were allowed in the facility and trained to perform certain tasks. Every last detail was reported and documented. Ashraf took special care to observe the robotic machinery as it dispensed the final culture fluid into vials to be frozen. Everyone in the company knew how important these last small steps were and trusted Ashraf and his team. It was imperative to freeze several hundred vials of the stock measles virus vaccine. One vial would then be taken out and grown when needed for each lot of vaccine each year the company needed to manufacture it. As he worked, he was very careful. The material he was freezing needed to be maintained in a sterile environment, which was why Ashraf was gowned and working in a biohazard hood. This was a critical step in the manufacturing process. Further, some stock vials would also have to be moved to a secondary GMP facility. In the event something happened to the primary storage, a backup was needed. All the virus was live and kept frozen in a −80 degrees Celsius freezer.

Ashraf had been a dependable worker for all these years and was proud of what he had done with the company. However, he was what one would call a worker bee. Yes, he supervised an important staff, but he had a bachelor's degree from the University of Maryland, Baltimore County. He had done very well in college and had all the technical skills needed to oversee and run any experiment in any biotechnology lab. Ashraf had not pursued an advanced degree, and he needed one to move up in the company. During the last several years, as Immunoviratherapeutics grew and its share price first quadrupled on the NASDAQ, Ashraf felt good with his one thousand stock options. However, most of his new coworkers had doctoral degrees or were physicians, and the company granted them thousands of stock options when coming aboard. Ashraf felt that he was working for nothing while everyone else was getting rich off his hard work in the lab. It was his time; he had not only helped develop the new MPV vaccine that caused the stock price to go crazy, but he actually made the point mutations in the key parts of MVoneshot. With the approval of the new measles virus vaccine, the stock price skyrocketed again and Ashraf felt left behind. It was always others—the rich, white, mostly Christian and Jewish corporate leaders who were advantaged. Ashraf was more than dissatisfied by his lack of participation in the upside of the company's growth. He felt he deserved a lot more for his role.

As Ashraf watched the robotics arm place the vials in the rack for freezing, he called to his assistant to come over to the hood. He instructed her as per the protocol to place the vials that were in a rack onto a cart. She was then to wheel them into another room and place them into freezers for long-term storage. All the freezers were maintained on a back-up generator. The next day, some virus stocks would be transported to a remote secure facility in another state in the event of some catastrophic event at the primary GMP location in

McLean. The future revenues from this product were dependent on a continued source of this virus stock.

Ashraf then left the hood and P3 area to an anteroom. An ultraviolet light blinked on for fifteen seconds; he then disrobed, taking off his gloves and total neck-to-feet laboratory covering, placing them in a biohazard garbage can. After taking off the outer lab wear, Ashraf showered. He then walked into the outer room, where he dressed in his street clothes. Before returning to his office—as he was one of few technical staff members to have an office—he walked to the research lab corridor. The labs were vacant by now, as it was well past six thirty in the evening. Ashraf took a few pieces of dry ice from a storage chest and placed them in a small Styrofoam container.

He then went to the freezer in the research wing, where he had stored many mutant measles virus strains he had developed over the years. He pulled three vials out of storage. They all contained the measles strain that had not passed the test for further development. This was the strain that had caused hind-limb paralysis in mice and a seizure in a monkey. It was actually the exact same strain he had just placed into production and had his assistant put into the freezer for growing as the commercial vaccine. He had made the switch months ago. No one was the wiser since the strains behaved identically in the lab—the only differences were the animal results.

After putting the vials on dry ice in the Styrofoam box, Ashraf walked briskly to his office. He was ready to leave his office after a long day. He slipped the small box in his large overcoat pocket. His work at Immunoviratherapeutics was done, but his day was not yet done. He was on his way to Baltimore that evening to meet his compatriot, Dr. Alan Mazer. Ashraf and Alan had waited two years for this day, and now he had just a short window of time to move forward with the plan long in the works.

As he pulled out of the parking lot, he thought about the very long, anxious, and exciting day at Immunoviratherapeutics. The rest of the day and evening—the paperwork and signing off on the work—could be handled by computer. He had observed his lab assistant freezing the vaccine seed stocks, and that was all he needed to see as he ended his day. He did not need to oversee the cleanup work for that area of the lab; he was not required to observe that process in person. His top assistant, however, could document all those steps, and her signature was needed for the regulatory purposes. He would then countersign on Monday morning.

The traffic was unusually sparse for the DC area as Ashraf headed east on the outer loop of the DC beltway over to 95 north. Traffic in this area was usually rated the first or second worst in the country, owing to the number of visitors, transients, diplomats, and of course commuters. Ashraf had even seen on multiple occasions drivers reading paperback books on their drives around the DC beltway. You never knew what you would encounter on your way to Baltimore, and Ashraf thought that making it to the Hopkins medical complex in ninety minutes was another victory of the day. Imagine—no Redskins games, no Orioles postseason games (of course, it was not the seventies), and no Ravens games made for a dream.

Ashraf called Alan on his office line as he exited 95 by Camden Yards so that Alan would know when he would be arriving. At this time of day, Alan estimated it would take Ashraf about seven minutes at most to arrive at Hopkins, so he finished reading a few emails. He then grabbed his overcoat and pulled on a ski cap despite the mild forty-five-degree weather. He scurried down the steps and went out the Monument Street exit of one of the hospital buildings. As expected, Ashraf was in his red 2005 Toyota Corolla, easy to pick out as he drove up to the door. Ashraf pulled over, briefly said hello to Alan, and handed him the Styrofoam box that contained the measles vaccine vials he had whisked away from the company. Ashraf said a few final words to Alan before he left and asked him if he had the cell lines up and growing in his lab. Alan confirmed that all was on schedule. Ashraf said he would return in two days, on Saturday, and told him to meet him at this door at 7:00 a.m. He needed an early start and wanted to make sure Alan knew his role. Alan headed back to his lab, and Ashraf rolled up his window. He headed east, cut over on Wolfe Street, and then retreated west on a parallel road that took him back to the highway and the DC area. It was a slower drive back because the skies opened up and the rain did not stop on his whole trip home to his apartment in Falls Church.

Ashraf was pleased it was a Saturday. Parking would not be restricted on the side streets on the weekend. He pulled into a wide space, easy for his small car. He grabbed his umbrella and a few files and hurried across the street as the downpour from the night before continued. It was a quick dash to the hospital entrance where Alan waited to sign him in to his lab as a visitor for the day.

The coconspirators took the stairs to the third floor neurovirology labs. Despite his radical Islamic views' leading him to design this terrorist plot, Alan was very proud of his scientific accomplishments and really wondered at times how he had gotten to this place in his life. The fact that he was one of just a few physicians working in this esteemed laboratory was a major achievement.

Alan's lab was not large but was suitable to run first-class virology and immunology experiments. He could also use the shared facilities farther down the hall if needed. They contained large, heavy equipment such as centrifuges, low-temperature freezers, overflow incubators for growing cell cultures, and radioactivity counters. Alan quickly showed Ashraf all the equipment but expected him to stay within Alan's individual space and not wander the hallways.

Ashraf and Alan stood by the window and planned the day. Alan wanted to continue to do experiments on this mutant virus even though the actual real work had been completed by Ashraf at company headquarters. They would inoculate the chick embryo cell cultures that Alan had prepared earlier in the week with the virus Ashraf had delivered from his freezer. This was the first step in producing enough virus to perform some additional experiments.

This was the virus mutant that had not passed all the tests to go through clinical trials. Ashraf had surreptitiously grown this virus in his lab and substituted this strain for the one that was approved by the FDA. This is the virus that the robot had placed in the vials earlier in the week. This was the mutant virus that was already now in the system at the company, ready for vaccine production. This was the strain that caused neurological problems in the animal models. The manufacturing group was none the wiser and was producing this as the real vaccine. Ashraf had made this mutant. Alan knew from experience that it had a very high likelihood of being problematic in humans. It might cause neurological issues in them as well, and if so, the company, its investors, and its leaders would take a huge financial hit. This would be one new way that Alan and his group could push their radical Muslim agenda—a new terror attack on the United States coming out of nowhere. It would be an attack on a company and a bioterrorist attack on the people of the country.

Ashraf opened one vial of the virus he had taken to Alan two days previously; he had infected the chick cultures. The infection started. It was nothing complicated. Alan had collaborated with the company and run a few experiments for them with other strains of virus, so it was not unusual for company personnel to be at Alan's lab. Here, however, the series of experiments Alan planned for the mutant virus were totally off the books. This work was not yet sanctioned; he had only hoped to do it. Nari had been totally misinformed. He never had worked with this neurovirulent strain before because the company wanted tight control of it. Alan had asked to work with it, and he waited anxiously for formal approval from the company's committee.

It was Saturday morning, and the collaboration began. Ashraf suggested that they attend the mosque in Baltimore where they had met. They agreed to drive over independently and meet for prayer time, around noon. After prayer, the two of them struck up conversation with several parishioners whom they both knew. They talked about world issues, and Ashraf clearly expressed his radical side.

Ashraf left Alan at the mosque and drove home. The next day, Alan returned to the lab to check the cultures. He carefully removed one of the cultures from the incubator; the culture fluid looked pink, a good sign. As he placed the culture on an inverted microscope, he examined the cell monolayer and saw some cells beginning to fuse. Clearly, the infected cells had begun to spread the virus from cell to cell. That meant that there were millions and millions of virus particles in the fluid above the culture. In the next two to three days, Alan would harvest the fluid. He had already prepared additional fresh chick embryo cultures for producing more virus before handling these infected cultures. Pleased with his progress, his day was done. Alan and Ashraf shared an email account, and Alan wrote a draft email that Ashraf could read in draft mode without its being sent. In that way, no one and no agency could intercept their communications. Alan knew it was possible that he was being watched. He had attended several radical mosques, and it was post 9/11. Even though Alan was a member of the community in good standing and a physician, any individual frequenting Muslim organizations would end up on someone's watch list. He was sure that at some point, national security agents would follow him.

Alan and Ashraf decided that this old-school communication method would work; number one, Alan did not want to make laboratory mistakes, and number two, he did not want to be taken into custody for questioning. It was a critical juncture. They had not done anything wrong; they were only collaborating on a project at this point, nothing else.

Ashraf responded later that Sunday afternoon to Alan's email, again saving a draft in the same account. He expected the type of cytopathic effect that Alan was observing on the cell cultures in just one day. This measles virus mutant, however, replicated in culture just as expected, just like the normal vaccine strain the company had selected. Ashraf expected that within seventy-two hours, on Tuesday morning, the cultures would be at peak virus production, and the fluid would be ready to harvest. He would have enough virus in these cultures to then inoculate and produce even more virus over the next several days. Alan's lab was becoming a small production facility. That was not their goal here; they wanted to produce concentrated virus for molecular study and further animal study to replicate the work done by the company. Ashraf was the key to the molecular biology work that Alan wanted to accomplish for his own academic interests.

Ashraf had other designs as well. He was a very intelligent man and knew his way around the laboratory. He had even shown some leadership skills. He was promoted to a senior manager position and began to oversee important aspects of the vaccine development process and scale up for manufacturing. This was a new area for Ashraf. His superiors wanted to see if he could handle a new set of skills, including management. On the other hand, Ashraf lacked some common sense. Having begun growing the measles strain that he and Alan were quite sure would be problematic as a vaccine in humans when placed into the manufacturing stream, Ashraf came up with his own way of making a profit. Since he felt all along that he had not been rewarded sufficiently for his work at the company, he had his own plan.

Alan was not aware of Ashraf's scheme. If he had been, Alan would have stopped Ashraf from starting his foolish plan. Ashraf figured it would be at least six months before the FDA would approve the new vaccine. Ashraf decided to meet with a few of his friends from the Baltimore mosque where Alan and Ashraf had first met. He revealed to Alan nothing of his plot, but he told several of his friends and stated clearly that he expected some very bad news out of the company in the next six to nine months. They could make some big money on this news. Now, he said, would be a good time to start "shorting the stock."

"You are betting on a company's stock to decline," he explained to them. Ashraf described what that meant and how to accomplish it. He told his friends how others he knew in the company had made bets on technology stocks and made big money when companies failed. He also knew that some had lost their shirts. But in this case, Ashraf told them, he controlled the cards, so to speak. Finally, he explained that they could keep some of the profits for themselves but must return some to the mosque and the Imam for investment into the American caliphate and the Baltimore cell.

He suggested buying "put" options on Immunoviratherapeutics for April and July of 2019. This was a strategy that bet on the share price of the company falling around that time. By using options, one could leverage and buy thousands of shares compared to buying standard shares in the company. There was a lot more risk but a lot more upside as well if the price of the asset fell. Ashraf was wise enough to not buy any himself but convinced his sister living in Toronto, who had a different surname, to invest close to $5,000. So with this in place, Ashraf felt he would finally receive some financial rewards for his work. He was particularly interested in the money for himself and the Baltimore cell. He thought he should have done well financially when the company big shots made millions. At least now, he could make some money for himself when the company failed. He also now knew that everything was on track with Alan to get things going in his lab. It thrilled him to have such a close ally in the war against the West. Alan Mazer was smarter than anyone he had met before.

Ashraf had concluded a long day in Baltimore and just wanted to return to his apartment and get to sleep. Once in his car, he tuned his radio to his favorite overnight talk radio show. The show's host was Gerri Nesmith. She covered everything from the paranormal to GMO foods to weird strangeness. He could not believe his ears when he heard they were discussing the measles virus and Alan Mazer was on the show. He had missed most of that hour.

"We have just a few minutes left tonight, so in the closing moments of our show, would you doctors like to summarize your thoughts on vaccinations?" Gerri asked. "I know that, for me personally, I always get my yearly flu vaccine. Some people tell me I'm crazy, that it doesn't ever work, but heck, it can kill thousands of us elderly folk every year. It killed millions in 1918. Might as well. Dr. Gregory, why don't you lead-off."

"Great show tonight, and your audience certainly had many interesting questions for us," Jim began. "First, you are right about the flu vaccine. It's an educated guess every year based on the circulation of strains in the Far East. We cannot always be right. And flu can kill the young and the old, especially. I definitely recommend the vaccine every year, especially if you're around lots of kids during the holiday season. I spend most of my time caring for sick children with a variety of infectious diseases. If we can prevent any of these common infections and their complications, I am of the mindset that we should try. I think there is sufficient evidence that vaccines developed in our country are safe and effective. Preventing the sickness and costs of hospitalizations associated with preventable infections is a blessing," concluded Dr. Gregory.

"Thank you, Dr. Gregory. Dr. Mazer, also from Baltimore, could you add your perspective?" requested Gerri.

"Of course. I am in agreement with Jim, but I have a different view. I have done quite a bit of field research, as have my colleagues at Hopkins, and have seen the devastation of neglected infections. Measles virus in unvaccinated populations kills thousand to millions—yes, millions—of children. It's hard to comprehend this number, but that is the truth.

I am very concerned about the groups of parents withholding this approved vaccination. Let me also add a comment, considering Jim's remarks, about our country's vaccines: we need to trust the machinery we have in place. A new virus could hit us, like a Zika or something more devastating. If we have a vaccine to stop its spread, let's use it. Our brave men and women fighting overseas have also been on the front line when it comes to fighting infections. They are sometimes the first to receive experimental vaccines because of necessity. They expect to meet the virus enemy as well as the combatant, so they are fighting multiple wars for us. Gerri, thank you for giving us some air time," concluded Dr. Mazer.

"Well, thank you both, and I reserve the right to draft you for a future show just in case we have a public emergency. I pray we do not, of course. Good night, good morning, and have a good day. See you on the air next time, and thank you for your ears and minds, everyone."

Alan felt great about his performance on this nationally syndicated talk show. The audience was somewhat over two million listeners, it was on satellite radio and terrestrial radio, and it would be rebroadcast on YouTube. He hoped his and Jim's word would spread just like an epidemic before the release of the new measles vaccine. The timing was perfect. He expected the new measles vaccine to be marketed shortly.

10

MEASLES MAYHEM

2019

"Good morning to all of you late-night owls all over the globe. This is your host of the early morning air waves, Gerri Nesmith, your humble lady of the night. Once again we have a great show for you this morning. We bring you the news that network and cable stations choose not to deal with. We focus on the out of the ordinary and stories that other outlets will eventually report.

"I hope you have all gotten your tax returns filed. If not, you have about twenty-four hours. It is early in the morning of the day we must face the music, so to speak. Tonight before we get to our first guest, who will discuss his book on the real pirates of the Caribbean, I'd like to have Duncan Johnson come on live. Duncan, affectionately known around here as Dunk, has some breaking news. Dunk, why the urgent call this early morning hour? We usually tape our reports with you."

"Gerri, thanks for taking my call. Yes, we do usually get together and tape some newsy events for the show. I hope you can trust me for an unscripted hot item that could devastate us all?"

"Dunk, I don't care about the unscripted part, but I am quite upset about the devastating part," Gerri replied.

"I just broke my arm."

"Not so devastating."

"Of course. But when I came out of the ER at San Ysidro Hospital, an area where I was covering another story, I saw five children in other cubicles or in the hall. All appeared to be dead or dying; another child was limping into the emergency room with parents on each arm. Several in the waiting area also appeared to be in a similar condition. The ones I saw had rashes covering their bodies. I believe something strange is in the air."

"We will have to follow up on this, Dunk," Gerri responded. "Sounds like something may be brewing down south in California. I will call you after the show for an update. I want you on the air tomorrow. Thanks, again."

Dr. Gregory, the head of Pediatric Infectious Diseases at Sinai Hospital, sent an urgent text to Nari Lee early Monday morning. He had wondered and wrestled over the past several hours how to handle a situation. Should he contact the company, the FDA, or the CDC? Or, for that matter, the hospital attorney? He had not slept all night and had been back and forth to the hospital emergency department. He also fielded calls from several pediatricians about unusual reactions to the new Immunoviratherapeutics measles live vaccine, MVoneshot. One problem he picked up on right away was that local doctors were not using the product as directed by the manufacturer. The panic over the recent rising number of cases of natural measles infections pushed docs to move quickly. Parents had delayed vaccinating their one- and two-year-olds with standard MMR vaccine, and now docs had started to give the new vaccine to older kids. He still was amazed that physicians in his own clinic were not giving the vaccine to appropriate patients. They had been educated multiple times on the use of this new product. The company had brought in experts on two occasions for presentations, and Nari Lee also provided an educational program. They perplexed him. One problem was evident to Dr. Gregory: MVoneshot had not been tested in older children. But panic had set in, and not just in the

United States. The number of measles infections in children and young adults in Western Europe rose more quickly than in the States.

Also, the injection was not to be given as a second dose after the standard MMR. So when Dr. Gregory heard about some unusual reactions, he also heard about the misuse of the product. He was shocked that his staff was dosing the new vaccine to the wrong population. But he could not believe the kids he saw. They were actually presenting in the ER with full-blown measles infections—rash, respiratory problems, and nothing like one would expect after a vaccine. Ever. One eight-year-old child who had not previously received the MMR received his first dose of the new vaccine. Afterward, he could not walk and had to be carried in to the hospital. The text to Nari was short: "Please call ASAP. We're having major problems with MVoneshot."

At 7:15 in the morning, Nari returned from a short half-hour run down the boulevard on the east side of Providence. That time of day, just after dawn had broken, was quiet, and there was nothing but her and her thoughts as she hit this familiar pavement. Living in an apartment near the Brown campus made her continue to feel young at heart. Although she was not old, it was nice to be around those ten years younger rather than those ten years older in a suburb. She was comfortable in this area even though a lot of her work took her to Boston, usually a quick trip on Amtrak to Boston's South Station. She could walk to Providence's Penn Station and had no car traffic or parking to worry about. Plus, there were plenty of trains. She could even take a local commuter train to the Providence train station on the way home from Boston. Further, an exorbitant public works project placing a little-used train station at Green Airport, the Providence airport in Warwick, had just been completed. This made commuting by air even simpler than if she lived in the Boston suburbs. There were plenty of nonstop flights to DC, Baltimore, Philadelphia, and any other smaller city that she had to travel to in the Northeast. Her only problem now was that other duties in the company were taking her west and across the country—not an easy trip out of Green.

She unlocked the door to her modest, second-floor walk-up and saw that she had a text waiting. *Unusual at this time of day*, she thought. Most of her contacts and colleagues worked pretty standard business hours, and she didn't have many friends, especially needy ones that would reach out so early. Further, her parents were three hours behind on the West Coast, and they rarely contacted her anymore. Nari was quite alarmed to see the text and from whom it was sent. She knew this was urgent and, perspiring heavily from her run, she did not hesitate. Nari pushed the number to Dr. Gregory immediately.

"Hello," answered Dr. Gregory, not recognizing the number.

"Dr. Gregory, this is Nari Lee from Immunoviratherapeutics, returning your message."

"Yes. Thank you. I was not sure which direction to go here, but there is a problem with the vaccine—the measles vaccine," declared Dr. Gregory.

"What is going on?" Nari asked. "This must be must be dramatic to be reaching out to me directly first thing this morning. We just launched this vaccine. Your docs should report these serious adverse events to the company or the FDA. We have a dedicated group that compiles and reports safety issues every quarter on a new drug to the FDA. If an emerging safety pattern or problems are occurring, we contact the FDA."

"I know! You are damn right!" he shouted back. Then he paused. "I am sorry, Nari. I'm not at all sure what's going on. It's a multifactorial problem. I know your vaccine is involved, but my docs may have dosed it wrong. I am calling for advice, and I am not sure what to do here."

Nari retorted, "Tell me what's going on. Regardless, you still must immediately report any serious unexpected adverse events."

"I'd like to, but it would be better for you to see some of these patients and for us to talk in person," Dr. Gregory replied in a somber voice. "Can I convince you to come to Baltimore today or tomorrow at the latest?"

"Just give me a quick overview. Obviously, it's bad. But I need to report what's going on, and I want my chief medical officer to meet with us," declared Nari, knowing that this was quite likely out of her league and a delicate situation.

"Of course. Suffice it to say I have seen full-blown measles in three children given the vaccine. Two others have been admitted with complications of pneumonia, and two others had neurological symptoms and are being worked up now. It is not a good situation." He continued, "I have received calls from local pediatricians who have administered the vaccine as per the company's directions, and some of these children are starting to develop early signs of infection. This does not at all look like the clinical studies on the vaccine."

"No. I cannot understand this at all," Nari agreed. "We are dealing with an attenuated vaccine given subcutaneously. We do not expect this at all. I will be there tomorrow and will have in tow at a minimum the CMO. I will get back to you with a time. In the meantime, could you please summarize all the cases for our review tomorrow?" Nari asked.

"Yes, and thank you for your rapid response," replied Dr. Gregory.

"No. Thank you, Jim. We have to figure out what's happening now. This is a critical issue for several thousand children out there who might have already received the vaccine."

The next day, Nari boarded a Southwest flight at 6:00 a.m. to BWI. It was not unusual for her to catch this early-morning flight to the Washington area. The TSA agents at Green Airport recognized her since she traveled by air at least once per week. And going to the DC area was a common trip. Nari hustled into the TSA Pre-Check line and was on her way through security with just her briefcase and laptop, not expecting this to be an overnight trip. Her company was located just fifty miles from this airport, and it was so much easier than flying into Reagan National or Dulles at this time of day. Both air traffic and ground traffic afterward would be tough around the beltway. Plus, on this trip, she would be on her way to Baltimore, not the home office. This trip made the circumstances of this morning's flight both unusual and scary. How could the new vaccine have caused these problems? All the testing had gone so well in both the preclinical and clinical stages. Nari felt panic as the plane accelerated down the runway, lifted off, and made its turn over Narragansett Bay. It was not the flight or the quick turn that induced the panic. It was that thousands of kids may have received their vaccine; that she had touted this vaccine in her educational talks to doctors and nurses all over the Northeast; and that who knew what could happen in a few hours. Nari grabbed the vomit bag in the seatback pocket in front of her and dry heaved for several seconds. Her seat mate looked distressed, but he did not say a word. In a few moments, she started to feel better and sat back in her seat.

"I am fine," she said in a whisper to the two people in her row.

Upon landing at BWI, Nari deplaned and immediately called her chief medical officer, Dr. George Robinson. He was waiting for her in the cell phone lot as planned and picked her up on the upper departure level. Within a matter of ten minutes from deplaning, she was in his car and stuck in traffic traveling north to Sinai Hospital north of the city. There was really no good way to avoid traffic at this time in Baltimore. But they had an 8:00 meeting with Jim Gregory, and he had slated the whole morning to go over what was happening.

"George, thanks so much for meeting me!" Nari exclaimed. "You have no idea how much it means to have you with me. You know all the medical—"

"Nari," interrupted George, "this is the highest priority for the company right now. All focus will be on solving this problem. As soon as you called me last night, it was my duty to inform Dr. Ickerson of what was going on. So all senior management, and I am sure some board members, know the issue as you described it to me. We will find out all we can and then head back to the home office this afternoon to meet with the team."

"I've told you everything Jim Gregory related to me. We will have to dig as deep as we can when we get there," explained Nari. "I am hoping he will be forthcoming because he did suggest his clinic docs gave this off-label."

As they passed the stadiums in Baltimore, they dodged their way through traffic around the Inner Harbor and found an entrance onto I-83 North. There was little traffic going in this direction. A quick jaunt up this highway a few miles took them to the exit for Sinai Hospital. They got there in plenty of time for their meeting with Dr. Gregory. Nari was already exhausted, having been up since 4:00 and not having slept much the night before. Despite the situation, she put on her happy face.

Nari and Sarge Williams went through their regular morning routine.

Nari said, "This is my colleague, Dr. George Robinson, who will be joining me on this visit."

George showed his ID, and they were whisked through to the waiting area where Ann, Dr. Gregory's assistant, waited for them.

"Thank you," they said in unison.

The three of them walked to the elevators at a quickened, focused pace. Despite her exhaustion, Nari did not think about stopping for coffee today.

Ann led them into a conference room. The table was piled high with several files, presumably records of patients to be discussed. Ann said that Dr. Gregory would be in shortly and to help themselves to the coffee, juice, and pastries on the credenza.

Dr. Gregory arrived with two others in tow. One was obviously a doctor, wearing a white coat with a stethoscope in the coat pocket. The other was in a gray, two-piece suit with a red striped tie.

"Hello, Jim," said Nari. "This is my colleague, Dr. George Robinson, chief medical officer at Immunoviratherapeutics."

"Thank you so much for coming and arranging all this on such short notice, and George, you as well. Nice to meet you, even under such unusual circumstances to say the least," acknowledged Jim. "Let me introduce my colleagues. This is Dr. Brian Harmon, one of our pediatricians who works in the infectious disease clinic, and this is Jason Kenilworth, counsel for the hospital."

"Should I get my attorney here as well?" asked George. "I thought we were here to review the records and adverse events you wanted to report. Why is Jason joining us in this meeting?"

"Adverse event reporting is new to us, and to Jason. I do not think we have had anything occur like this in the past, and if so, maybe it has been an isolated event. So I want to be sure we are doing this right to protect our institution and doctors," explained Jim.

"Well, I think we are off on the wrong foot," George said. "This is not a legal matter at all, and it is not about protection of institutions or doctors. Right now, it's an investigation, and it's about protection of patients. I have no objection to Jason's sitting in as we discuss all the cases you have brought to our attention, but this is adverse event reporting. We as a company need to understand what is happening with our product, if anything. This is a real-life, real-time, investigation. I would like to start all over if it is okay with you, Jim," George more or less demanded.

Nari was taking a back seat to all this, which is why she had brought George to the table.

Jim responded, "I understand fully, and as a doctor I am very worried about the children who might be at risk. Let us get to the task at hand and look at these records together."

George had brought with him a form that he had used previously in his career to evaluate common denominators among patients in his investigations. Eventually the data would be entered into a database, but as they worked together on these ten or so patients who were the source of the events today, they might get some idea of what happened. On the form were obvious demographic and medical data from the patients' charts, such as age, gender, prior vaccination history with another measles vaccine, race, allergies, date of injection, vaccine lot number, and type and onset of reaction.

They all sat around the table for an hour or so pulling the data on the patients and putting the information into tabular form. Three children had been admitted to emergency departments with full-blown measles rash, two had measles pneumonia, and two more had measles encephalomyelitis, inflammation of the brain and spinal cord. Finally, three others came in just with the beginnings of the infection.

Jim looked at the data as it stood. "I do not see any common features as of now. This is very frustrating."

George agreed. "Yes, it is, but I have a couple of follow-up questions. How many vials of vaccine have you ordered, and how many have been administered? Also, do you know if more than one lot number of vaccine was received? These are important questions. You see on the data table that these kids all received vaccines from the same lot. However, many also received it off label here in the clinic, so that is something that needs to be looked at separately. They did not receive the vaccine according to manufacturer's instructions."

"Yes, that is true, and some were not administered here. Some children were admitted after receiving the vaccine at a pediatrician's office. We tracked much of that information yesterday," said Dr.

Harmon. "Also, both Dr. Gregory and I are getting calls from local pediatricians that the vaccine is actually *causing* measles and not preventing it! There might even be spread to secondary individuals. Parents called reporting that siblings showed signs of measles seven days after a family member received MVoneshot."

George responded, "That is more than a little disturbing. Jim, could you get more information on the sibling you referred to; maybe the family traveled and the child contracted natural infection elsewhere. Also, I am thinking these other reactions might be specific to one lot number. Nari, can you please call the safety group in Regulatory Affairs and see if anyone has reported any serious adverse events in the last couple of days on this lot?"

Nari quickly dialed the company while the rest of the team continued to review the clinical data. Attorney Jason Kenilworth was not pleased about the off-label use but seemed to breathe a sigh of relief that this might have been a company problem with the vaccine.

Nari got the information she needed and spoke quietly to George.

"We thank you for pulling these charts and reviewing them with us," George began. "We will file these adverse events reports with the FDA since we now have all the data we need for the time being. If we need any follow-up information, our safety group will be in contact with you directly. In the meantime, we are pulling this lot from commercial use. Please call your pharmacy immediately. An emergency notice is being sent out right now to anyone who ordered this lot, and we will direct them on what to do with the vaccine. They will also be given information on what to tell patients if they should develop any adverse events or signs of measles infection," he summarized.

"We are headed back to Virginia," Nari added. "If you think of anything else that could help us, please feel free to call or text me anytime. I will respond as soon as I can. Jim knows that I am very responsive. Thank you again for your cooperation."

They headed out of the room, and after dropping their IDs off with Sarge, they headed back to McLean as fast as they could. A major meeting with senior management was about to take place, and in all likelihood all hell was about to break loose.

Nari and George spoke briefly on their ride back to the company, reviewing what had just happened, but after about ten minutes the ride was silent. Both of them were lost in thought as they went back to the home office from Baltimore. How could something like this happen? The company had a 100-percent-perfect quality-control track record with its first vaccine for MPV. So many infants were being protected from severe lung infection. No one thought that such a vaccine could be produced successfully, but they had done it and now they were onto their next big project—a new measles vaccine. Yes, measles had been "conquered" in the United States and Europe. In the 1990s, measles all but disappeared. Then parents became complacent, and measles began to crop up again. Anti-vaxxers reared their heads, and measles reappeared. If all the anti-vaxxers knew that worldwide measles had killed over one million children a year in the eighties, then maybe they would not be so quick to skip the vaccine.

The company's MVoneshot was a big step forward—one dose. During the clinical studies, the only adverse events seen were local skin reactions and a few mild fevers, really nothing close to what was being reported now. As Nari and George entered the parking lot, an early DC-area afternoon spring thunderstorm began. Nari hoped this was not a harbinger of the meeting, vaccine, or company. Thankfully, George had a covered parking space, and they headed into the building and to the sixth floor boardroom running on empty. Nari had consumed only a donut so far this day.

The CEO, Colonel Arnold Ickerson; chief operating officer; chief research officer; George and Nari; VP of Regulatory Affairs; VP of Marketing; senior counsel for the company; VP of Finance; VP of Clinical Development; and VP of Manufacturing were all present and accounted for. Arnold was a man of action and just wanted the answer, plain and simple. But he and the others did not have all the information that George and Nari had collected in the morning. Red-faced with anger, Arnold did not try to hide his irritation.

"George, what in the hell is going on?" Arnold roared.

"I can only tell you what we observed in the ten patient charts at Sinai Hospital in Baltimore. I think it was enough, along with the several reported here, to decide to pull the lot. All the subjects received the same lot of vaccine, and none behaved as subjects in the trials. They all either experienced full-blown measles infection, with or without complications, or were just starting to develop infection. We also are investigating the possibility of transmission of the virus to siblings of recipients. This is not what we saw at all in the trials. We saw complete protective antibody and cellular immune responses," replied George.

"Okay, now that we know that one of these lots was fucked up, what does that mean?" shouted Arnold. "Are we cooked? Now what?"

"We have a call with the FDA at 4:00 p.m. We have pulled the one lot we know caused these problems. They might demand that we pull everything until we determine the source of the problem," said the VP of Regulatory Affairs.

Arnold's face turned darker shades of red as he listened to the response.

The VP of Finance spoke up. "We also have prepared a statement to be released after close of the stock markets. It will read differently depending on the FDA decision. It will indicate that the company had to withdraw from marketing its measles virus vaccine."

Arnold stewed in his chair. "Do you know what this will do to the market cap of our company? It will be whittled down by at least 50 percent! If we can't keep our products clean, no one will trust us!"

George interjected, "Sir, it was the only thing to do. And if we had not acted, we could be at larger risk with other children being injured."

"You're right, but haven't you heard of the National Vaccine Injury Compensation Program?" Arnold shouted. "The government pays for injuries from covered vaccines! Where's our head of sales?"

"He's not here. He's in the field today, sir," said the COO. "But we do not yet have coverage by the NVICP. That is still under review."

"What the fuck!" yelled Arnold. "The other measles vaccine is covered by the NVICP!"

"Yes, it is, but we are not on the docket until next month," the COO explained. "We took a risk with limited launch a month early. There was—"

"You're fired! Clear out your office and tell your head of sales not to show his face in here again. You are idiots," Arnold ranted. "And you, Mr. Head of Marketing, you're gone too. You should have known we needed the government's vaccine insurance before launch. I mean it! All three of you. Thank you for your service. Goodbye. I want to be on the 4:00 p.m. call with the FDA. Dismissed."

The conference call with the Center for Biologics Evaluation and Research (CBER) Division of the FDA started at exactly 4:00 p.m. On the call representing the company were the CEO, chief medical officer, chief research officer, and the VPs of Regulatory Affairs, Clinical Development, and Manufacturing. The deputy director for CBER took the unusual step of joining in on the call. She started the call by reading a brief, concise statement.

"We at CBER have seen your preliminary report regarding the lot-specific adverse events for your newly introduced measles vaccine, MVoneshot. We agree that you should immediately withdraw this lot from commercial use. Furthermore, given that alternatives are available for measles vaccination, the FDA is withdrawing its approval for MVoneshot until the company can provide additional safety data and assurance that the product will not harm the public. All lots should be withdrawn from commercial sale immediately. If you have any questions, you can direct them to your contact at the FDA. Thank you for your prompt action on this important matter."

The team at the company thanked the deputy director, and with that the conference call abruptly ended. Regulatory Affairs would follow up one on one with the safety group at the FDA to determine the timeline for a safety report, but for now the company employees knew what they had to do. It was not pleasant.

Soon afterward, Arnold went into action mode. He gave an order for the press release to be written and issued as soon as possible. From the clinical and safety side, all distribution channels had to be notified to halt further shipments. All offices and practices with product on hand of any lot had to suspend administration of the vaccine and return any remaining vaccine to the company as soon as possible. The sales force would be called upon to help track the material at offices and return it. A safety follow-up study had to be developed with the FDA on those children who had received the vaccine. A full-scale in-house investigation with FDA input was needed.

How could such an event happen? Arnold wondered. Manufacturing was tightly controlled at every step in the process. The share price of the company would plummet in after-hours trading and continue after the opening bell. Calls and meetings with key institutional shareholders and analysts would be needed. The company was not a one-trick pony. It already had one success on the market and others in the pipeline. To keep the company running, key officials would need to explain this event and spin any positive news they could. This mess was going to be a huge mountain to overcome, and public perception and safety problems in kids were the worst.

Before Arnold left the room, he had a few more terse words. "We have a lot of work left. I expect to see everyone back in this board room tomorrow at 8:00 a.m. sharp, with plans of action."

With that, he left the room. Everyone else remained to discuss next steps but found it hard to maintain focus. They were all dumbstruck by the lack of concordance of the studies and the real-world experience. The head of Regulatory Affairs took point on the rest of the meeting. She laid the groundwork for what had to be done from a legal and regulatory viewpoint. Number one was to get every vial of vaccine back. No one else could receive it. She placed a call to the sales organization and told sales reps to go out and grab all the MVoneshot vials at every office and location in the country. A coordinated effort with the wholesalers and distributors began immediately. It was a good thing this was a limited product launch and had not yet made it to the pharmacies. Such a large-scale start would have resulted in chaos and been even more damaging for the children and the company. The company, at the request of the FDA, needed to get identifying information on anyone who had received the vaccine.

"Nari, could you please pull together an intake form and have George and drug safety review the form?" the head of Regulatory Affairs asked. "We want to collect any data that we might need on other children who have received the vaccine and had adverse effects. This will be useful for follow-up with the FDA."

"I will start that right away," replied Nari.

Many other activities started. A consulting group hired by the head of human resources came in to review all the internal personnel records and anyone else associated with the measles virus vaccine project. Regulatory Affairs started its own external audit immediately. This group investigated and interviewed all the individuals responsible for MVoneshot production, from initiation of vaccine growth to the final stage of vaccine shipment. If there had been any problems along the way, either mistakes or otherwise, this group would find them.

"I don't think we will have anything for the colonel by 8:00 tomorrow, but we seem to have some good plans going forward. Does anyone have any questions or anything else?" George asked. No one spoke up.

"Okay then, let's get to work with what we have and present what we've done tomorrow morning. I will be in my office until at least ten if you have questions. Thank you," the chief research officer said to finish up and then walked out. Everyone left and went to their offices.

While all this was going on, CEO Arnold Ickerson had returned to his office and took action on his own. Despite the fact that he acted like an asshole and was often vulgar, like in the earlier meetings, he took in all the information and knew that additional action was needed. He was a genius. He had isolated and discovered the origins of many viruses during a short term at the United States Army Medical Research Institute of Infectious Diseases, where defensive vaccine research was performed, in Frederick, Maryland. He worked there on loan from the air force during his active duty career. Arnold had even stayed on in Frederick for a few years after he finished his military commitment. He thought out action plans that needed to be taken like chess moves, which were several steps ahead of anyone in this group. When Arnold heard the news about the vaccine, he surmised that the wrong vaccine strain may have been released or that the initial vaccine had mutated. And at this point, it was likely being transmitted from person to person, something that was very problematic. This, he hoped, was clear to everyone. But what was probably not clear was that this was a scenario that called for national security action.

Arnold still had connections with high-level authorities in the Pentagon, but his best connection was with the director of the National Institute of Allergy and Infectious Diseases. Carlos Annetti, a physician, had served in the air force with Arnold and then moved up the senior military ranks with him. The two were quite different and had different goals. Carlos did not want to sign himself up with

Arnold at USAMRIID and chase viruses all over the world. He wanted to settle down, so he took a research position at the NIH in one of the immunology labs. Over the years he had worked with many fine scientists, had built a great reputation in the infectious disease area, and was happy to have a stable family life in Bethesda. In time he was named director of the NIAID and remained in that position for years. Carlos was seen on CNN and Fox at least once a month talking about the most recent viral epidemic or possible cures and vaccines for AIDS. But what most did not know about Carlos was that he had lofty political connections. He always kept close to the director of the NIH, who is a political appointee, and he was close to the current president. He could call him at any time—at least that was what he had told Arnold at their last dinner. This was the time to find out, This was a potential national emergency. Arnold's plan was to make sure that Carlos briefed the president on the potential danger of measles virus spread and particularly this agent. He rang him up on his cell phone.

"Carlos, Arnold Ickerson here."

"Colonel, nice to hear from you. To what do I owe this pleasure?" asked Carlos.

"Carlos, to put it bluntly, we have a problem here, and this is not Houston!"

"Okay, go on. This sounds serious coming from you," Carlos responded. "I thought life was nice and cushy in the swanky Virginia suburbs in your board room and plush CEO leather chair."

"It is serious, and life is not so cushy. You will see a press release this afternoon. The FDA just withdrew our new measles vaccine from the market."

"God, what happened?"

"Let me tell you. We don't know exactly, but there has been a terrible mix-up or mutation or something. Several children have developed measles encephalomyelitis. Others have gotten measles. It looks like the subcutaneous injection has even spread to and is replicating virus in the lung, causing some secondhand infections," continued the colonel.

"This is a catastrophe," said Carlos.

"Don't I know it," said Arnold. "And, as we both know, if this virus is spreading like natural measles, there are so many unvaccinated people.

Thousands of people deferred or refused vaccination because of some of the studies linking the measles vaccination to autism. We know those studies are not strong or well done. I don't care one iota about the stock or share price, but I am very worried about the future and how we can halt this. I think if everyone gets the standard measles vaccine, we could be all right." Then he added, "One thing that did not come up yet in my brief discussion, however, is immunosuppression."

"Of course," Carlos responded. "Measles virus suppresses the immune system of anyone for many weeks after natural infection. This is an observation that goes back over a hundred years. Many people could have problems with superinfections if infected with measles. Even vaccinations suppress the immune system to some degree."

"I think this could be a national emergency, and considering your connections to the president, I am asking you to make a call. We could be in a serious situation here. If this spread cannot be stopped, we are talking about many millions of people at risk, including those who have been previously vaccinated. I just do not know," added Arnold. "It may even be a pandemic."

"Look, I will call the president, and I will visit him if possible," Carlos said. "This is a shit storm. There is not enough standard vaccine available to protect everyone, and you don't even know if it can stop the spread of the new vaccine that has run amok. What else is going on here? How could this have happened?" he asked.

"I do not know. I have my whole team on this, and we are bringing in outside groups tomorrow to review every person and process in the manufacturing scheme. I am hopeful.

"I am just not sure, and I am calling you to suggest that we pull together a national program," said Arnold. "I am hoping that you can persuade the president to elevate this to the level of a national emergency. I think at this stage we need to try to protect him, his staff, and at least those in his cabinet. There must be a prioritized list of government officials in each of the arms of the government that make our country operational. They all might need to be read into this scenario and protected at some point in time. That's his call."

He added, "As for the alternative medical treatments, unless you have something, all I can think of is immune globulin. That is how we treated infection in the old days—you know that. We can start having plasma-collection centers screen donors who have high levels of antibody to measles virus. But we both know that may not be a workable treatment," he concluded.

Carlos responded, "Well, you certainly have added to my workload, Arnold, and I will do my best to speak with the president tonight or first thing tomorrow. I know he is in DC, so getting to him should be easier than usual. And it is just before Easter break, so there's not much politicking this week."

Carlos hung up his phone and immediately dialed the White House. It was two o'clock in the afternoon, and he got through to the president's personal assistant. As he expected, he did get a short, five-minute phone appointment. The president, she said, could call him back around six o'clock. Carlos knew that the call would last longer, but at least he got on his calendar. He sent a text to Arnold confirming his call to the president later in the day. He told him that he would call with a summary after he spoke with the president.

Nari Lee could not believe what had happened. The FDA and the company had found no evidence during the trials of MVoneshot of any significant adverse events. No problems had occurred other than a few local reactions and low-grade fevers. The full-blown measles infections and kids with pneumonia and neurological complications suggested that this was not the same animal. This was a different virus altogether—and it was spreading.

Nari was not a virologist, but she had plenty of experience. She knew from having worked in this field long enough that the company had to procure serum and virus isolates from affected patients and check the molecular signature of the virus. If this virus was different from the virus tested in the trials, then a mutation must have occurred spontaneously. It was now being transmitted in the population from vaccine recipients to susceptible individuals, those who had never received any vaccine. Nari also had another horrible thought: the company might have manufactured the wrong virus isolate when making the vaccine. *Unlikely, but possible*, she thought. Several measles isolates were tested, and only one passed all the preclinical tests and animal tests to make it into the clinical testing phase. *Could someone have slipped and mixed up the strains? Could this have happened when every step of the process is so tightly monitored?* she thought.

After a very long day that had started at Sinai Hospital and ended with the withdrawal of their company's product from the market and a blasting by the CEO, George dropped Nari at the Tysons Corner Marriott on Route 7. The hotel was near the huge Tysons Corner Mall, and Nari knew she could pick up a quick bite at a number of places nearby. Unfortunately, she did not yet have time to dine. Her day trip to Baltimore had turned into a nightmarish multiple-day trip to Maryland and McLean. She rented a car from a local Hertz desk at the Marriott and headed to the mall. She did not have much time, but she needed clothes. Her day trip had now extended into at least a few days, at a minimum, so clothing, toiletries, and other items were required.

Nari knew that Nordstrom's was one of many anchor stores at the mall. She was in the store twenty minutes later. She picked out two outfits and undergarments and left the store in about thirty minutes. She was a buyer but not much of a shopper, especially tonight. At least that was one easy part of the day. She also did a bit of walking around the mall and finally settled into a California Pizza Kitchen. The place had emptied out by a quarter 'til nine on this Tuesday evening. She ordered a salad and an IPA beer. Anything quick was good after this long and disastrous day. Nari completed her meal within another thirty minutes. After finding her car in a few minutes, she headed back to the Marriott. She went to the hotel hoping to sleep, rise early, and help solve the mystery of the vaccine problem.

Nari realized she had forgotten to pick up toothpaste and other odds and ends in her rush to get back, so she asked for a personal sample pack from the front desk and headed to bed. She had a restless night at the hotel. She did not sleep well, pondering her future and that of the company. The next morning, Nari had coffee and read the headlines of the *Post*. She skipped her morning workout and breakfast for the first time in days and drove over to the office. The place was hopping at only 7:45.

At the 9:30 opening stock market bell, the news of the company's press release from the previous evening reporting the MVoneshot withdrawal affected its share price greatly. After what had happened, every financial analyst was strongly bearish on IVTP. Before trading opened, huge sell orders were in, and the company share price plunged 45 percent in the first five minutes of trading. Trading was halted at 9:45. The company did not expect any additional information during the day, and sell orders significantly outweighed buy orders. The market suspended trading for the rest of the day.

Meanwhile, back in McLean, the remaining executive team was frantically piecing together its plan. The investigation was two phased. First, the group needed to determine what had happened to the safe vaccine in the trials approved by the FDA. Second, they needed to develop a campaign to prevent what would amount to a long-term financial and public relations disaster. The company was known as a giant among biotechnology companies in the Washington, Virginia, and Maryland areas. Immunoviratherapeutics was just the beginning of the biotechnology boom in the DC area. The company put Virginia on the map and put the I-270 corridor in Maryland between DC and Frederick to shame. Maryland had poured hundreds of millions of dollars into that area, and with the exception of one or two companies, nothing had sprouted from the State's investment. The company had, with its success, now brought millions and millions of dollars of venture capital to Virginia and hundreds of start-ups in the biotechnology sector. And with that, many IPOs had followed. The company never had any problems, but now it was facing charges from "murder" to "infanticide" splashed on the front pages of newspapers across the nation.

It was clear to Nari and George what had to be done. As they sat and had their second cups of coffee the morning after the product had been withdrawn from the market, they saw only limited possibilities. They both had gone through them independently the previous night and couldn't sleep a wink. They then reviewed them together.

Others started to join them in the conference room before their CEO arrived. Arnold obviously was not showing up at 8:00 a.m. Other company business was keeping him occupied. Nari was not the senior person by any stretch of the imagination, but for some reason she just stood up and started writing possibilities of what had happened to the measles vaccine on the large white board. She said to the group assembled as she wrote them down, "I am sure many of you have been tossing and turning all night like I have. Here is what some of us think might have happened.

1. There was a deliberate switch of a mutant measles virus—internal.
2. Sabotage of some sort—external.
3. A mutation occurred with this lot during production.
4. The vaccine strain mutated or recombined once in the field.

Can anyone think of any other events that could have accounted for this drastic effect? We know that none of our kids in the trials had reactions to the vaccine as seen with this commercial lot," Nari said.

She sat down, now facing the group, surprising even herself at taking the lead over all her superiors in the room. As a student, her confidence had shone through; she always stood out from the crowd. She knew it was her frustration coming out in flames at having seen this great development and company reputation scathed and damaged. She hadn't noticed Arnold entering the meeting room as she was writing on the board.

"Nari, thank you for taking the lead this morning," he said. "I'm glad we're all assembled here and you've got the ball rolling for us. As we all know, this is our only priority. Also, I want to apologize for my outbursts yesterday. Please accept my apology, and I hope you understand how raw we all were and still are and will be until we sort this out. With that said, we have much to do, and I hope you are ready to attack this huge hurdle," Arnold added.

"We are," all in the group chimed in.

"Okay, Nari, continue leading this first part, and then we will look for solutions," Arnold said.

"Thank you very much, Dr. Ickerson. Okay, does anyone have any other possible ideas of what happened to our vaccine, or should I take any of these four off the list?" Nari asked.

"I know there are huge numbers of adverse events," George offered. "We just have to check the profiles of the children being injected to see if they are similar to those who received the shots in the clinical studies."

"Good point. Let's add that as number five. Our drug safety team is capturing that information now. We should be able to have that resolved today. Any other suggestions?" asked Nari. No one added any comments, and after a pause of a minute, Arnold broke in.

"All right, then. That appears to be a good start. Now how do you propose we determine if this was internal or external sabotage? How do you investigate these possibilities?"

"Are we qualified for this piece?" asked George, the medical director.

"I think so," Arnold said. "This is a scientific or forensic inquiry first. Let's ask ourselves a simple question or two. Is the virus the same virus used in the clinical trials? Is the virus isolated from patients who are having adverse events the same virus that was injected into those patients? Just answering these two questions can answer all Nari's questions. It can tell us whether sabotage or a virus mutation occurred. However, it cannot tell us where or how these events occurred. It is just a start."

"I want to add one thing in our thinking here," George said. "When I think of sabotage, I ask another question: Who benefits? Are there any other companies developing measles vaccines to compete with us? And if so, that would be a pretty daring and drastic move. The answer is yes, but no one is anywhere close to us. There are some small companies in very early preclinical development. We are light years ahead of them."

"Good points, George. So our thinking should be open but maybe looking more at ourselves, potentially, or a mutation. That's why we have to do the research," Arnold said.

"I think that's a quick way to get us going. We are already collecting clinical samples to try and isolate virus from patients who have early symptoms," Nari interjected, "but the research group can get going right away and test samples from the clinical trial lots and compare them to the lots just released for commercial sale."

"This is already in progress," said the chief research officer. "We started to grow up the virus last night so that we could get a pool of virus to evaluate RNA and protein sequences where we made the two changes in these strains. We will have an answer in tomorrow."

"At some point, the company selected the measles virus to be used for commercialization, then it was grown up in a large quantity," Arnold said. "I remember distinctly watching our robot machine dispensing small portions of the virus solution into vials for freezing. Ashraf was in charge of loading the machine with the solution. Then, at some point, hundreds of vials were frozen here and at another facility so that we would then be able to take these out and grow them up to make batches of vaccine."

The chief of research was right. It took only two days total. The virus in the vaccine that was returned from a local pediatrician office had the same molecular profile as the stock virus used to grow the vaccine. This eliminated proposition two: there had been no change to the vaccine after shipment. But the research staff also conducted additional comparisons. They removed other viruses, including the mutant that had not been developed. MVoneshot, the approved vaccine shipped out by the company, turned out to be identical to the mutant virus that the company had deep-sixed for development. *How did the wrong virus get into the production pipeline?* the chief wondered. It certainly had not been used in the clinical trials approved by the FDA.

One more test was required. The chief of research needed two more days. He took the commercial vaccine lot that was causing all the problems and compared it to the lots used in the clinical trials. Two days later he was sure: the two were totally different, and they differed in the areas that made the bad vaccine neurovirulent. Someone had definitely switched virus stocks and produced the wrong virus for commercial use. But the questions still remained: Who did this? And why?

Measles infections were spreading rapidly, and company employees' morale plummeted. Measles virus infections hit hundreds of communities. Alan had never expected such an outcome from this mutant vaccine. He thought some children would be hospitalized with neurological disorders or would die and that, after a month or so, the company would withdraw the vaccine. Then a video would be sent from an anonymous source in Afghanistan or the Sudan— somewhere to throw any investigation askew—claiming that a radical Islamic group was responsible. Now measles was being spread by the vaccine and the glut of unvaccinated children. These were kids who had been unvaccinated largely because of hysteria caused by the "fake news" about autism-like problems caused by measles vaccines drummed up by Alan's colleagues in Pakistan, London, France, and elsewhere around the globe. This was no time to announce responsibility. *Let it ride*, he thought. Just one lot of vaccine had been distributed, and several thousand shots of vaccine had been administered. In two weeks, problems had surfaced everywhere, and the government didn't have answers. And with parents not sure what to do and not able to trust the government on vaccine recommendations to take the original vaccine, the new mutated virus from Immunoviratherapeutics would circulate and cause even more problems—not just medical but economic as well. Parents began to stay home from work. Productivity suffered. This was a huge bonus for the jihad. All was going well, and Alan would need to congratulate Ashraf. Alan hoped to convince him to work with him on further projects.

MVoneshot had been presumed to be the next great vaccine, but it now spread measles virus rapidly across the country. Spring break and the Easter holiday season did not help. Families and college students were traveling across the nation and to international destinations as well. What began as something thought to be a relatively limited incident was that no more. Those in the know were traveling with face masks, but most masks would be of little help filtering out small viral particles. Measles virus is one of the most highly contagious respiratory infections. One person in an air terminal could spread measles infection to multiple locations across the nation.

This virus had taken on a life of its own. Doctors had limited knowledge of how to handle measles. Most physicians had never seen a case in their entire lives. In the United States, the Centers for Disease Control had declared measles eliminated in the year 2000, with only a few imported cases before that.

The CDC quickly convened a meeting with top infectious disease experts, pediatricians, and virologists. With this group, they developed a detailed measles treatment algorithm and sent it out to all physicians in the country. The World Health Organization coordinated a similar effort to combat any spread in the continent and the rest of the world. This was an excerpt from the CDC release to the community:

The best medical treatment at this time is first isolation of anyone with mild symptoms. Persons with symptoms should stay at home and be treated according to doctor's orders. Anyone who has been exposed to someone with symptoms should also remain isolated at home. If a child develops severe symptoms such as difficulty breathing, very high fever that cannot be controlled, problems walking, or other problems, head to the nearest hospital emergency department. For anyone who has not received a standard vaccine, centers have been established at local firehouses in many communities. Do not go to these facilities if you have any symptoms or have been exposed to someone with symptoms. At these locations, the standard measles vaccine will be administered. This vaccine has been used for decades and is safe and effective. We do not know if it will protect against the current outbreak, but we are hopeful it will help reduce symptoms. We recommend that anyone leaving the country receive a booster vaccine.

The CDC had developed additional protocols for health care workers and for treatment of patients with severe symptoms.

In Washington, DC, Carlos Annetti finally connected with President Frank Chapman, a longtime friend. They talked very briefly by phone, but it was an intense conversation. It did not take long for the president to understand the urgency of the situation. He agreed that this was quickly becoming a national emergency. He also agreed with Carlos that he and his entire cabinet and staff should be revaccinated with the currently approved measles vaccine. President Chapman asked that Carlos work with his agency and the CDC to put together a list of recommendations that he could lay out to assuage the country immediately. He gave Carlos two hours. Chapman planned to present his plans to the country on live television that evening. He understood the seriousness of this event.

At 9:00 that evening, all eyes were on President Chapman. It did not matter that this was Tuesday night or that the president's speech broke into one of the most-watched television shows to hit the air recently. The country turned to hear Chapman. They knew something was in the air, and it was serious.

All stations announced, "Live from the Oval Office, the President of the United States of America." Chapman began,

> Good evening, ladies and gentlemen. I did not expect to be addressing you on this beautiful spring evening. However, a crisis has literally infected our country. It came from within, but we do not know how. You might have seen some of your children or your neighbors' children become very sick or even die from the measles virus. This virus had been previously eradicated from the States years ago but has now cropped up here and there because of poor adherence to vaccination procedures. One of our young, great biotechnology companies, Immunoviratherapeutics, developed a new measles vaccine requiring one injection for protecting our children—an innovation that the FDA agreed was a safe and effective improvement and approved for distribution last year. Something unexpected happened. When the vaccine was distributed and given to children, it did not behave at all like the vaccine tested in the thousands of children in trials. Children got sick, very sick; some are dying and passing the virus to others. Many of your own children have been devastated by this event. Measles virus is the most highly contagious virus we know of. We are working very diligently with other vaccine companies to produce more of the standard vaccine to get everyone revaccinated and hopefully protected from this new virus that is now circulating in the community. Beware—this new virus is not the run-of-the-mill measles virus. It is dangerous. It is a killer. We need to take major precautions now.

I am invoking a national emergency for the next ten days. The experts at the CDC tell us that is all we need, just ten days for the flame of this virus to die out. After that we can go back to living our normal lives. For now, however, it will not be easy for any of us. Unless you are a sanctioned health worker, police, fire, or first responder, you will have very restricted mobility. The only way to stop the spread of the virus is to avoid contact with others and to get protected by vaccination. The National Guard will be called up in all states and the District of Columbia to enforce my orders. All schools, public and private, as well as colleges and universities will be closed. There will be no public gatherings allowed. All theaters will be closed. You will not be going to work. Work from your computers at home if you can. Spend some time with your family. I know this will affect our economy in the short term, but our actions today will save thousands of lives and our country. We have been attacked by many methods, but this is an invisible threat that must be stopped in its tracks.

The National Guard will distribute food supplies from federal repositories to families and those individuals sequestered within campuses. Do not leave your homes and current locations. The National Guard will also bring food and dried milk to neighborhoods. Again, it is imperative that you do not leave your immediate homes to go to stores. They will not be open. I have ordered the guard to keep you from leaving, and they will help you if you need supplies or emergency transport. We have plenty for all and have planned for such contingencies in our country in the past. The world is watching; let us show them how we respond to a crisis. Looting and destruction will not be tolerated. It will be punished with a quick and mighty force.

Details of the plans I have laid out will be published online and will be broadcast many times on television and radio. Listen to and read them and abide by them. Please pray with me as I know we will be a stronger nation for living through this ordeal. God bless you, and God bless the United States of America.

As the TV camera turned off, the president turned to Carlos, who had come to the White House to prepare the president before his speech.

"Mr. President, I must say, that was perfect. And I am not blowing smoke up you know what," Carlos said.

"Thank you, Carlos. I think we got our message across. We can only pray that panic does not set in," said President Chapman. "Is there anything else we should be doing at this time?"

"I cannot think of anything else," Carlos said. "Let's just hope this burns out like most epidemics."

"Thank you for being on top of this, and please send my regards to Arnold Ickerson for being forthright and open," said the president. "He's a good soldier."

"Of course. Good night, sir." Carlos turned and left the Oval Office.

11

ASHRAF'S PROBLEMS
ERUPT
MAY 2019

Sabina set out the breakfast dishes and poured coffee for Alan, who was getting a late start on the day.

"Good morning. You slept in today. I am glad to see you are taking a little time to yourself," Sabina said. "It is nice to have you around even though this world is upside down."

"I am not attending this month. I am just writing and doing lab work. More time for you and the kids," Alan responded. "I assume they are up to date on their measles vaccinations?"

"Of course. It is terrible what's happened with that company's vaccine. I hope they can stop this," she said.

"Yes, me too," Alan said.

"I would like to see what you think about another topic altogether. You know the schools in this district are not the best, and our kids start first grade next year. I think we should think about moving to the county. The schools—"

"Wait a minute," Alan interrupted. "You want us to sell this beautiful condo in the city so close to work and mosque?"

"We cannot afford to send both our children to private school and pay the mortgage on this place," Sabina answered. "What are we supposed to do—send our kids to substandard schools?"

"Why do you think the schools are substandard?" Alan asked.

"Test scores bear it out. Plus, I think we are living above our means here." Sabina continued, "If we sell our condo, we can live in a nice neighborhood in the county and not worry as much about how to pay our bills."

"You just sprung this on me, Sabina. Let's talk about it again later. It is a big lifestyle change. I know you're thinking about what is best for the children," he said.

"I am glad you are open to talking. We can pick this up when you get back tonight. I love you." Sabina gave Alan a kiss on his way out the door.

Ashraf could not believe how quickly the aftermath of the vaccine switch was happening. He seemed to have been hit from so many directions in the last week. First, the whole company turned upside down and inside out. Following the withdrawal of the MVoneshot vaccine, the COO was fired. Then the next week, without one of its major products to market, half the sales and marketing team was let go. Then the proverbial shit hit the fan. The manufacturing processes, including everything that Ashraf oversaw, was being scrutinized by an outside consulting team brought in from Alexandria, Virginia. Every step of every process, from walking in the door to shipping the product to the doors of the recipients, was being evaluated with a fine-tooth comb. The outside contractor began inspecting all personnel records, work records, performance appraisals, and interactions within the company as well as collaborative arrangements with outside investigators or contractors.

A conference room was set aside for interviews of all employees involved in any part of the manufacturing processes. The company counsel, as well as two of the consultant team members and each employee, was brought into the room one at a time. This process started almost immediately after the withdrawal of the vaccine. The CEO wanted answers yesterday.

The interview room was set up with a screen facing the interviewee. At times during the interview process, various images flashed upon the screen. These images stimulated various physiological responses in the subject, including blood pressure, heartbeat, and pupil diameter. Hidden sensors measured these evoked responses immediately. It was a high-tech security system invented by the Israelis and used to detect terrorists at airports and other venues. It seemed like this would be a significant piece of the investigation and could be a key cog and important task in the investigation project. As Ashraf started to hear about these interviews, their length and depth, and the unusual electronic screens set up in the rooms, he became very apprehensive.

Ashraf now clearly remembered the memo sent out to all employees that stock-trading activity in the last ninety days was to be investigated. It was not unusual for top management to be in a blackout period most of the time, as they had inside information about the company. They were restricted by Securities and Exchange Commission regulations and could trade shares or options of their holdings in the company only after certain disclosure periods. However, 90 percent of the employees had the freedom to buy or sell at most times. This was an unusual time, however. Close to approval and launch of MVoneshot, more than 50 percent of the employees, including all the sales and marketing team, their in-house support team, and the manufacturing team, were included in the blackout period. They had inside information or were close to people in the company who could have provided them information. Ashraf knew it would be unlawful to make any trades on his own during this time. He went around the system, he thought. But Ashraf did not know the full extent of the law. Providing information to outsiders was just as bad as acting on his own behalf.

Something else was going on as well, and Ashraf was not sure he could handle much more today. He had received a call from his sister, Nadirah, in Toronto. She had been questioned by the Ontario Securities Commission (OSC). His company was also traded on the Ontario exchange. The OSC questioned her about the short sale of IVTP she had made. She had bet on a huge fall in the stock price of

IVTP even though she had never before invested in the stock market. This was certainly not the way a new investor typically started trading in the market. Plus, it was a windfall. Her investment of less than five thousand had turned into fifty-five thousand. Plus, she had an additional set of options that would expire in July and would be worth at least that amount. She had never traded in this type of issue before, and now suddenly she happened to hit on some of the worst news any company can get.

"Ashraf, I am in trouble!" Nadirah shouted trough her phone.

"Nadirah, what has happened? Are you all right?" questioned Ashraf.

"No, I am not. Remember when you asked me to buy your company stock in October?" she said.

"Yes."

"Ashraf, I just got a call from the police!" screamed Nadirah.

"The police? That cannot be," said Ashraf. "You have done nothing wrong."

"Well, someone from the Toronto OSC—whoever that is—called me and said I just did something bad," Nadirah said meekly, starting to weep.

"Let's talk tonight. I am sure you did nothing bad," Ashraf said comfortingly as he googled *OSC*. "Go home from work and relax."

"Okay. Please call me as soon as you can. I love you. Goodbye." She hung up.

Ashraf could not believe what he saw. The first hits on his search were related to SEC and OSC cooperation on investigations of fraud and illegal trading across borders. Now he was upset that he had Googled anything on his work computer related to the SEC and OSC. This was an additional electronic footprint besides the call he had just taken from his sister. Ashraf felt like things were unraveling in his world.

Alan desperately needed an inside update from the company. He of course knew all about the problems with the vaccine, and Hopkins had admitted a few children who had been affected. He had even seen one child with encephalomyelitis, an inflammation of the brain and spinal cord. He had never before seen a patient with such a complication since it occurs in only one in every thousand natural measles virus infections. Alan did not have to wonder what their altered vaccine strain might do now in the community. Based on the president's address, he knew things were out of control. They had unleashed a virus that was spreading wide and fast. The prior version of the vaccine might not even protect against it. If so, this was working toward the goal of his people much faster than he could have imagined.

He called Ashraf from his office using one of the burner phones he had previously purchased at a corner store. He had always kept several on hand for calls he did not want traced. Even though he was collaborating on projects with the company, Alan did not need any calls traced back to him. Ashraf did not recognize the number and did not answer the phone. At this point he was paranoid. He figured the next call he would receive would be from the SEC, FBI, or some other three-letter bureau. Alan left a message on Ashraf's company voice mail: "Ashraf, this is Dr. Mazer at Hopkins. I would like to speak with you about the antiserum we have been using in our studies. Please give me a call as soon as possible."

Alan thought this bogus message should get Ashraf's attention and a call back. And at least now he would recognize his number.

Within about thirty minutes, Ashraf called him back from his home. He had clearance during the national emergency to go the office but had stayed home on this day.

"Alan, this is Ashraf, calling you back. What's up?"

"Ashraf, I am calling you to get an update. A lot of crazy things are going down. I am seeing a lot of sick kids. I know the vaccine is off the market, and we all heard the president last night. What is going on at the company? You must tell me all you know," pleaded Alan.

"Things are crazy here, but I did not go to work today," Ashraf said. "We are basically shut down. The CEO is batshit crazy. He and everyone else here have lost half their wealth. Every person close to the vaccine is being investigated and questioned. I will be too very shortly. Every procedure will be checked, and every vial will be also. I am certain they suspect me. I made the switch, and I left before signing the records. My assistant signed them first, and I countersigned the next day. They will hang me out to dry. Not you, of course. We just tested the virus in your lab to make sure it was still neuroinvasive and caused disease in mice. I also have another problem."

"What do you mean you have *another* problem? Everything is perfect. The virus is spreading into the community just like we wanted. I laid the groundwork with papers from Europe and around the world on problems with vaccination to keep vaccination rates low. What is the problem?" Alan shouted through his phone.

"No, Alan, not that. It is not a problem with our goal. I was trying to raise money, and I told several of my brothers in the congregation and my sister in Toronto to short sell my company," Ashraf explained.

"Now that is a problem. You gave inside information to your Muslim friends? That is crazy. If the SEC does not find you or your friends, the CIA will!" bellowed Alan through his tiny flip phone, feeling his blood pressure rising. "And you have a blood relative in Toronto. That's international law we are dealing with. With all the Arabic names associated with these transactions, this could shut us and the caliphate down fast. This is only the beginning of several biological attacks in my long-range plan for the program. You were just one piece of this, and you do have a big problem. You have just now put this cell and everyone at the mosque at huge risk."

After a pause, Alan added, "Get yourself to your office. You look guiltier than ever by not being at work. You are one of very few people allowed out under the emergency. You are expected there to figure out what went wrong."

Alan closed his phone and walked down the stairs and outside. He decided to head around the block a few times for a rather long walk. He knew that he was restricted from walking too far or the guard would stop and question him. He broke his phone in half and tossed it in the first garbage can he came across. He was not hungry. He just needed to think for a few minutes away from the Hopkins campus. He wanted some exercise and time away from the buildings and activities inside. Alan needed to figure out how to eliminate Ashraf from the equation. If Ashraf were taken in on SEC charges for providing inside information, that would not be enough. He would only be squeezed for more information and possibly questioned by extreme means about terror cells by other agencies. Ashraf would talk. Alan had to eliminate

Ashraf for the cause, but how? He was one of them. Ashraf had helped so much for the jihad. But he was just a weak link now. These were many of Alan's thoughts as we walked around the block for the third time, this time eyed by the guardsman on duty. Alan entered the hospital through the Wilmer Eye Institute.

12

JOINT TERRORISM TASK
FORCE INVESTIGATES
JUNE 2019

The Securities and Exchange Commission lead investigator, Harvey Goodman, received the report at the team meeting Monday morning. He had heard just about all he needed to take the next steps in this case: file the case with the commission for review and then file in federal court. A group of individuals in Baltimore and Howard County, all living in and around the same zip codes and never having shorted a stock before, had bet heavily in late 2018 on Immunoviratherapeutics to drop precipitously in the spring and summer of 2019. There had been little such activity by other investors. Having obtained a warrant for phone records for each of the suspects, the investigators found a common thread. Each of the investors had spoken with the same person several times in October of 2018. That person lived in Falls Church, Virginia. This, they thought, sounded like a typical insider-trading ploy. This insider and the investors acting on this knowledge could go to jail for a long time. Another individual investor in Canada was also involved. All parties had Muslim surnames, and the international involvement brought the attention of the National Security Agency and CIA. There could be major intelligence and terror threats associated with this transaction and possible international terrorism. Harvey would not wait long in getting the Joint Terrorism Task Force involved in this investigation. But then, he thought, informing this group directly was way above his pay grade.

As the day moved along—and this was no ordinary day, being under a national emergency—and with no sign of his superior in the office, Harvey was in a quandary. He could wait to inform his boss and go through all the correct government channels. But he knew this was the time to be bold. Harvey couldn't wait for paper trails or the right channels. His high level of concern about what had happened in years past when silos of the government didn't communicate well brought the current issue to a whole new level. Now at least agencies spoke to one another. Before 9/11, many groups did pieces of the same task that might have prevented that disastrous day. Communication was dismal. Harvey took it upon himself to reach out to the Joint Terrorism Task Force. Specifically, he knew now that there was a memorandum of understanding among several government agencies and within his own agency. Treasury was taking the lead, along with the FBI. Harvey also knew that the Terrorist Tracking Financing Program was now a US and European effort to catch the flow of cash to terror groups. Most of the groups, like Hamas, were funded by nongovernmental organizations, which made tracking extremely difficult. The TTFP had been operational for many years and curtailed several terror operations across the globe. Its aim was to identify, track, and pursue terrorists.

Harvey seemed to have come across a group that had made a boneheaded move. And they were at his back door in Baltimore. It seemed as if the task force, if they wanted, could pull in a cell or a whole group of potential terrorists right now. *That's their job*, he reasoned. He called Martin Erlich, his contact at the task force, and summarized what he knew for him.

"Martin, good afternoon. I have some information for you, a story for you. I hope you have a few minutes," Harvey said.

"Well, hello, Goody. Go ahead. We've got nothing to do here—just counting some big bills," he said with a chuckle.

"Good one. Funny. My group and I noticed a number of unusual transactions recently. A biotechnology company, Immunoviratherapeutics, heavily traded, had a major sell-off at the end of March. One of their two products, a measles virus vaccine, was withdrawn from the market by the FDA after just two or three weeks. Several children had died and many were sickened."

"That's horrible," Martin interrupted. "You'd have to have your head in the ground not to have heard about this. Thousands of people are getting sick, Harvey, and we are all in a state of national emergency. Of course we all know about this. What the fuck can you tell me about it?"

"It may tie to a terror plot. Maybe. I don't know. But please hear me out," Harvey pleaded. "The bottom line is that a group of individuals all with Muslim surnames had invested in the company in October and had bought put options, betting on the stock to dive. None of these people had ever invested previously in this type of instrument. And a sister of an employee at the company, also Muslim, in Toronto, likewise invested," Harvey finished.

"I take it they all cashed in after the stock tanked?" Martin asked.

"Yes. And they cleared a pretty penny. Hundreds of thousands of dollars. That doesn't sound like much, but it goes a long way to fund a local cell and pay expenses. Plus, they have July contracts that would be worth close to a million or more. No one else in the investor community was betting on this company to fail. By the way, the symbol is IVTP. It is down about 50 percent and going nowhere since the disaster. The whole market has taken a huge beating," Harvey added.

He continued, "The clinical trials were nothing like what had happened in the patients who received the vaccine when distributed in the marketplace. No kids were injured or hurt in the trials."

"Well, from this brief explanation, it sounds like I may want to do a site visit to the company, do a little poking around. Let me pack my bags. Where are they located again—Bethesda?" Martin asked.

"Close—McLean. You can jump in your car without any bags and can actually take the metro if you want. They're near the Tysons metro."

"This is all very interesting. We definitely need to follow up on this. Anyone else within the company selling anything?" Martin asked.

"No. They were all blacked out. I believe Canada will get back to me with the name of the sibling investor in Toronto. I think the Canadian authorities have questioned the sister already and may have information for us shortly," added Harvey.

"Goody, thanks for the information. Can you send the file to me? We will get working on this immediately. Lots of things going on here. First, it looks like there could be external forces at play to move the stock price. Are these forces affecting the vaccine? Did the Muslim investors know about these or have something to do with it?" Martin questioned. He paused. "We have a lot to investigate. I will lean on you, Goody. Just because you brought this to me doesn't mean you're out of the loop. I'll speak with you soon. Thanks." Martin ended the call.

Harvey Goodman was doing his job. He may have jumped the gun by not going through correct Treasury channels first, but he needed to step up this investigation as fast as possible. He would tell his boss now and let him handle the other connections in the government. To someone looking in from the outside, it still looked like a spider web—two groups in the same agency, Treasury, working on the similar but different goals led by different directors. No wonder coordination was still not great. The relatively unknown but important Office of Terrorism and Financial Intelligence stood at the ready within the Department of the Treasury. One of its major functions was weeding out terrorists by following financial activities, but its main goal was safeguarding the financial systems. Harvey figured his boss would get them into the mix as soon as possible. He would get a slap on the wrist for going directly to the Joint Terrorism Task Force, but he would let the boss have credit for this one.

As Martin got off the phone, he had high hopes and lots of questions that went way beyond insider trading. Iran was the major financier of worldwide terrorism. A link to the Baltimore group and Iran was what he was hoping to find. Especially after the US knee-jerk response bombing of Iran in 2012 by President O'Malley, it would be nice to find something to tie back to Tehran, even if it was years later. Most people had tunnel vision; Martin did not. It was just a thought in the back of his mind. Was there anyone in the Baltimore area involved with the company? Maybe Iran had seeded this group. Or, possibly, Iran had funneled monies to Hezbollah, the most dangerous terrorist group lurking in the United States, or other such organizations. Who knew where this investigation might reach? Ever since the administration had sent billions of dollars in cash to Iran in 2015 when a nuclear deal was struck, it seemed as if more and more money was funneled to terror groups around the world. Iran was and continued to be the greatest sponsor of terror groups, and this influx of cash could only help the funding of Hezbollah, Hamas, the Syrian Revolutionary Guard, and who knows what other terror cells around the world.

Finally, based on some solid interdepartmental communication, the Joint Terrorism Task Force was called into action. A financial hiccup and trading by some amateurs all with Muslim surnames might have led to the source of the problem, but then again it might just be a coincidence and some good luck. The virulence of the measles vaccine was undoubtedly unexpected. And furthermore, the attenuated virus— or at least what the company had developed as an attenuated virus— should not have spread to secondhand recipients in so many cases. In maybe two cases in the archives of medical history had a vaccine for a respiratory agent like measles been injected in the skin, spread to the lungs, and then infected another person. And in these one or two cases, the vaccine had been given to a person who was immune compromised.

The medical and research teams at the company had their work cut out for them. It would not be a simple task to determine where things had gone wrong. They desperately needed to find it, fix it, and somehow try to earn back the confidence of the medical and consumer communities. During this hiatus from the market for MVoneshot, the company's communications and investor-relations group tried to explain as much as possible. They were severe but tried mightily to right the ship.

Executive management needed to rethink its next move for the measles vaccine. Should they start from scratch after finding out what went awry? Relaunch this product that had already killed and maimed?

Rename a modified product and do minimal studies to get it back on the market? They had already invested over $300 million in this product. It didn't seem wise to throw it down the drain. They could eventually have a global market. So many questions and a lot of frustration had built up with this disaster.

Martin Erlich arrived at Immunoviratherapeutics headquarters early Tuesday morning, June 4, a week after Memorial Day. He timed his arrival for a week after the holiday, figuring many employees had taken advantage of the short week for vacation, one they all needed. Most would be back to work this week. He had called the CEO, Dr. Arnold Ickerson, during the week of Memorial Day to introduce himself. He told Arnold that the SEC had discovered rather clear evidence of an insider-trading ploy and that his terrorism task force from Treasury would now investigate. Arnold was livid given the strict company rules and communications, but he understood orders and knew what had to be done. Martin had requested an assembly of all employees. Arnold told Martin to split them up into two groups because they would not all fit in the largest meeting room. Arnold also told Martin that HR and a consultant group had already begun to interview employees who had worked on the project to discuss work issues. Arnold was direct and spoke his mind to Martin. Before meeting with the employees, Martin knocked on Arnold's door and entered.

"Good morning, Dr. Ickerson. I wanted to speak with you before I speak with your assembled masses," he said.

"Good. Martin, I know you need to do your thing. But let me give you two names of people I think you should speak with first. I know we all need to move on this fast. Ashraf Khaleed has worked for us for many years, and I did put lots of trust in him. He runs the manufacturing group now. And I think he is Muslim. Furthermore, we have asked him to do some work with one our colleagues, a Dr. Mazer in Baltimore at Hopkins," Arnold finished.

"All right, so we have three or four pieces here that I might have to follow up on," said Martin.

"Yes, but I have no concerns about Alan Mazer. He is a top-notch scientist and is world renowned. In fact, I think he's Jewish," remarked Arnold.

"Is there anyone else with a company-Baltimore connection I need to investigate?" asked Martin.

"Not so much investigate, but you should speak with our top medical science liaison, Dr. Nari Lee," said Arnold. "She has just recently been able to get some meetings with Dr. Mazer. Even though we collaborate, he has been a tough nut."

"What does she do?" Martin queried.

"She travels in his region, the Northeast, speaking with opinion leaders, like Mazer, and giving them updates on what we are doing here. She also gets information on what they might be doing—sort of our internal spy network. But more than that, she keeps us up to date on the pulse of product perception from a scientific point of view," Arnold said.

"Fine, I will try to get to them both tomorrow. But honestly, it sounds like Ashraf might be my best guess. His sister in Toronto is connected, and all eyes are on the mosque in Baltimore right now. Thanks for taking time. I will debrief you if I can before heading up to Baltimore this afternoon," Martin concluded. "Can I speak with Dr. Lee briefly before we begin?"

"Of course, I will have my assistant get her. You can use the vacant office next door," Arnold said.

"Thank you." Martin got up from his chair. Arnold couldn't help but notice Martin's sidearm in his shoulder holster. It was a little unnerving even though he was a former soldier. He was now leading a top biotechnology company in the Washington, DC, area, not a battalion of three hundred soldiers in the field.

Nari Lee walked confidently into the large ex-COO's office and sat comfortably on the side chair across the desk from Martin.

"Good morning, Dr. Lee," he began. "I am Martin Erlich. I head up the Joint Terrorism Task Force and wanted to spend a few minutes with you before I head into the company meeting."

"Very nice to meet you. Please call me Nari," she said.

"Good. I just have a few questions. I understand you have been on top of the measles vaccine from the beginning. Correct?" he said.

"Well, I have been following its progress from my position and giving updates as I can to doctors I work with," she said.

"That's what I wanted to ask you. You recently met with Dr. Mazer in Baltimore, one of IVTP's collaborators?" he asked.

"Wow, using the stock symbol?" she said. "Yes, he has requested some of our mutant virus stocks, especially the neurovirulent strain, and I think Ashraf Khaleed has gone to help him a few times to work on other measles strains."

"I am tied to the SEC—that's the reason for the stock symbol. Anyway, that is excellent information. Tell me about your meetings with Dr. Mazer, please," Martin requested.

"Very short, succinct, and to be honest, not very helpful," Nari responded. "I would have hoped to develop him into an advocate for our products, especially since we have supported him with a grant, but he has basically not given me the time of day."

"So you have been disappointed?" Martin asked.

"So far, but it takes time to get to know some of these younger docs. I am hopeful. He seems busy and distracted much of the time I drop by to see him," she said.

"Okay, thanks for that insight. I hope we can talk later," Martin said.

"Anytime," Nari replied as she got up from her chair and hurried off to the assembly location.

The meeting with the company employees would not be easy. Martin had suggested to Arnold that the group had been traumatized. Most didn't know what had hit them. From what he could figure, the company had been on a wild ride. It had marketed two fantastic products—lifesaving products—for infants and children in the past five years. Many employees had become rather wealthy on paper and then seen it all disappear overnight. Hundreds of employees were undoubtedly over their heads in mortgages and car loans. Most had never known failure their whole lives, and now their lives were collapsing. Desperation was just around the corner unless upper management could turn the company around.

In the last two months, their new and innovative vaccine for measles virus had been revealed to actually be just the opposite. It was spreading disease and destruction to toddlers and children. Their neighbors were furious that they had been locked down for ten days in their homes because of this "new and improved vaccine." Martin, along with the VP of Human Resources, now had the first group assembled. The HR head introduced Martin as an agent from the Department of the Treasury. At this time, Mr. Erlich and his agents were here to speak with several individuals in the company. Martin then took the stage. He was very charismatic and tried to put the group at ease. He told them that no one was under arrest but that he had several sets of handcuffs in the car. He got a few nervous laughs and continued. He told the assembled employees that he understood the history of their vaccine and was truly sorry. Further, he said that another consultant group was looking into details of employee behavior and technical aspects of vaccine production. Martin said he was there on another mission. "As an agent of the Treasury, you might ask what in God's name am I doing here. Well, I'm with the Joint Terrorism Task Force," Martin explained. A huge gasp could be heard across the meeting room. Martin noticed many people looking around at others, not sure what to think.

"Let me continue and explain. It is all right if you do not understand what's going on. It came to the attention of the Securities and Exchange Commission that there had been unusual trading in Immunoviratherapeutics just around the time the awful problems with your vaccine came to light and patients suffered," he stated. "We at the task force have reason to believe this is not a coincidence. There might be terrorist involvement. The Treasury Department is tasked with investigating these types of activities." More gasps were heard.

"As of this moment, you are all potential witnesses to a crime or crimes. And you must not discuss any information related to these inquiries with friends, family, or coworkers, whether employees or consultants or contractors. These discussions would be considered obstruction of justice. Let's not go down that road. Just as a little education, I've put up on the screen a summary of the law. This is a definition of obstruction of justice and what it could lead to. Don't memorize this. It's not something you have to worry about. Just discuss nothing at this point. I have left copies of the law for you on the table at the back of the room. Take a copy on the way out and sign the form showing that you received this information. I took this verbiage directly from the code of federal regulations."

The paper copy of the law read in part,

> Whoever, with intent to avoid, evade, prevent, or obstruct compliance, in whole or in part, with any civil investigative demand duly and properly made under the Antitrust Civil Process Act, willfully withholds, misrepresents, removes from any place, conceals, covers up, destroys, mutilates, alters, or by other means falsifies any documentary material, answers to written interrogatories, or oral testimony, which is the subject of such demand; or attempts to do so or solicits another to do so; or
>
> Whoever corruptly, or by threats or force, or by any threatening letter or communication influences, obstructs, or impedes or endeavors to influence, obstruct, or impede the due and proper administration of the law under which any pending proceeding is being had before any department or agency of the United States, or the due and proper exercise of the power of inquiry under which any inquiry or investigation is being had by either House, or any committee of either House or any joint committee of the Congress—
>
> Shall be fined under this title, imprisoned not more than 5 years or, if the offense involves international or domestic terrorism (as defined in section 2331), imprisoned not more than 8 years, or both.

"So do not discuss the ongoing investigation with anyone, as that would be included in the definition of obstruction of justice above," Martin continued. "You should only speak to me or other federal agents under my command about this. When we meet with some of you individually, you will have an opportunity to ask any questions you would like. If anyone has any information they wish to bring to our attention before we get to you, please see me immediately. Anything that could help us to get our answers more quickly is better for everybody. It might have been something you heard in the workplace that sounded trivial but now in this context might not be so innocent. Come forward and talk to us. I will have an office set up in the executive suite for the next week. That is all for now. Thank you all very much. Oh yes, just one more thing. We will have the exact same meeting with the rest of the staff in the next hour. We just couldn't squeeze everyone in here. Thanks again," concluded Martin.

One of Martin's first meetings was with Ashraf. "Mr. Ashraf Khaleed, please have a seat. Nice to meet you. As you know, I am Martin Erlich, Treasury Agent and head of this Joint Terrorism Task Force." Martin noticed that Ashraf's respirations were quickened and his eyes were dilated, both signs of anxiety and stress—not unusual in this situation. However, in his experience, if these physiological responses continued for more than a few minutes, he would have concerns about this witness.

"Okay," Ashraf responded.

"Ashraf—may I call you Ashraf?" asked Martin.

"Please do."

"I have a few minutes here before I have to drive up to Baltimore. We will record this interview for our records. My agents will perform most of the questioning. But I understand you have been one of the key players with the company for many years, is that correct?" Martin asked.

"Well, I think I have played a pretty important role. I do not want to brag too much, but I did do a lot of the genetic manipulation on the virus strains and selection of the mutants we used for the vaccines," Ashraf replied.

"I think that is a great accomplishment. Congratulations on your work," Martin said. "What do you think happened to this vaccine that caused all the problems?"

Ashraf seemed rattled by this question. He had not expected the fastball so quickly.

"I—I d-don't know," he stuttered.

"It seems that you worked on developing these mutants, and then you were put in charge of manufacturing, a big promotion. Give me some ideas that I can investigate," Martin prodded.

"I am thinking. Maybe … maybe the trials were a fluke, and this is not a good vaccine. That is one possibility?"

"You mean over five thousand children received the vaccine in the trials without any major problems, and now after just a few weeks on the market all these problems occur?" asked Martin.

"That's probably not likely. The virus may have mutated to a virulent form when we grew it up for production," Ashraf added.

"Help me understand that. How would you know if that happened?" asked Martin.

"I think our chief of research is probably already on this, but the first thing you have to do is grow up a batch of virus from the lot of vaccine that was shipped out and a batch of virus that was originally placed in storage to be the vaccine. The next step is to do a genetic analysis and compare the RNA and proteins of the two viruses. If they match, then they are the same. If not, then we have a different virus in the lot that was shipped out," summarized Ashraf.

"If they are different, how could that have happened?" Martin continued.

"I do not know, sir," Ashraf answered.

"No idea whatsoever?"

"I can only guess, and I don't think that's a good idea," Ashraf added.

"Humor me. I do not have a background in this area. This will help me as I speak with others," said Martin.

"I am only hypothesizing, and remember, I am not the scientist," Ashraf said. "It might have mutated when it was grown up for production. The batch of cells used to grow the vaccine might have something in them, a contaminant that is causing the problem, or maybe there was a switch by accident. The wrong virus could be in production."

"All very interesting. Thank you. Okay, Ashraf. That's enough for now. Either one of our other agents or I might be questioning you further down the road. In the meantime, do not discuss this conversation or anything about the company and this incident with anyone, as we discussed earlier today at the meeting. Understood?" said Martin.

Ashraf nodded his head.

Martin added, "Could you please say that you understand and that you will not discuss this with anyone, for the transcript?"

"Yes, I understand."

"Thank you, Ashraf, and have a nice week. Good day."

Ashraf got up and left the room with slumped shoulders, his eyes still quite dilated.

Martin sat back in his comfortable chair, not used to such nice accommodations. Arnold told Martin he should occupy the now-vacated office of the recently fired chief operating officer. He had several thoughts as Ashraf Khaleed left the office but was interrupted by a call from his administrative assistant in Washington. He had asked her to cross-check terrorist databases looking for the names of all the company employees. She looked at two major sources: the no-fly list and the Terrorist Identities Datamart Environment (TIDE). The TIDE is the US government's central database of known or suspected terrorists. It contains extremely classified information on over 1.4 million people, provided by worldwide members of the intelligence community, such as the FBI, NSA, and many others. She entered in the names of all employees and consultants, as well as any of the people who had traded options of the company during the time of the drop in the stock price. No hits came up. This shocked Martin. Could this be just a bunch of stupid people trying to get rich at the same time there is a horrible accident? This did not add up, and Martin did not believe in coincidences. Martin decided he needed to make time to see one more person before heading to Baltimore. He asked his assistant to find Nari Lee. She was not usually in the home office, so she could have staked out an office anywhere while working to help clean up the mess that had developed. After a few minutes, he heard a soft knock on his door.

"Come in," Martin said.

Nari entered the office.

"Ah. Good morning again," said Martin. "Please have a seat, and make yourself comfortable."

"Yes, Agent Erlich. I imagine you want to speak with me because I am heading home tomorrow," Nari replied.

"Well, that is news to me. And since we are on an informal basis after our early-morning session, please call me Martin. So I guess it is good timing. Where is home?" Martin asked, trying to start the inquiry in a relaxed manner.

"I have lived in Providence for about fifteen years now. I am originally from the West Coast but am now comfortable out here despite the fact that everyone seems to be always leaning on their horns," she said.

Martin chuckled. "Nari, I understand that you spend most of your time on the road meeting with researchers and physicians. Is that correct?" he asked.

"Well, that's pretty close to what I and a few of my colleagues do. I hope to learn from the people I meet, and in return I provide new information to these scientists. Hopefully over time they will be advocates for our company's products," said Nari. "I also provide grants and set up new research projects with some of the scientists around the country."

"Great. Can you tell me about your work with doctors other than Mazer—in Baltimore in particular," Martin inquired.

"Sure. I am there often to see Dr. Jim Gregory at Sinai Hospital. He is the head of the pediatric infectious disease division. He was a strong supporter of our first product, our MPV vaccine. Initially, before the product was approved by the FDA, he was quite dubious. But when he saw the trial results, he was on board. This was a first-of-its-kind product, and as a company we were proud and excited to launch this vaccine. It was a novel and innovative product," Nari excitedly explained.

"Your enthusiasm must be infectious. You probably don't want a vaccine for that."

"Thank you. No, we don't. Anyway that product put us on the map," Nari continued. "MPV was the orphan virus in babies. RSV was the big daddy, so to speak, and everyone failed previously with RSV vaccines. When we succeeded with our MPV vaccine, our company took off. Dr. Gregory was not really enthusiastic about the measles vaccine because the standard vaccine had been in use for years. I had told him that when ours was approved, we hoped to eliminate the need for a second injection, as any child would love not being stuck twice.

But the major benefit was the improved immune response to the virus. In the meantime, we would meet to discuss the ongoing progress as the committees and FDA reviewed our data."

"Is there anyone else in Baltimore that you met or continue to meet with?" Martin asked.

"Yes. I try to get in to see Dr. Gregory and several docs on his staff to discuss the measles vaccine. You should know Jim was the first to call me directly about adverse events in his patients. He first made the company aware of the problem."

"This morning you said Mazer was almost impossible to meet with. Why is that?" Martin asked.

"If we'd had more time this morning, I would have gotten into that. Here's what I could not understand. He has been to our company to lecture in the past. Plus, we had given him a small grant and some of our mutant measles virus strains that we are not developing. He also wanted to get hold of the strain we did not develop for the vaccine because it was neurotropic and had severe effects on the nervous system in animal models," Nari summarized.

"Okay, now you've gone way over my head," Martin interjected. "You will have to give me the fifth-grade version."

"All right. We developed a battery of several measles mutants. Our goal was to find one that could induce a rapid and sustained immune response in animals, with no adverse events. We wanted to have a vaccine that would require only one injection. The current vaccine requires a booster, a second shot. Are you with me so far?" Nari asked.

"Yes, got it."

"So, the scientists made changes in two areas of one of the measles proteins that controls our responses to the virus. They tested several for their ability to grow in the lab and to produce a good immune response. Once that was accomplished, the next step was to evaluate whether or not these strains were problematic in animal models. We tested three in parallel, if my memory serves me. Two were going along nicely. One did great, and that one was chosen and eventually became MVoneshot. A second passed all the tests, except it caused neurological problems in a mouse model and in one primate, the rhesus macaque. That is the strain that Dr. Mazer wanted to examine in more detail because of his interest in neurovirology," Nari concluded.

"Finally, how does Ashraf Khaleed fit into Dr. Mazer's work? Do you know anything about this?" he asked.

"I don't know any specifics; this is really not in my area of the organization. I can only guess. Before Ashraf moved into the supervisory role in the manufacturing area, he was in research. He played a big role in developing the mutant strains that were used in our selection of the final vaccine," Nari explained.

"Please, continue."

"So, Ashraf might have been helping Dr. Mazer grow the mutant measles virus in his lab or showing him some of the tricks of the trade to get high yields of the virus in culture. Once you have been shown a few of these hints, it doesn't take much to do it on your own. I will say from my experience and talking to others who work in this field that growing this virus is not easy. It takes time, patience, and commitment," she said. "It is more of an art than a science sometimes."

"This would not have been something that required a full-time or long-term commitment by Ashraf?" Martin inquired.

"I would doubt that the company would have allowed something like that. The company might allow him to go to Mazer's lab once in a while to help him out, but that would be it," she explained.

"Nari, you have been very helpful, and you have given me a good education. Thank you for your time, and good luck. I may be asking you further questions by phone or on your next trip here," Martin said. "By the way, have you ever thought about working in the government?"

"Not really. Most of the opportunities for me were at low-level jobs at the NIH, and I was not willing to start that far down on the pay scale," she said.

Out of his usual character, Martin spoke quickly, excited for the possibility of recruiting Nari to the Agency. "Let's talk soon. I am on loan to Treasury from the agency for the Joint Terrorism Task Force. I believe we can use someone with your background. I think the pay will surprise you. It might not be exactly what you're making now, but you might like the challenge."

"I will get back to you. I always keep my options open, especially now." Nari turned and left the office.

Nari did not feel at all uneasy personally but worried about everyone around her. She wondered why Martin had not asked her anything about what she thought had happened. She was knowledgeable about the product, more so than most in the company, yet he did not even ask for her theory. Maybe that's not how the investigation works. She had no idea. Right now Nari's only thought was that something was screwed up in the manufacturing group. There was no way that a vaccine with no similar adverse events in over five thousand children in the trials all of a sudden had a changed profile when commercialized.

Martin stepped out of the office and knocked on Arnold Ickerson's door, the office adjacent to the one he was using.

"Come in," boomed Arnold.

"I wanted to catch you before I head up to Baltimore today," Martin began. "I just had my assistant check all the employee and consultant names against our terrorist databases, and you will be happy to know that everyone comes up clean."

"Well, I didn't know if we had a problem there. I thought we might have a criminal issue," Arnold responded.

"I cannot rule out anything. I am checking out all possibilities and would bet you had that on your mind, no?"

"To be honest, Martin—and let's keep this between the two of us right now—I have taken some unilateral action. Yes, I know that we cannot rule out terrorism. And I know it's prejudicial to say that just because a group of Muslims had been involved in the trading there might be a tie here. I have a lot of power in the capital, my friend. It was my call to our head of the National Institutes of Allergy and Infectious Diseases, Carlos Annetti, that got our president moving so quickly. Carlos has close ties to the president. I think that without that national emergency declaration, we could have all been in a different place right now. Forget about ISIS, Hezbollah, and every other ingrown terrorist group. Our citizens would have been looting and rioting in the streets for food and water. We needed to protect our president, necessary staff, secretaries, and heads before everything was lost."

"So you *do* think this is a terrorist action!" Martin exclaimed.

"I really do. And I am very concerned that we will not be able to control other events like this. Hell, *this* might yet not be controlled. Kids are still getting infected. It is just not a peak phase. Can you imagine the outcome if we were tested by an unknown agent or a virus with no vaccine? We have a lot of brain power here. I do not think this was an accident. The vaccine tested in the trials did not in any way resemble that sent out in our commercial lots. Someone screwed with this," Arnold concluded.

"I just finished questioning Ashraf Khaleed, your lead man in manufacturing. Do you think he could have something to do with this?" asked Martin.

"Listen, at this point, it could be anyone. You said no one in my company is on the terrorist watch list," Arnold replied.

"Yes, I did. That doesn't mean we don't have a new cell or a new group to deal with," said Martin. "Ashraf was quite nervous, as most would be during questioning. But let's just forget his background for a minute. He was nervous the whole interview and did not calm down despite my trying to ask him calming questions, congratulating him on his work, and asking him how to do certain things in his area of expertise. I have some suspicions. He attends a radical mosque in Baltimore. In fact, all the traders attend that mosque. It doesn't take a genius to put two and two together. Plus, Ashraf's sister invested in this scheme. She lives in Toronto and has already been questioned by the Ontario Securities Commission in Canada. We have enough evidence to arrest Ashraf Khaleed on several charges related to insider trading."

"But what about changing the vaccine that went into the market?" Arnold asked. "Do we have evidence that Ashraf did that?"

"No, we don't. Ashraf had some ideas on how it could have been done, which leads me to think he might have played a role—maybe, maybe not. I think if I question some of the other traders from the mosque, they might tell me something about Ashraf and his connections," said Martin.

"Well, go to it, my friend. Your other agents may get some other information here, and meanwhile my research team could turn up something in the lab," said Arnold.

"I am on my way to Baltimore. I will visit the mosque that Ashraf prayed at occasionally with his coinvestors. I will either call you or see you tomorrow," Martin announced. "And one other thing. Your Dr. Lee—she is very bright. We might want to take her off your hands and put her in the agency."

"Don't go grabbing my best people, Martin, especially now in our crisis!" Arnold protested. "Now get yourself up to Baltimore and find out what the hell has happened."

"I hate to tell you this, Arnold," he said, "but Dr. Lee and I are already working on this together."

Martin hightailed it out of the office and jumped into his government-issued black Ford sedan.

Thankfully Martin's assistant, Amy, had quickly added all the company employees and consultants to the Computer Assisted Passenger Prescreening System. Arnold had also given Martin the names of the research groups in Baltimore that had done any work on measles virus in the last five years. Amy added the names of any people associated with these labs to the CAPPS just to be all-inclusive.

After his less-than-fruitful visit to the Baltimore mosque, Martin had a brief call with his agent in charge back at Immunoviratherapeutics. She had gleaned very little information from thirty interviews of manufacturing employees. One sad outcome was that an employee had admitted to insider trading. A young woman told her parents she was blacked out but thought the company was going to rally and the share price of the stock would increase in the spring, when the MVoneshot was approved by the FDA. Unfortunately, for her parents, who took out a second mortgage to invest in the company, the gains in the stock were already built into the share price by investors. Share prices fell. The woman's parents sustained a huge loss and now will have a long-term debt to repay. It was likely as well that they would visit their daughter in jail for three to five years. Sadly, the terrorist the task force was looking for was someone other than this woman.

Martin summarized his afternoon. Nothing. No one with whom he had met talked. No one admitted to knowing Ashraf very well. Oh, yes, they would see him at some evening prayer sessions, but he was not from the area. His mother lived here, but he was from the Washington area. That was about the only information about Ashraf that Martin could scrape up from anyone. They had been tight-lipped, and his badge and title had not seemed to bother them. Maybe a different venue or, more importantly, getting in touch with the six "investors" might be a different matter. Martin confirmed with the Imam that these six individuals had been in contact with Ashraf. The Imam also mentioned that Ashraf was friendly with a doctor from Hopkins who also prayed there occasionally. His name was Mazer. The Imam indicated that it was a strange name for a Muslim. *Indeed, it is,* thought Martin.

Martin took the opportunity to head over to Hopkins to see what he could dig up on Dr. Mazer and anyone else associated with him. His name had already come up earlier in the day when Nari had discussed the mutant measles virus collaboration and Ashraf, so things were starting to get a little messy in his mind.

Martin found it was easy enough to gain access to the hospital by flashing his badge at the security desk. He hated the unsecure buildings in the country. If terrorists only knew what harm they could do. Martin headed to the elevator of the neurology wing and found the neurovirology labs. He spotted the sign for Mazer's office on the third floor and headed directly to it. No one could be seen anywhere. The lights were off, and the desk was clean—not a paper or a pen on it. *Rather odd*, he thought, *for a doctor's office.* He then headed down the hall and asked someone in a white coat where Mazer's lab was. The white coat pointed down the hall, three doors down. Martin walked in and found no one in the lab either. All the fluorescent lights glimmered and several machines hummed in the background, suggesting that operations were ongoing. But, again, no people were in sight. Martin retraced his steps, looked one more time back to Mazer's office, and then headed back to the elevator. He rode up to the sixth floor. By now it was close to five in the evening, and he was hoping to drop in on the chairman of the Department of Neurology. As luck would have it, he was in. With government badge in hand, Martin was taken right into the office by the chairman's executive assistant.

"Sir, excuse me," the assistant said. "This is Martin Erlich, head of the Joint Terrorism Task Force. He would like a few minutes with you." She backed out of the office.

"I have never in my life thought I would be ... not sure what the word is ... not *entertaining* ... talking with, whatever—hello, I am Dr. McMaster," he said.

"Hello, I am Martin Erlich, as your assistant said. I really hate to barge in like this. But I was in the area, and we are investigating a possible ongoing terrorist attack that could be tied to Hopkins Hospital. I need you to keep everything I say in total confidence and not discuss anything with anybody or you may be obstructing justice under federal law. Understood, doctor?" Martin said.

"Yes. This sounds serious!" Dr. McMaster exclaimed.

"Oh, very. You no doubt have followed the news of the unfortunate measles vaccine cases and spread of measles virus in the country, which fortunately now seems to be under a little better control. We think the attack may have been linked to the new vaccine," Martin said.

"Yes, we could hardly miss that. A couple of children with neurological problems were seen here," he said.

"Well, that's where the mystery begins, we think. The trials of the vaccine were clean. The company saw no such events in thousands of children in the clinical trials. And now it appears that the virus spread after vaccination. From what I have learned—and I am no scientist—this is unheard of for an attenuated vaccine," Martin said.

"Yes, it is," McMaster confirmed.

"I'd like to ask you a few questions about Dr. Mazer, if I could," Martin said.

"Sure. Do you think he could be involved? I cannot believe it, but go ahead," he said.

"First, tell me about him."

"Alan has been here for years," McMaster said. "He was a neurology resident, chief resident, and then a neurovirology fellow before coming onto the faculty here. He is a fine clinician. He spends a lot of time with his patients and is an excellent diagnostician. And I cannot say enough good things about his abilities. He puts out an enormous number of academic papers and pulls in lots of money in grants for the department. Again, I can't see him being a problem."

"Where does he live?" Martin asked.

"He lives in the Harbor Moon Condo and Marina complex, down by the Inner Harbor. Nice location. I have not been there, but it is a nice place from what I understand from others who live in the area," McMaster said. "Honestly, I guess he must have some family money because that's a pretty classy place for someone on an assistant professor salary."

"What else can you tell me about him?" Martin queried.

"Honestly, after all these years, I cannot tell you much about him as a person. He is a loner. Except for interactions with colleagues in the doctors' dining room, I rarely see him with anyone else. I know he is married and has two children—twins, a boy and a girl. I have not met them. They have never come to my yearly holiday parties. He is a hard worker and a solid physician scientist. And one of his grants takes him to Egypt twice a year to study a virus or two over there. Also, Alan took a month without pay to go to Syria and work for Doctors Without Borders a few years back after some of the chemical attacks," said McMaster.

"Really. Would it surprise you to learn than Alan Mazer is Muslim?" said Martin.

"I am shocked. He does not practice any rituals around here, so yes, I struggle to believe this," McMaster responded.

"Well, that's the reason I am here. He was working on measles virus strains that Immunoviratherapeutics did not develop. He was interested in neurotropism, I believe the correct term is. He wanted to determine what caused these properties, if I have that right. And he was working with an Ashraf Khaleed from the company, also a Muslim. We think Ashraf might have been involved in a scheme to switch the good vaccine with the neurotoxic vaccine. And at the same time, he told members of this mosque so they could bet on the stock price to tank," Martin summarized.

"This is an amazing story," McMaster said.

"Unfortunately, we don't think it's a story. The president implemented the national emergency, and we have done a good job in slowing the spread of the virus through that program. Now we have to find Mazer, who is not around. I have questioned Ashraf today already, and I think he may give me more information soon. Thank you for your time. If you can think of anything else, Doctor, please call me. Here's my card. Remember, please do not mention any of our conversation with anyone, including your assistant or family members. I may be back to you a little bit later to follow up on the Egyptian connection and Doctors Without Borders trip. Thank you again," Martin said.

"Of course," said McMaster.

Martin had just stepped out the door of the hospital when his phone vibrated in his pocket. It was Nari Lee.

"Dr. Lee, I didn't think you wanted to come on board that quickly," he joked.

"Ha! You wish. I had a new idea when you left and mobilized the staff, with Dr. Ickerson's blessing of course," Nari continued. "You remember that I told you that our research group determined that the vaccine that was produced was not from the same stock of virus that was used in the clinical trials?"

"Yes," Martin responded.

"We now know that the neurovirulent virus must be the culprit. And, further, the facility must account for each vial of virus in every laboratory. I asked each lab to account for their virus stocks. Every vial was counted," Nari said. "And it will not surprise you to learn that this was a major undertaking. Freezers in multiple labs had to be searched and compared to notebooks across several teams. Lots of frostbit fingers in this exercise."

"Nari, get to the punchline already," Martin pushed.

"Okay, three vials turned up missing—from Ashraf Khaleed's lab," she said. "I think you need to lock him up and throw away the key."

"Hold on, Detective Lee. First off, I like your initiative and counting skills, but let's not jump the gun," Martin said. "We have to consider not just a few missing vials but who might be behind the plan, how it got into production, was the count correct—"

Nari interrupted, "I had everyone triple check their counting, and it was clear. The box of vials in Ashraf's lab had three vials missing, and there were no notations in his lab notebook of their whereabouts. I am sure he put that virus into production several months ago, and that is the stock virus from which our team has made commercial vaccine. He is a murderer!"

"Calm down, Nari. Let me do my job now, with my team," Martin said. "I want you to go back to Providence, as you planned. If we need you for any further work on this, I will call you. Okay?"

"Okay, but I am infuriated. And the more I think about it, I might be calling you sooner than later," Nari responded. "The money in big biotech does not mean that much to me anymore. I think I can be a help, and not just a counter of crap."

"Oh, we—I know," he said.

"So you and your agency have done your due diligence on me already?" Nari asked.

"You could say that," said Martin. His mind raced with thoughts of recruiting Nari to the Agency. Her talents could be of great help to the country.

"Well, I will have some thinking to do on the flight back tonight," Nari said before clicking off her phone.

DEMISE AND UNDOING
JULY 2019

Although hundreds of children died, and thousands hospitalized, thank goodness the measures instituted during the national emergency worked. The National Guard did their job, the public cooperated, supplies were delivered as promised, and the economic impact of the epidemic was eventually minimized. Now the emergency was over, and the country was back to relative normalcy and routine. The virus was still out there simmering, but the public knew that summer was now upon them and that virus spread was less likely. Schools would be closing soon, and that would help. Those with infections were kept isolated, while those who were getting sick were still awfully ill.

The country did not want to face this type of strike again. Answers were needed. Congress was on the hook for investigations. Was this an FDA issue? Homeland Security? Everyone had questions, and no one at this time had the answer. Who was responsible? In time, answers would be forthcoming. The country might not want to hear all of them, but they would be coming.

Martin Erlich had spent his career on many investigations. He was not a paper pusher or a desk jockey. His twenty years at the CIA spanning several international assignments had given him insights into how his investigation at the company would proceed. Because of his vast global experience, he had been a perfect choice to head the Joint Terrorism Task Force in the Department of the Treasury. Martin had done his homework and knew that he would need to spend some time in Baltimore as well, checking out people and places. Arnold Ickerson told Martin that Baltimore had more measles expertise at the University of Maryland and Hopkins than the rest of the country, and many of these scientists worked with the company on measles and other virus candidates. Arnold provided Martin with a list of all these collaborators and researchers, and he took action. Martin placed these names and all company employee names in the exit travel data base. This was not the no-fly list, but rather a separate database, the Computer Assisted Passenger Prescreening System.

The government and airlines had developed and put this updated system in place after 9/11. Its purpose was to find "individuals known to pose, or suspected of posing, a risk of air piracy or terrorism or a threat to airline or passenger safety. The list was used to preemptively identify terrorists attempting to buy airline tickets or board aircraft traveling in the United States, and to mitigate perceived threats." Martin was not necessarily concerned about an air event. He wanted to know if someone involved with the company or stock transactions was about to leave the country. Any airline, rental car agency, or rail-ticketing group could instantly notify the task force about any targeted individual intending to buy or buying a ticket or leasing a vehicle. That's exactly what Martin worried about. Was someone with ties to the company or an employee involved in this disastrous plague? His job went far beyond the stock sale issues. He and his agents were now on the trail of a terrorist cell or a money connection to major financiers of terror. This could be just the beginning of a massive terror plot. He hoped it was not. But his job was to protect the homeland. Right now his thoughts were on whether there were any other bioweapons aimed at the United States or its allies. The MVoneshot measles vaccine could have just been a test. Were the country's reactions being watched?

In the meantime, Harvey Goodman at the SEC had already taken it on the chin from his boss at Treasury for not calling him first and going through proper channels, but he did not give a shit. Harvey had done the right thing, and the investigation was in full swing. He had not wanted to wait an extra day. It could have taken days more than that for his boss to get it on his plate.

And, as Harvey knew would happen, the terrorist task force brought Canada and other allies up to speed on the investigation. He felt great about his communication, and now he could see what would happen. He hoped that it was just a greedy man in the company who was trying to get rich quick—and nothing more.

Now Alan was in full swing. He had to meet with Ashraf. He decided to bring him back to the lab under the guise of destroying any evidence of the neurotropic virus remaining in his lab. Alan, of course, could do this himself easily enough, but he had bigger plans for Ashraf. Alan knew of a colleague who was working on the detailed mechanism by which batrachotoxin from a South American frog killed its prey. It had both neurotoxic and cardiotoxic effects and killed its prey rapidly. The professor had large quantities frozen in his lab for research use. It was easily accessible to those who knew their way around. Alan was just that person, and there was no antidote once injected into the body.

Alan called Ashraf on one of his burner phones.

"Ashraf, I know your lab is shut down, so I need your help in my lab. We have flasks of virus still growing, plus hundreds of frozen vials of the neurotropic virus. In addition, we injected some adult animals last week in a follow-up experiment with a larger dose to see if we could reach a dose that was lethal," Alan explained.

"So what does that have to do with me?" Ashraf retorted. "I am under tight scrutiny right now. Everyone is watching everyone's moves. I have my own issues and plenty of them."

"I know, but please—I need help in cleaning up my lab. You and I are the only ones who worked on this agent. I am not supposed to have this strain here yet. We have to get this out of the lab now. This may take your mind off some of what's going on down there. You have to get up to Baltimore now," pleaded Alan.

"I cannot get up there until Saturday. In two days."

"What's wrong with Friday evening? The place will be cleared out of most of the staff, and we can work more freely," Alan replied.

"Okay, if you insist, but the animal work is all yours. I am not going down to that mouse vivarium. It usually stinks to damnation," Ashraf insisted.

"Deal. Thank you. I will see you Friday. Call me when you are close, and I will meet you at the door as usual," said Alan.

The lab was empty by five thirty on Friday evening. At about six thirty, Alan went into the shared facility room where the low-temperature storage freezers were kept, along with other heavy machinery such as huge refrigerators and ultracentrifuges. All this equipment was kept together on back-up generators. He knew exactly where the batrachotoxin was stored since the professor working on this project had borrowed spaced from this department. He grabbed a 1 cc vial of the toxin from the −70 degrees Celsius storage freezer and took it to his lab. On the way to his lab, it started to thaw. That was not of concern to Alan, as the toxin was extremely poisonous, and even if it lost some of its potency it would still be effective. It was a thousand times more potent than cyanide, and the equivalent of just two grains of its salt would kill a 160-pound man. Alan had learned most of this during lunches with his colleagues. The toxin was originally isolated from various frogs and some insects and was used by many native tribespeople on their poison darts. Just by rubbing their darts on the skin of a frog before using them, the dart would then kill their prey or enemies in less than ten minutes after penetration. Alan donned a pair of latex gloves and, under a laminar flow hood, pulled up the solution of toxin into a 3 cc syringe, with a 25-gauge needle attached. That was enough toxin to kill many hundreds of people. He left the syringe on a bed of ice and waited for Ashraf to call.

Ashraf arrived without any extraordinary problems on Friday evening at around seven o'clock. He made his usual call on his way to Hopkins when he passed the stadium complex at the exit ramp of the highway. About five minutes later, Alan was outside waiting for him.

By that time there were plenty of parking spaces on the side streets by the entry door.

On their way up in the elevator, Alan reviewed with Ashraf what their goals would be. Although Alan now had permission to work with the virus, he did not want to have any of this killer measles strain left in his lab. It was crucial to wipe out all evidence of its existence here. Alan assigned Ashraf the removal of all cultures from the incubator and pouring all fluids into a concentrated solution of bleach so that the final volume would be 10 percent. He also told Ashraf to add a 10 percent solution of bleach to all the culture flasks.

Ashraf interrupted Alan. "I have been doing this for a long time, Dr. Mazer. Please do not insult me."

"You may have, but you have not been in this situation before, and I want to make sure you do everything my way. Please," Alan pleaded.

"Okay," Ashraf agreed.

"Then, after you leave the bleach in contact with the culture material for thirty minutes, please double bag the material in autoclave plastic bags and place them in the autoclave. We will then destroy all the material," Alan continued.

Ashraf proceeded to the incubator to pull some cultures and bring them to the lab bench. Alan put on a pair of latex gloves for his work in the vivarium with the animals.

"Ashraf, I will be headed downstairs to the vivarium and will euthanize the remaining animals from our experiment!" Alan shouted from the front of the lab.

Alan then turned and picked up the syringe of toxin that was sitting on ice in the hood. As he did, Ashraf was distracted by pulling culture flasks from the incubator in the back of the lab. Ashraf backed away from the incubator with each hand holding two flasks. He was startled to see Alan still in the lab and right behind him. Alan quickly jabbed the needle and plunged the full 1 cc of toxin into Ashraf's right upper arm. Alan quickly capped the syringe and put it in his lab coat pocket.

"What the fuck!" Ashraf screamed at Alan. "What are you doing?"

"You gave me no choice. You put jihad, our plan, our cell at risk. The SEC and the CIA will be on our back. I cannot trust you." Alan grabbed the four flasks from his hands before Ashraf dropped them.

Ashraf started to shake and then fell to the floor.

Alan casually left the lab and continued to the animal facility. He went to the basement and completed his job, including incinerating the syringe he had used to inject the lethal toxin into Ashraf's arm.

In about thirty minutes, Alan returned to his lab. Ashraf was on the floor, dead. Alan still called a code blue. Alan pulled off Ashraf's coat and shirt and started chest compressions to put on a show for the team that would arrive shortly. In a matter of a few minutes, a resuscitation team arrived to his lab. They realized almost immediately that Alan's attempt to resuscitate the patient was hopeless. The patient was not breathing. The team leader pulled Alan away and took over. Ashraf was cold to the touch, indicating that he must have been deceased for at least twenty minutes.

"When did you find him?" the doctor asked Alan.

"Just before I called you, not more than five minutes ago. We spoke twenty-five minutes ago, then I left Ashraf in my lab while I tended to my animal experiments for a while in the basement facility," Alan replied.

"Well, it looks as if he died during that time," the doctor said. "I'm calling this: patient pronounced dead at 8:23 p.m. I will get the authorities and someone up here to handle the body and any follow-up questions as soon as possible. I am sorry, but you will have to wait around. The police will have some questions before this is wrapped up." The doctor stepped away from the body.

Ashraf was placed on a gurney. The team left quickly.

"Dr. Mazer?" an unkempt but nonetheless gentlemanly individual in a tie and coat called as he entered the research lab along with two uniformed officers. "Dr. Mazer, police!" he shouted to get some attention, not seeing anyone.

"Over here, in the back of the lab. I am just resting here at a desk. It has been a long day. I am Alan Mazer."

"Dr. Mazer, I am Lieutenant Johnson from the Baltimore Police. I am sorry but in all situations like this where there has been an unexplained death, we have to investigate," Johnson explained.

"I am aware of that necessity. I have no idea about Ashraf's medical conditions. He was a colleague who helped me out occasionally by working in the lab. He came up from a company in Virginia," said Alan.

"Well, as you may or may not know, since he died outside the actual hospital, there needs to be some forensic work to determine the manner of death. It was not an expected death, as you know, and depending on what the external investigation finds, an autopsy may be required to determine cause of death," Johnson continued.

"I am also aware of all this," Alan added. "Is there any reason I have to stay around much longer? I saw patients early this morning, and now it is late in the evening. I would like to get home. This has been a very upsetting event."

"Of course, Doctor. Just a few questions, if you don't mind," said the lieutenant.

"Yes, I will answer all your questions. I just want to make you aware of the fact that this young man is a Muslim, and according to his tradition, he would want to be buried as soon as possible after death," interjected Mazer.

"Okay, then let's get on with it. When was the last time you saw Mr. Ashraf alive? Is this his name?"

"I saw Mr. Khaleed—Mr. Ashraf Khaleed—alive just before I went down to the animal facility in the basement. It was around seven thirty. I am not sure of the exact time. We had spoken just before that about what we were going to do with about our ongoing project," replied Alan.

"And can you tell me what that project was?" Johnson asked.

"I can, but I'm not sure what that has to do with anything," replied Alan.

"Humor me," said the lieutenant as he took a seat on the corner of the lab bench next to the desk. "But before you do that, let me take a quick look at the body, and then my colleagues here can take the body down to the morgue, okay?"

"That's fine with me."

Johnson lifted the sheet off Ashraf's body and took a cursory look at his face and chest. He saw nothing that was suspicious to him, but he of course was not medically trained. He was looking for gaping wounds or bruises and the like.

"All right, boys," he said, "take this body down to the morgue. Please make sure you collect and get proper sign-off all physical property on his person and make sure the staff here stores it appropriately. Thanks. I will see you downtown later."

The two officers quickly rolled Ashraf out of the lab and down the hallway to the hospital wing toward the building that housed pathology.

"Dr. Mazer, let us continue. What were you and Mr. Khaleed working on so late on a Friday evening that brought him here from Virginia?" asked the lieutenant.

"Well, sir, science is a lot about timing. Ashraf was doing some work on my cell lines in which he had specialized training. It was time to harvest those cells and do further work on the virus growing within them," replied Alan.

"Aha," said Johnson, "and you need someone to come all the way from Virginia to do this while you tend to animals? Honestly, this does not make too much sense to me, Doctor."

"I am sorry if it makes little sense, but it is the truth," Alan responded. "Ashraf has been working on the measles virus for years and knows the molecular ins and outs of this agent. I am more comfortable with my animal experiments."

"Oh, is this the company in McLean that had the vaccine recalled? The one that caused the national emergency?" asked Johnson.

"Yes, it is," replied Mazer.

"Wow, I didn't think I would be so close to that. Well, I think I have enough information for now, Dr. Mazer. Why don't you get some rest? If pathology comes up with anything requiring more information from you or if I have more questions, I will get in touch with you. In the meantime, here is my contact information. Please feel free to reach out to me if you can think of anything that might help, such as if Ashraf had been sick recently or taken any vacations to foreign locations. That sort of thing. Thanks again for your time." With that, Lieutenant Johnson slid off the lab bench, not waiting for any answers. He did an about-face and quickly headed out of the lab.

Martin Erlich was informed of Ashraf Khaleed's death by Dr. McMaster at Hopkins. He immediately called the Baltimore City Police and learned that a Lieutenant Johnson was handling the case.

Martin called him at once to bring him up to speed on his investigation. This was not just an ordinary death in a laboratory, as per McMaster's call. Martin recounted the whole episode. The lieutenant was familiar with the measles tragedies but had not known the linkage to Mazer's lab. He also did not know that Mazer was Muslim and had worshipped at the same mosque as Ashraf. Some of the pieces were fitting together. But the financial end of the picture—the short selling of the company for gains when the company share price collapsed—had no connection to Mazer, as far as either of them could tell at this time. It was possible that Mazer might have been the brains behind the attack and pushed Ashraf into making the moves at the company. But what had Ashraf been doing at Mazer's lab this evening and why was he dead? Had he been killed? Or was it a natural death? Was there any motive for Mazer to kill Ashraf?

Alan put his head on the desk and closed his eyes briefly. He had to take time to work out in his mind what his next steps would be. Should he stay put? There was a high likelihood that someone would follow him. Who knew what connections had already been made to Ashraf and the stock transactions and him. And now, Ashraf had keeled over in Alan's lab. This may have been a blunder, an irreversible blunder. It had taken just five minutes for a Baltimore city Columbo-esque cop to put together the company with a vaccine and Ashraf. Alan already had spent months overseas with his jihadi brothers; he had connections in Egypt and Pakistan. Was it time to run now?

Alan had worked hard his whole life. He could have been one of the top neurologists and virologists in the world, developing medicines for patients with multiple sclerosis, Alzheimer's, ALS, and other disorders. But he had long since developed a personality disorder. His devotion to Islam and now to jihad did not reconcile with his love for and dedication to medicine and science. In Alan's mind, he had found the only way to integrate the two. He used his brilliance to develop weapons of destruction. He felt a bond to the Palestinians. He felt they had been robbed of their land by the Jews of Israel with help by the United States. And now he wanted to help all other Muslim brothers burdened by past Western imperialism. Alan saw the great success that his knowledge contributed to in working with Ashraf, spreading disease and destruction with the mutated measles vaccine. He knew that he could do more, targeting bioweapons to enemies of his people. He made his decision. He could no longer continue hiding in plain sight in the States, at Hopkins, or anywhere else. He needed to leave and head to his laboratory in Egypt. As much as he loved his family, he loved his cause even more and needed to escape.

Alan had chosen his exit plan. He was not sure if could leave the country under his own name. He had surmised that police or other agencies might have his name on a list somewhere that would block him from leaving the country. He had a postdoctoral fellow in his lab primed and ready to leave with him on his next journey to Egypt, scheduled in the next two weeks. The fellow resembled Alan in height, weight, and complexion. All Alan had to do was shave his beard so that he could pass quite nicely for his student. It would be easy enough to change his fellow's ticket to tomorrow evening's flight and fly out of the country with his documents. Alan dialed United Airlines from the fellow's landline. The student's passport was in his desk, along with his visa for thirty days of work in Egypt. The receipt for his airline ticket had been processed already and reimbursed, so Alan had the credit card number in his file. He had pulled that and had it ready in case the agent needed a card for change fees. Everything went smoothly. Tickets were switched, and Alan was booked under his new name, David Forman, MD.

Alan Mazer, now traveling as David Forman, was clean shaven. He felt very strange. He had had facial hair and a full beard for almost twenty years. His hands continued to touch his face; it was a strange feeling. And to be honest, the clean-shaven look was not bad—he looked younger. That was the idea. Of course, Alan was not looking for self-perfection. That would be contrary to Islam. He needed to appear as the photo in the passport and other papers.

Alan did not go the university that day. He left at his usual time but did have other things to do. His plan was simple. He would empty his bank account in the morning, getting travelers checks that he could use anywhere. He planned to carry any valuable items with him in a carry-on onto the plane. And finally, in the late morning, he would pack all his clothes, which was not much, in one suitcase to check all the way through to Aswan. He then would take a ride-share car to Dulles, leave his car at his apartment, and say goodbye to the United States and his family. This sounded easy, but he knew that the last item on the checklist would not happen. He would just leave his wife and twins behind with no explanation. He was sure that this was best decision.

He had a quick bite to eat at the Inner Harbor and took a short walk along the water. No one recognized him. He then went back to his place. At two o'clock he pulled up his ride-share app, and a car was there in six minutes. An hour and ten minutes later, he was dropped off at Dulles in northern Virginia. The lines were quite long for the coach check-in at United. Alan, now David, wasn't going to make a stink about traveling coach; he just wanted to get out of town. After thirty-five minutes, he had finally crawled up to the front of the line. He handed his documents to the agent.

"Good afternoon. I'm Dr. Forman. I'm going to Aswan via Frankfurt today," said Alan.

"Good afternoon to you, Doctor," the agent replied cheerfully. "Let me check everything here."

She typed in a few keystrokes. "Will you be checking bags, Doctor?" she asked.

Alan responded, "Just one."

"Great. Oh, not again." She pushed some keys on her computer to print and frowned. "I have run out of luggage tags on my printer here. Let me go in the back and get a new roll. I will be right back," she said.

Alan smiled back and waited patiently. Everything seemed to going well to this point. The cover as David Forman was working well. Next, he thought, were the security checkpoints, but the ticket agent had already looked at the passport, he reasoned. Alan looked at his watch. The agent had not yet returned, people behind him were stirring, and he started to worry. *What could take so long to get printer paper for the luggage tags?* he thought. Just when he thought that, the agent reappeared and Alan felt a sense of relief for a millisecond. But then two men grabbed him from behind. One cuffed him, and the other quickly said, "Dr. Alan Mazer, you are now under arrest for violating the United States laws of domestic terrorism. You are charged with being involved with acts dangerous to human life that are a violation of the criminal laws of the United States, and you are further being charged with murder under federal statutes."

An anxious crowd just wanting to get to Germany and beyond in the line backed up several steps behind Alan. They watched in awe as the activity progressed. The men took Alan into custody.

"Hey, you did not read me my rights!" screamed Alan.

"Let's go, Doctor," one agent said as they pulled him toward the exit doors at the front of the departure area, where two unmarked cars were waiting for him.

"A couple of things about your rights, Doctor," one agent explained on the way. "You are an imminent threat to the public. You represent fear of continued or another biological attack. I may question you right now. I am not going to read you your rights." The agents walked him outside and put him in the back seat of the waiting black Lincoln. Alan faced federal terrorism crimes and could be put away for at least thirty years, maybe more. If they connected him to the Olympic Games ISIS attacks and convicted him, he would not get out. If convicted of Ashraf's murder, a more likely scenario, he would be in prison for life. Others at the mosque would take prison terms for the insider trading but would have no connections with Ashraf or Alan for the devastating vaccine attack.

Leesa Mazer Khorasani woke up early that summer morning as she did most days. She opened her apartment door and picked up the *Washington Post* expecting to see the normal political nonsense splashed on page one. But that day, she got her chance see her beloved son, Alan. She hadn't seen or heard from him in over ten years. Occasionally, Sabina sent her a picture of their beautiful twins, but Alan himself never made contact. He did not exist. She read the headline and almost collapsed in the doorway.

Her son could hurt no one, except her with a broken heart. She couldn't believe what she read. The police had arrested her son the previous night for terrorism charges, murder, and the horrible measles outbreaks.

She closed the door. Neighbors could hear her wailing off and on for hours. None of her friends could console her.

Unknown to the agencies involved in capturing Dr. Mazer, they had just seized a pawn in a larger jihadist plan. Yes, the government would determine that Mazer and his diabolical work were behind the lethal and malicious virus attacks on the United States as well as the Olympic Games in Jordan, thanks to the investigative work of the Joint Terrorism Task Force and the Mossad. But a key person, who provided the impetus and funding, was close to Dr. Mazer. One major culprit, so close to the center of the cell, remained at large and just out of reach. Mrs. Sabina Hassani Mazer had quietly volunteered first for the Imam in Cambridge and then for the Imam in Baltimore and worked with the American caliphate and the ISIS jihadist movement. Alan did not know of Sabina's involvement. She was deeply embedded in and involved in all the day-to-day strategies for the American caliphate and jihad in America. In fact, as a young teen, she had traveled to Libya and trained for two months with leaders before returning under cover through Egypt and Europe on her way to the States. She was well hidden from any intelligence organization and would not be discovered. She was outside the religious organization but well inside the deep plans for the ending of America. Her parents never knew what was going on. She "studied" in Europe in high school and then continued to work with the Cambridge mosque. The marriage was a setup to get Dr. Mazer working with them. Sabina grew to love Alan immensely and loved their twins, but the goals of jihad were always number one. Someday she hoped to explain all this to her children. Right now, both Aamir and Najah were confused. They had no idea of either parent's role in any terrorist activities. Their father's fate was sealed. Sabina's fate was undetermined, as were those of her children.

NOTES FROM THE AUTHOR

During my career I have worked with many dangerous pathogens. I have also had the privilege to work with some of the top virologists and immunologists in the world. It has been exciting to develop and then see state-of-the art, first-of-their-kind, lifesaving products come to market. These products have saved babies from dying of severe respiratory viral infections, have prevented transplant recipients from losing their organs from devastating organ infections, and have provided vaccines to prevent outbreaks of severe infections. On the other hand, I have witnessed firsthand the devastation of widespread measles infections in a country where vaccination was not available. Huge population growth and immigration of thousands of unprotected children resulted in widespread epidemics each year with predictability. Every year hundreds of children were hospitalized and died. In the States, the measles virus was eliminated; only now we are seeing it reemerge. It is shameful, and everyone must do their part to reeducate Americans about the importance of vaccination.

Influenza is another virus to which we need to pay close attention. Every year in the United States alone, thirty thousand to fifty thousand people die following influenza infection, and two hundred thousand are hospitalized. That's an average number. In high years, it can be much,

much greater. The vaccine available every autumn is usually a trivalent or quadrivalent (for three or four viruses) one. The CDC meets each spring and attempts to determine what viruses will be circulating the following winter. Based on its best guesses, companies produce vaccines that summer for the next fall and winter. It doesn't hurt to stem the tide and get vaccinated. Most vaccines are inactivated and cannot cause the flu.

The use of viruses and other human pathogens as biological weapons is not a new potential threat to the world. What is important to note is that new and horrible mechanisms to unleash such diseases become available at a rapid pace. The technologies are developed for good, but unfortunately they can be twisted and used for evil. That we cannot control. *We can,* however, protect ourselves. One important message I hoped to convey here is that when protection is possible, we should avail ourselves and our children of it. If a safe and effective vaccine is recommended, we should take it.

Solid scientific data on measles vaccination in children shows that it protects children from natural infection. Unfortunately, data published years ago suggested that measles vaccination caused autism and related disorders. This drastically reduced the rates of measles vaccination in several countries, notably the United Kingdom. These data were not reproduced. As a result, over time, in both the United States and Europe the rates of infection increased. At one point before the autism scare, measles was actually eliminated in several countries, including the United States. Many parents think measles is just another childhood infection and is not serious. Their kids get a fever and rash and recover in one to two weeks. For many, that is true. But one to two people in each one thousand will die, and another one to two in each one thousand will have neurological complications after infection. Many children will have infections that affect their hearing; many will have acute gastrointestinal problems from the infections. Those who are malnourished or immune compromised will be prone to pneumonia and will die. Without a certain large percentage of children obtaining protection from vaccination, there is a loss of herd immunity, and the virus can spread in the wild from child to child, such as what happened in this novel. Dr. Mazer, the antagonist in this novel, planned for this in this story. He played both sides. He encouraged publication of false autism data by his foreign associates, encouraging low vaccination rates. When he was back in the States, he encouraged vaccination to make sure that his bad vaccine would get injected into the naive population, spreading destruction.

If you have enjoyed this book, please leave a review on Amazon and Goodreads and recommend it to a friend.